Date: 5/18/22

GRA KIKI V.3
KiKi,
Roll over and die. I will fight
for an ordinary life with my

Flum Apricot

Milkit

Leitch Mancathy

Welcy Mancathy

Hallom Yandoura

Kleyna Yandoura

Dafydd Chalmas

Susy Chalmas

ROLL OVER AND DIE

NOVEL 3

*I Will Fight
for an Ordinary Life
with My Love
and Cursed Sword!*

STORY BY

kiki

ILLUSTRATED BY

kinta

Airship

Seven Seas Entertainment

ROLL OVER AND DIE: I WILL FIGHT FOR AN ORDINARY LIFE
WITH MY LOVE AND CURSED SWORD! VOL. 3

©kiki 2019
Illustrations by kinta

This edition originally published in Japan in 2019 by
MICRO MAGAZINE, INC., Tokyo.
English translation rights arranged with
MICRO MAGAZINE, INC., Tokyo.

Seven Seas press and purchase enquiries can be sent to
Marketing Manager Lianne Sentar at press@gomanga.com.
Information regarding the distribution and purchase of
digital editions is available from Digital Manager CK Russell
at digital@gomanga.com.

Follow Seven Seas Entertainment online at
sevenseasentertainment.com.

TRANSLATION: Jason Muell
ADAPTATION: Brock Wassman
COVER DESIGN: Nicky Lim
LOGO DESIGN: George Panella
INTERIOR LAYOUT & DESIGN: Clay Gardner
PROOFREADER: Jade Gardner, Stephanie Cohen
LIGHT NOVEL EDITOR: Nibedita Sen
PREPRESS TECHNICIAN: Rhiannon Rasmussen-Silverstein
PRODUCTION MANAGER: Lissa Pattillo
MANAGING EDITOR: Julie Davis
ASSOCIATE PUBLISHER: Adam Arnold
PUBLISHER: Jason DeAngelis

ISBN: 978-1-64827-088-8
Printed in Canada
First Printing: June 2021
10 9 8 7 6 5 4 3 2 1

CONTENTS

4 · The Lies and Losses of the Necromantic Memories

EPISODE

4

The Lies and Losses of the Necromantic Memories

ROLL
OVER
AND
DIE

The β Girl Overcomes Incongruities

WHENEVER SARA CLOSED HER EYES for even the shortest of naps, the nightmares came flooding back: All the sights, sounds, and smells, like she was right in the thick of it again.

The endless eyes.

The creatures her beloved brothers became.

The thought that Ed and Jonny threw down their lives just for her.

Despite their sacrifice, the creatures had still cornered her. Her back up against the wall, surrounded by eyes, with nowhere left to go. A single touch would be the end for her: they would worm into her, everything they touched twinning and proliferating until she was an unrecognizable tangle of heads and limbs.

Sara breathed heavily.

"Ed...Jonny...I'm so sorry. You gave up your lives for me, but I think this is it. I'll be with you guys soon."

She could go no further.

The eyes showed no sign of hesitation as they relentlessly moved in on her. One by one they made contact and seeped into her body through her skin.

"No...no!! I...I don't wanna...I don't wanna die...!"

Alas, her cries were completely ignored as they wriggled deeper. Sara scratched at the wall in desperation, though it held firm. There would be no escape.

"Nnngaaaah! This...eugh! This is awful! I don't... I can't become a monster!!"

Her nails ground against the brick, and her fingertips began to bleed. A new leg sprung from her torso, and her body began to bloat. She felt bile rising in the back of her throat, but instead of vomit, organs began to bulge out of her mouth.

Her body was transforming just like her brothers' had a short time ago.

"No...nnngaauh... I...d-don't...gaaaaugh!!!"

"Noooooooooo!!"

Sara sat up with a start.

"Haaah...haaah...haah..."

Her shoulders heaved, and her blonde bangs clung tightly to her face from the sweat covering her body.

"Waaaaaaugh!!!"

This wasn't just any nightmare, though. She experienced all these things firsthand. Sara brought her hands up to her face and sobbed, shuddering in time with her cries. The people she held the dearest were dead, leaving her the only survivor. The guilt alone was nearly unbearable.

A blue-skinned woman—the Demon Chief Neigass—pulled Sara into a warm embrace as she cried.

Neigass's fact-finding expedition into human territory hadn't paid out well, turning up little about the church's activities or the Origin cores. Infiltrating the capital was the last thing she wanted to do, but she was out of options.

She happened across Sara completely by chance. The capital wasn't safe for them, but they'd run into Gadhio on their way out of the city, trusting him to pass along their message to Flum. Several days had passed since then, and the two were now holed up in a small mountain cabin.

"Shhh...shhh. You're okay, they can't find you here." The eyes had stopped following them the moment they cleared the wall. "Even if they do come back, I'll protect you."

Sara wrapped her arms tight around Neigass and buried her face against the older woman's chest. Her initial misgivings had completely melted away. This didn't mean she trusted the demons now—Neigass was simply all she had left to rely on after the church's betrayal and her separation from Flum.

Sara sobbed hard against Neigass. "What did I do to deserve this??"

"You didn't do anything wrong at all, Sara."

"Then why did this have to happen?!"

Neigass had no answer for her. All she could do was continue to stroke Sara's hair.

She could have written it off as the church's fault, of course, but Sara, Ed, and Jonny were all members. The institution itself was blameless. The fault lay with Origin, the will directing the church elite.

Sara's sobbing subsided, replaced by a reflective calm look. "Th-they really excommunicated me?"

"That's what I've heard, yes."

The church excommunicated Sara on charges of heresy to ensure she'd never be welcome in the capital again. Should a member of the church ever find her, she would be immediately detained, tried, and likely sentenced to death.

"But you know," Neigass said, "I hear whispers on the wind that there are members of the church who are still dearly worried about you."

"R-really?"

"Not everyone is convinced by the church's account of things. They showed too much of their hand with you, and people are starting to ask questions. So, don't you worry. Your name will be cleared, and you'll be back in the capital in no time."

Neigass's kind words brought a smile to Sara's lips. Suddenly she jerked her head back to look straight up at the demon woman. Neigass smiled slightly.

"Oh? What is it?"

"Wh-why are you bein' so nice to me, Neigass? I took an oath to oppose you in all things."

"I couldn't turn my back on a child in need."

"Yeah, but even when I have a nightmare, you're always right there to comfort me. No matter how bad I break down, you're always kind and gentle. Not everyone could do that."

"Hmm. I guess you have a point." Neigass would be lying if she said she had no ulterior motive. She wasn't eager to discuss the details, but there was another reason behind her visit to the capital.

Sara fixed Neigass with a pointed gaze. "Are you keeping something from me?"

Neigass thought it over and determined it would be dishonest to avoid the young girl's question.

"Promise you won't be too upset?"

"Is it something to get upset over?"

"Remember when we first met at the cave, and I said I thought you were cute?"

"Yeah, I guess."

"Well, I was kinda thinking maybe I could see you again."

"Huh? You came to see me?"

"Well, I mean, that was only half of it. The other half was to uncover the church's plot. Hey, w-wait a second! You don't need to back away like that!"

Sara started to scoot back from Neigass. "So you had some kind of ulterior motive?!"

"No, not at all!! I would have helped anyone in that position, whether it was you or not. I'm telling you the truth here."

"I don't doubt that." Sara knew well that Neigass was completely sincere in that regard. If she was faking it, Sara would certainly be able to tell.

"I mean, you told me you wanted to know everything, didn't you?"

"Well, I guess I just dunno how to react. Is that it? You're not hiding anything else?"

Neigass hesitated.

"Why did you go quiet all of a sudden??" Sara demanded.

"Well, umm...you know how you said Flum was like a sister to you?"

"Yeah, I guess. But I've spent my whole life hating demons."

"Well, it seems like some of that's kinda lightened up now, so maybe you could try thinking of me as something of a big sister, too. You can even call me Sis!" Neigass tried to sound cool, but she was breathing just a little heavier than before. Sara found something altogether odd about her reaction.

Her answer was simple and to the point. "No."

"Why noooot??"

"It's just too weird! You're Neigass, and that's fine."

"But...! Just try it out, see how it feels to call me Sis!"

Neigass was beginning to sound like a pleading child. The image Sara had built up about demons over the years began to crumble as she watched Neigass stand there pouting.

After a few moments, Neigass's expression went serious as she seemed to recall something. "Well, I guess that's fine, too. At least we're on a first-name basis now.

I've always kind of dreamed of having someone look up to me like a big sister, but this is probably the closest I'm going to get for now. Aww, it's all so heartwarming, I feel like I could cry."

The look of surprise was apparent on Sara's face as she took another step away toward the door. "Hey, I'm heading out. On my own."

Neigass reached out and grabbed Sara.

"Let me go! I don't want to be here with a freak like you!"

"Listen, I'm sorry! I guess I went a little overboard there for a second, but I'm really sorry about all that! Please, just don't leave!"

"A little? You think that was just a little overboard??"

"I got it, okay. I promise I won't make too big of a deal over what you call me."

"Really?"

"I... I'll try."

"I still don't know if I can completely trust you, but I guess I'll believe you for now."

Much to Neigass's relief, Sara abandoned her plan to leave, and the two returned to bed. Sara sat down on Neigass's lap and leaned back against her ample chest.

"I wish it were under better circumstances, but at least this got my mind off that dream."

"My plan worked, then."

"You're an awful liar." Sara pinched Neigass's thigh.

"Ow owww!"

"I guess I must trust you. I wouldn't be able to open up like this if I didn't. I'm a pretty simple girl, to be able to just turn around and contradict everything I've learned."

Flying over the capital in Neigass's arms, Sara had realized the tremendous mercy demonkind was extending humanity; they could have flown over the border and leveled the kingdom whenever they liked. That alone was enough to start her questioning the idea of demons as humanity's natural enemy, as she had been raised to believe.

"Maybe if we're lucky, someday the rest of the humans will come around like you, Sara."

"I dunno, with weirdos like you letting your shameless side show to little kids like me, this might be an uphill battle."

"Wow, you wound me, Sara. Are you always so harsh?"

"Depends on who I'm talking to."

"Not sure if I should be happy about that."

"Your spirits could use a little lowering, to be honest."

Alas, despite all Sara's rebukes, Neigass still seemed over the moon. Until, that was, her expression went dark. "To be fair, I'm not personally acquainted with every

demon out there. There may very well be some who think it a mistake to spare you."

"Are...are there?"

"I'd hope not, but if it's a choice between that and Origin's power getting free..."

"Getting free?"

"Listen, Sara, I want you to know I fully intend to continue investigating the church. I can't head back to the Demon Lord without anything to show for my efforts."

"Oh? Well..."

"I can take you someplace where you'll be safe. Given your situation, that can't be anywhere inside Origin's sphere of influence."

"That pretty much covers the entire kingdom, though."

"Exactly. I was thinking the safest place would be in my country."

"So...I'd be the only human among demons?"

"We're generally forbidden from going out of our way to interact with humans, but we don't *hate* them. I'm sure you'd be well cared for—it's in our nature."

Everything Neigass said was true. Human or not, "child" and "enemy" were not categories that overlapped in her people's worldview.

None of this really helped to reduce Sara's suspicions of demons in general.

"All right, if you're not hot on that idea, I guess you could just stick with me? You'd have to face off against the church. Probably fight all kinds of creatures. It really would be safer to hunker down in my domain."

"Well, I...I only really know recovery magic, and I'm not even all that strong. I dunno if I'd really be much help."

"No need to worry about that. Having you by my side is all I need to inspire me! Your cuteness is more than enough!"

"Yeah, that really doesn't make it any better."

"Listen, if you want to be humble and talk about whether you're 'useful' or not, it's very helpful to have someone around who can patch me up. I'd be honored to have you by my side, Sara."

Sara had no reason to refuse such a warm invitation.

"All right, I guess I'll come along. Besides, I'd like to know more about what's going on with the church, too."

"Great! Then I guess we're off on this journey together, then! Yaaay!"

"However!! Keep all your weirdo talk to yourself, okay? Try it again and Imma punch you."

"Hmm, that's a tough one. It's hard to bite my tongue in the company of someone as utterly adorable as yourself. I am a demon, ya know."

"That's got nothin' to do with being a demon! So I'm just telling you now that I absolutely won't forgive any... nnngaaahhh!"

Neigass pulled Sara in close, pressing the younger girl's head tight against her chest.

"Aww, you think I've got some sort of weird fetish? It's not my fault you're such a cutie, Sara!"

Sara gave in and let herself sink against that warm, soft, sweet-smelling blue flesh. Loathe as she was to admit it, there was something oddly comforting about being held in such a warm embrace. It took her mind off the tragedy in the capital.

After all, she had no memory of the devastation the demons had supposedly wreaked on her hometown eight years ago. Right now, the bulk of Sara's pain, sadness, and anger could be traced directly back to the church's machinations. The church had set in motion the events that took Ed and Jonny from her.

"Pffffbt!" Sara excavated herself from Neigass's cleavage and looked up at the older woman. "Didn't I just tell you not to do this?! I'm gonna let you have it the next time you do!"

"I'll just have to make sure you get used to it, then."

Sara's cheeks puffed out in annoyance, though she finally acquiesced. "I don't need to get used to it! Gah...

Anyway, I'm pleased to have a chance to work with you, Neigass."

The church—or rather Elune, her substitute parent—had taught her to always be polite.

"Me too. Let's hope for a good, long journey."

They were unlike each other in every aspect—their birthplaces, the color of their skin, their eyes—but the warmth their bodies shared was undeniably similar.

Sara was confronted with the realization that demons and humans were kin, as all living creatures were.

The α Girl Learns of the Incongruities

THE PARTY, now down to just Cyrill, Jean, Maria, and Linus, continued their great journey. Cyrill was still in a dark mood and spoke little, which exacerbated the gloomy atmosphere hanging over the group.

Though something was different this time: Jean was in surprisingly high spirits.

"Don't be so grouchy, guys! This is great marching weather!"

"What the hell's got into Jean?"

"There's nothing wrong with being motivated. We should hurry up too, Linus."

Linus sighed. Maria was also in a surprisingly good mood and even more talkative than usual. He knew that he should be happy about this turn of events, but he found himself maintaining his distance and keeping a close eye on Jean and Maria.

It felt like a cold, icy hand had gripped his heart. Something was amiss. It didn't feel like they'd overcome some sort of immense challenge, but rather, that the party was somehow heading in the wrong direction.

Suddenly Maria turned around and looked at Linus. She looked annoyed—a look quite uncommon for the usually reserved woman.

"Hey, didn't I tell you to hurry up?"

"Uh, I... Yeah, sorry."

She grabbed on to his arm, her warm chest pressing against his side, causing Linus's mind to go blank. Linus was no stranger to interactions with the fairer sex, but things were somehow different with Maria.

"Why do you look so worried?" she asked.

"I dunno, you just seem to be in such high spirits. I was wondering if something changed."

"No, nothing in particular. I just feel really energetic today."

"Well, I guess that's good then."

She was definitely hiding something. She didn't want to tell him, either because it wasn't useful for him to know or because she didn't trust him.

Or, just maybe, she didn't want him wrapped up in whatever it was?

A few days prior, Maria's smile would have been more than enough to wash away his concerns. All it did now was deepen his worry.

Maybe I really should just bring this journey to an end, he thought, *even if I have to force her to stop. Then the two of us could live in peace, somewhere far, far away from it all.* Maria would likely resist this with all her might. Linus just couldn't bring himself to unquestioningly support everything that she so fervently believed.

Maria looked up at his serious expression, and her face clouded over. "Linus, why are..."

"Hm?"

"Never mind, it's nothing. Let's get going." The concerned look on her face quickly faded, and she intertwined her fingers with Linus's as they walked on side by side. Despite their closeness, Linus was all too aware of the impenetrable wall between them.

◇ ◇ ◇

After pressing deeper into demon country, Tsyon showed up again to put an end to their progress. They'd fought him several times at this point, each time managing to push him back.

"You guys are downright chilly! I've got just the thing for ya... Flare Meteorite!!"

Tsyon summoned up a massive ball of fire. Wary of how deeply it would cut into his magic reserves, he didn't use the Illegal Formula to make it any bigger or more powerful than usual this time. The party of heroes had been diminished to a point where he could afford to hold back.

Linus, the one member of the party whose combat skill remained unaffected, launched a volley of three arrows from just outside of Tsyon's range. The arrows split off shortly ahead of their mark and flew in toward Tsyon from different directions.

"Looks like one of you is still red hot!! Still gonna have to up your game to scratch me, though!" Flames enveloped Tsyon's body like a suit of armor, incinerating Linus's arrows on contact.

Linus wasn't ready to give up so easily. He drew his bowstring and let off another three arrows. *CRACK!* They flew through the air at immense speed, hinting that this was an entirely different type of attack from his previous attempt.

"Mighty impressive. But still not good enough!" Tsyon shot off a volley of flaming arrows of his own.

Jean took this as his opportunity to launch a spell. "Blue Flame!" The azure fire flickered through the air like a floating spirit as it closed in on Tsyon.

"Heh, you're going to use fire affinity magic against me? Have you gone mad?"

It was a rather weak attack. So weak, in fact, that Tsyon didn't see any reason to even address it. Instead, he focused his attention on Linus's arrows.

Tsyon's fire arrows collided with Linus's barrage and exploded. A moment later, Linus's shattered volley pushed through, wrapped in a protective barrier of wind.

"Huh, those were no normal arrows."

"That there is Telemessenger! Even if you destroy the arrows themselves, they'll still pursue you to the ends of the earth!"

Linus was more than a gifted archer—he could also draw on his wind affinity to imbue his arrows. Though he was weaker than most dedicated mages, it combined with his natural skill to make for a powerful attack.

Tsyon tried to shake the arrows trailing behind him, with little effect. Even if he could destroy them in a powerful blast, that would only increase the projectiles chasing after him.

Jean's Blue Flame continued to slowly close in.

"Try this!" He stopped in midair, letting the attacks converge. "Blaaaaaze Fiiiiiiiiire!!"

Tsyon's body was enveloped in a massive ball of fire that incinerated everything it touched. Linus's arrows were reduced to ash in an instant, though Jean's Blue Flame remained unaffected. The blue ball of fire wormed through the inferno, and the Demon Chief clicked his tongue in annoyance, reaching out to snuff out the attack.

Ordinary fire posed no threat to him. But this blue flame quickly wrapped itself around his arm and began to sap the heat from his body.

"Wait, this...this isn't fire? I can't move my arm! Is this ice? My Blaze Fire should have burnt that away!"

Jean smirked at the sight of the bewildered Tsyon.

"Oh, Blue Flame is definitely a fire attack...blended with an ice element. I imagine it must be hard for a simpleton like yourself to truly comprehend. Ha...gyaha-hahaha! Anyway, now that we've come this far, it's time for my next attack. Medusa Wind!"

Jean put his hands together, though it didn't look like anything actually happened.

A moment later, Tsyon felt a blast of wind against his face. He winced, brought his hand up to his cheek, and was surprised to feel stone. He tried to pluck it away, but it clung tight to his flesh.

"You... Did you turn my skin to stone?!"

The blast of wind clearly had something to do with this. Now rattled, Tsyon took off at high speed.

"You're up, Linus."

In the same instant the words left Jean's mouth, an arrow made contact with Tsyon's shoulder.

"Nngah! Damn you little buggers! Promethe..."

Tsyon was done holding back. He began to summon his most powerful attack, but Maria was quick to put a stop to that.

"Sacred Lance!"

A radiant lance shot toward Tsyon. In spite of his attempts to twist his body out of the way, the lance still found its mark and pierced his right arm.

"Graaaaugh!! Why you little...!!"

Alas, Maria wasn't done quite yet.

"Spiral!"

The lance of light began to spin within the wound.

"What the hell? It's...gaah! Spinning?! Ngyaaaauh!!"

The lance spun like a drill, boring deeper and deeper through flesh and muscle before piercing straight through the bone. Tsyon's arm was reduced to little more than shredded pieces of meat.

"Haauh...nng...you...bastards...!!"

He wasn't ready to call it quits. Under no circumstance

could he let them get close to Sheitoom, but Jean and Maria both had their next spells ready to go, while Linus sighted down his bow at his target. Cyrill stood by with her sword slumped in her hand and a dejected look on her face. Even without her, though, they were still powerful enough to put his life at risk.

Tsyon imagined Sheitoom's tear-streaked face. He had to stay alive. No matter what, he just couldn't die yet.

"Dammit, I...!"

Overcome with grief, he picked up the remains of his severed arm and turned to flee.

"Element Burst!"

"Judgment Storm!"

Jean and Maria both unleashed their most powerful attacks at the escaping Demon Chief.

Element Burst was a special attack that combined all four affinities into a powerful beam which could destroy nearly anything it touched. The beam of white light could easily be mistaken for a light affinity attack, though this was just a side effect of the four affinities mixing together.

Judgment Storm was a massive blade of light meant to enact holy judgment upon its targets. The blade spun toward its opponent at high speed, incinerating anyone within its range of effect due to its powerful shock wave.

Tsyon dodged out of the way of the Judgment Storm, though not completely. It still caught part of his shoulder, but so little remained of his right arm that this wasn't cause for concern. The Element Burst, however, caught his left arm. The powerful spell quickly overcame his own magic defense and began to spread throughout his body.

"Hnnngaaaaaaauuuugh!!"

After coursing through his body, the blast of light finally curved and shot up, sending him straight up into the sky, through the clouds and beyond. Though badly hurt, Tsyon somehow managed to make his escape.

Tsyon entered the castle and went immediately to his room, where he collapsed to the floor.

"I need to heal this up before Sheitoom sees me...hnng. Man, gaah...I can't let her see me like this..."

The problem, though, was finding someone to help. He'd need to find his way out of the castle unseen and stealthily make his way to a suitable accomplice.

Tsyon heaved for breath as he grabbed ahold of the wall to pull himself back up to his feet. Just then...

"Oh, you're back?" The one person he'd been hoping to avoid called outside his door.

"You can't be serious..." Tsyon slumped back down to the floor.

For the briefest of moments, he clung to the hope that she'd leave if he just stayed quiet, but alas, that wasn't to be. After all, he and Sheitoom often barged into each other's rooms without bothering to ask permission.

"I know you're in there, ya know. I could hear you! I'm comin' in!"

Sheitoom's voice took on a petulant tone—she clearly resented being ignored—as she pushed the door open, not bothering to wait for a response. She immediately let out a gasp as she laid eyes on Tsyon.

"What happened to you?! Did the heroes manage to injure you this badly?!"

"You could say that. I'm really not much to look at right now."

"Wait, is this why you were quiet earlier?? You know, I already knew you weren't much of a looker!"

"You wound me, Sheitoom."

Sheitoom immediately went about healing his physical wounds, though it did little to help his injured pride. Even his arm, torn from his body moments ago, quickly regenerated to reassume its proper place. Sheitoom had a rare affinity that gave her domain over both light and dark magic. Tsyon liked to tease her about how unlike a Demon Lord it was for her to use curative spells.

"Thanks."

The way he locked eyes with her brought a pink blush to Sheitoom's cheeks. "Don't keep secrets from me, okay? Just tell me when you need help."

"Hey, I just wanna be cool, okay?"

"Grow up and get over yourself. You and your stupid popped collar."

"No way. That's—"

"Who you are, right. I know what you're going to say, so don't even bother. I just think you'd look cool without that stupid thing."

Sheitoom's annoyance was clear in her voice. In reality, she didn't like the idea of other demons finding him attractive, but of course, she would never admit that out loud.

She stood up and plopped down on Tsyon's bed. "Anyway, what happened back there? They really did a number on you."

"I dunno. They just whipped out some spells I'd never seen before and completely overpowered me." Tsyon got up off the floor and sat down next to her.

"They got more powerful, huh? And here I was, hoping we were about to be done with all this now that they've lost so many members."

"You were definitely right about the humans coming to realize they'd been lied to, but the reduction in their numbers didn't quite turn out as expected." Tsyon ruffled Sheitoom's hair, and she scooted closer.

Demons weren't warlike by nature. Sheitoom took after her mother in that she believed in the inherent goodness of others and had led a relatively carefree life. She had already evacuated the demons directly in the path of the heroes up north to minimize casualties. Most of her subjects obeyed readily, though a few had defied her orders. She had originally appointed the Demon Chiefs and sent them out to harass the heroes to appease those people, but even that simple act weighed heavily on her.

"But how could they get so much more powerful with such little training?" said Tsyon.

"My only guess is that they have Origin's power backing them up."

"They were using rotation, connection, and even growth-based magic, so it would make sense. Hey, are you sure your seal is still holding firm?"

"The book outlining the sealing technique is in a place only the Demon Lord can access. Besides, Dhiza and I are the only ones with any knowledge of its contents. I'm confident there's been no change in the seal."

"Well, the humans back in the capital have been acting strangely for at least fifty years or so now."

"Right, back during Mother's time. I've heard we were on good terms until then."

"I don't imagine she could have screwed up that bad... so what happened?"

Ritus—the previous Demon Lord, and Sheitoom's mother—fell ill and passed away shortly after the human-demon war thirty years prior. Compared to how long demons usually lived, her life was cut incredibly short. Sheitoom and Dhiza had cared for her right to the end. At her deathbed, Dhiza held her hand tightly as Ritus asked her faithful aide to keep watch over her daughter. With that, she fell into an endless slumber.

Shortly thereafter, the young Sheitoom took on the mantle of Demon Lord. With the support of Dhiza, Tsyon, and Neigass, she continued to watch over and maintain the seal. But despite their efforts, the humans had somehow managed to obtain the power of Origin. Neigass had embarked on a journey to try and uncover how, though she hadn't turned up anything noteworthy.

"If things keep going this way, the heroes will make their way to the castle and break the seal." said Sheitoom.

"I guess we have no choice left but to kill them."

"But that's almost certainly what Origin wants! If we kill the heroes, then we're only going to anger the humans even more and further this feud!"

"Sorry, I got ahead of myself."

"No, I'm sorry. I got a little too emotional there. Besides, you only wound up like this because I underestimated the humans." Sheitoom leaned back against Tsyon. That one simple act only drove home what he already knew: he had to protect Sheitoom at all costs. "So, how can we stop them?"

"We have to stop the church and the kingdom," Tsyon said. "They're the ones supporting the heroes."

"We're far past the point where they might listen to us. Our letters go unanswered, as do our requests for a meeting. All of the nobles who were even remotely sympathetic to us have either fallen from grace or been arrested on trumped-up charges."

"We can't overthrow the church or the royal family all on our own. We'll need human allies. But who?"

"Every human alive today has been raised believing that demons are terrible abominations."

"Well, what about the people who left the hero party?"

"Gadhio, Eterna, and...Flum, was it?" Sheitoom never actually met them personally. She only heard of these people through Tsyon and Neigass's stories. "It might

be worth reaching out. Didn't Neigass run into them a while back?"

"That's right. She's been away for quite a while."

"I imagine her investigation isn't going so well. Anyway, we can ask her when she comes back. It can't hurt to try."

"You're right."

With the pressing matter settled, a calm silence fell over the room. Sheitoom pressed her cheek against Tsyon's newly healed shoulder. She felt a tinge of worry come over her as she caught a whiff of the freshly dried blood.

"Wh-why do people have to fight?" she murmured.

"They want to get their way, I guess."

"They could still have what they want without fighting, though."

Tsyon wrapped an arm around Sheitoom in a tight embrace. As she felt the warmth travel from his body into hers, she whispered to herself: "I wish this time could last forever."

After their battle with Tsyon, the party continued on to their planned destination, using a teleportation stone so Cyrill could cast Return and take them back to the waypoint in the castle's basement.

"Well, well," said Jean, "I'd say that went swimmingly. What do you say to a celebratory pint, Linus?"

"Sorry, I've got plans."

"How rude. I finally invite you out and this is how you respond? Whatever, I'm not going to let you spoil my wonderful mood!" Jean's high-pitched cackle echoed off the walls as he made his exit.

Cyrill frowned slightly as she watched him leave. Something was clearly bothering her, though Maria didn't seem to notice. She, too, was in a great mood.

"Hey, Maria..."

Maria walked out of the room before Linus could finish speaking. Fortunately, it didn't look like she was ignoring him, exactly; she just was too caught up in the moment to hear him.

Linus's face screwed up in concern. It was all he could do to just stand there.

"I wonder what happened to them." Cyrill finally broke the silence, asking the question hanging heavily in the air.

"Beats me. They've been acting pretty strange for a while now."

"Maybe it's because I'm just no use anymore..."

"Don't worry too much about that. It'll come back to you with time. We need you on this journey, and we all know that."

"I guess."

Linus's words had little obvious effect on Cyrill's mood. She left the room without another word and made her way to one of the castle's balconies for some fresh air.

There must have been something especially approachable about her, because ever since she became a hero, Cyrill often found herself swarmed whenever she was out. Every attempt to take a moment to herself was a battle to avoid being backed into a corner. Standing on the balcony, she looked down at the people milling about below. Up ahead, she could see the confectionery she and Flum had visited so many weeks ago.

Cyrill closed her eyes. The memories came flooding in as if they took place mere moments ago.

"Now this is city living! Sponge cakes with cream filling, more fruits than you can shake a stick at...this is great!"

"Mmm, everything's delicious!"

"Tee hee. You should pace yourself, you know! You won't even taste it going down."

"No problem, I'll just eat another one. What about you, Flum?"

"Hmm... Sure, I'll have seconds, too!"

They'd licked their plates clean in a matter of seconds and then returned to the menu to order another round.

43

After the waiter took their orders, Flum had turned back to look at Cyrill.

"I'm so glad we had a chance to meet, Cyrill."

"Huh? What makes you say that all of a sudden?"

"You know, I've just felt so anxious ever since I learned I was chosen. You guys are all so amazing, and I'm, well, useless. If you weren't here, I probably would've just run away a long time ago."

"Oh, Flum..."

Flum had blushed slightly as she spoke. *"I'm glad we met. I really, truly mean that."*

The truth, however, was exactly the opposite. Cyrill had felt like she might go mad from the mounting pressure and the anxiety it was causing her. If not for Flum, she might have had a complete breakdown. She should have just said so, at the time. She should have thanked Flum, but her throat seized up with emotion, and she couldn't get any words out.

Cyrill cursed herself for her lack of skill at communicating.

Her trip down memory lane continued, the scene in her mind's eye changing to another event that occurred shortly thereafter.

"It's all your fault that someone got hurt. How do you plan to make up for it, huh?"

"I... I'm sorry..." Flum sat in the dirt, her knees held close to her chest. She looked absolutely miserable as Cyrill and Jean looked down at her.

"You have no idea just how useless you are, you little scum! You think saying you're sorry will make it all better?!" Jean raged.

"Hnnph!"

Jean grabbed the collar of her shirt and yanked her up into the air. He only really yelled at her like this when no one was around.

Flum looked desperately to Cyrill, the only one left who could help her out of this situation. But Cyrill averted her gaze, pretending she hadn't seen anything.

There were plenty of excuses she could offer for her behavior: the pressure of being a hero was just too great, she was tired of worrying about others all the time, Jean was too terrifying to stand up to... None of them were sufficient to explain why she would turn her back on Flum like that.

Flum couldn't take the pressure and disappeared, never to be seen again. Now Cyrill was without her dearest companion, the person who brought her such happiness and supported her in her time of need.

Now she had no one.

She had dug her own grave.

"Oh, Cyrill."

Cyrill heard a gentle voice call out from behind her. She turned around and caught sight of a familiar figure. "Maria?"

The look on her face was so warm and compassionate, like a buoy to a man lost at sea. Maria stepped closer and took Cyrill's hand. She pressed a black crystal into her palm. "This is a core."

"A core?" Looking closer, Cyrill felt almost as if she were being drawn in by the spiral moving inside it. A chill ran up her spine; she knew instantly that whatever this was, it wasn't good.

"Jean and I both used these to power up," Maria explained.

Cyrill had seen the effects of that power-up for herself earlier that day. *If only I had some of that power. I might be able to help the party and get over this funk. But...*

Could something like this really grant you such immense power with no repercussions?

"Don't you want to be a useful member of the party?" Though there was no detectable change in Maria's voice, the pressure behind her words was apparent. "Just give it a try. I'm sure you'll be impressed with the results."

"Is...is it really okay to use?"

"I'm using it, and besides, it was made by the church. You can trust it."

She had no reason not to trust Maria.

Cyrill thanked Maria and slid the core into her bag. With that task done, Maria bid her farewell and made her way back into the castle.

As Maria walked through the castle halls, a blonde woman in a white lab coat approached her, causing Maria to stop. The woman readjusted her glasses on the bridge of her nose and smiled. "So, how did it go?"

"Ah, Echidna. Cyrill took it, just as I thought she would."

"Glad to hear it. I'd hate for all the time we spent creating the core to go to waste."

The voluptuous woman with the pouty face was Echidna Ipeila, a high-ranking researcher within the church. Only Mother rivaled her in influence.

"And how do you find the core? Any side effects?"

"None thus far. I've heard nothing but great things about the Chimera core, so I don't anticipate any issues."

Echidna laughed. "Good to hear. I have no intention of being outdone by the Children or Necromancy projects, after all. Still, I was a touch worried about what might happen to you. It's pretty rare to use the cores on a living person."

"I appreciate your concern, but I have places to be."

"Ah, right, sorry. I guess we'll talk again later, then." She shot Maria a quick smile before heading off down the hallway, leaving Maria alone once again.

Maria closed her eyes and focused on the voices echoing in her head.

"Not bad."

"Just a little bit more."

"You don't need it."

"I'm worried."

"Need to recover as soon as possible."

Countless voices all spoke at once.

"I understand, Origin. My master." Maria perked up.

"Combine."

"Connect."

"No, kill."

"We must crush the will of the stars first."

"What to do about the next possibility?"

"We must connect."

"Kill, we must kill, kill, kiiill."

The core only served to amplify these voices. They were usually all in alignment, but lately, they seemed to break apart and take on a life of their own.

It was all Flum's fault.

"First and foremost, we need to get Cyrill to the castle."

They could still pull the plan off once they achieved that. Maria needed to make that happen in order to make her dream of releasing the seal on Origin a reality.

"And then everything will die," she muttered to herself as she turned to look out the window. "I hate them, I hate all of those demons. And that's why I need to make sure they're eradicated."

She could only be her true self when no one was watching.

"Hate...hate them..."

A distracting thought began to break through the noise. A smile, an image of a man.

She shook her head to clear her mind.

I need to forget about him.

She had no time for such distractions.

I can't leave any room for hope.

Trust would only lead to betrayal.

"Humans are awful. All life is awful. That's why it must be destroyed."

She bit her thumb until she tasted the metallic tang of blood.

Her heart was consumed by hate. This had become her whole reason for being; even her life in the church was built around fulfilling this goal. There was no one she would not betray, no compromise she would not make, no course of action whatsoever she would not take.

There was no room for uncertainty.

There was nothing—or at least she told herself as much—to tie her down to this world.

ROLL
OVER
AND
DIE

001

That Which He's Lost

THREE DAYS HAD PASSED since the whole incident surrounding Ink came to a close.

The West District was surprisingly calm, and the church still hadn't come looking for Flum or any of the others involved. It was possible they simply didn't know Ink was still alive or that they'd decided to give Flum some breathing room.

In any case, Flum tried to ease her heart as she and Gadhio made their way through the eerily quiet town. The wind blew through the narrow alley and kicked up the familiar, musty stench of the West District. Flum scowled and ran a hand through her golden-brown hair.

Gadhio adjusted his coat. "Sure is quiet." Earlier that morning, he'd shown up at Flum's house and asked if she wanted to accompany him to the guild.

Flum looked up at Gadhio. "It seems like the church hasn't come after us yet, either."

Over the past two nights, Gadhio had managed to discover where Mother and her cronies were hiding out. By combining the information he already gathered with the additional facts Ink was able to provide, he was able to track them back down to the church. The facilities were already abandoned when he got there, but it was still a victory, considering they deprived the opposition of a research lab. Mother and the Spiral Children were probably on the hunt for a new hideout elsewhere in the capital.

"Things may have calmed down quite a bit now that Dein's gone, but I doubt this peace will last very long." Gadhio closed his eyes and shook his head in annoyance. "I can feel a headache coming on just trying to imagine what those thugs will try without a leader to keep them in line."

Dein had ruled over every scapegrace and outlaw in the West District once. Without him around to exercise some control, they were running rampant.

"Someone's gotta step up to try and usurp Dein's place," Gadhio said.

"I can't imagine that'll be easy," Flum said. For all his shortcomings, Dein had had charisma. Your average street punk couldn't easily fill his shoes.

"I figure they'll break up into different factions and vie for power. That's why we need to get to the guild and start putting our own plans into motion."

"At the guild?"

Flum hadn't bothered to ask Gadhio why he was taking her to the guild, assuming it would become clear when they got there. A few moments later, she led the way through the doors of the West District guild. Y'lla, the receptionist, was resting her cheek in her hand when she caught sight of the newcomers. A scowl instantly took over her bored expression.

"Heyaa! Shop's cloooooosed for the day!"

"For a receptionist, you sure hate to work."

"Ever since Dein disappeared, things have been nice and calm. I'd really appreciate it if you don't ruin this for me."

"Isn't there such a thing as being a little too independent?"

"Hardly. I'd love to take this as far as I can. So why don't you go on and scram, dirty little slave girl. Shoo, shoo!"

"You're just as petty and annoying as ever."

Y'lla turned her head to the side at Flum's comeback, as if she had nothing more to say.

"C'mon, you sent a brand-new adventurer who didn't even have her license yet to go take down a pack of were-wolves. I bet if the Central District guild caught wind of this, you'd be out of a job for sure."

"Heh, you best take off your rose-colored glasses, kiddo. You think they'd take some D-Ranked slave at her word? Move along and go play with your little bandaged-up doll to your heart's content."

"You'd really be in for it if the guild master were ever around!"

Y'lla laughed. "Just let it go and stop holding onto dreams, kiddo. Our guild master is a super important S-Ranked adventurer. He's got better things to do than deal with the West District guild!"

Before the argument between the two women could heat up any further, Gadhio finally stepped in and made his presence known. He looked Y'lla dead in the eye.

"You called?"

She froze instantly in place, as if she'd found herself face to face with a dragon. The color drained from her cheeks instantly, and she started sweating.

"G-G-Gadhio Lathcutt? But aren't you out on the great journey??"

"Some things came up, and I had to step down. Anyway, it sounds like you called me. So what exactly is going on here, Ms. Y'lla Jerishin?"

"Ah, uh, right. Hey, Slowe? Could you come out here for a moment and help me with something?"

No answer. Slowe usually leapt to her beck and call,

but apparently, even he was smart enough to know better than to stand up against Gadhio.

Y'lla scowled, her shoulders slumping forward. "Well, looks like you're no help."

She turned toward Flum in a bizarre, last-ditch grab at salvation. Obviously, Flum had no interest in coming to Y'lla's aid. She just stuck her tongue out at her, instead.

"You brat!!" Y'lla shot an angry glare back at Flum, once again letting her anger get the better of her.

"Hey, so you're the guild master of this place, Gadhio?" Flum asked.

"You could say that. They pushed the role on me years ago. I never really did much about it."

"Aah! So that's what you meant about needing to put together a plan of action at the guild! Since you're the guild master, you can crack down on all the shady business here in the West District."

"Speaking of which...it sounds like this woman here almost got you killed, Flum."

"That's right. They had me hunt D-Rank monsters for my trial assignment."

"You're supposed to be given an F-Ranked task in order to get your license. Going two whole ranks higher could easily get a novice adventurer killed. We can't be having that."

"N-no, it was all Dein's doing, you see! I tried to stop him, y'know! Really! And, besides, just look! She managed to complete the task anyway. No harm, no foul. Flum agrees, don't you?"

Flum brought her hand up to her mouth to stifle a laugh. The look on Y'lla's face was just too comical for her to resist. Y'lla squeezed her hand into a tight fist underneath the counter. The gall of a slave to make fun of her...

"I have no qualms against firing you right here on the spot. What do you think, Flum?"

"Hmm..."

"W-wait a second! You're not really thinking it over, are you??"

"I mean, would it really be so bad if you got fired?" Sure, Flum had managed to survive her encounter, but that was only after having all her limbs severed. Anyone else would never have made it out alive. "It's not like we're friends."

"W-well, how about we start getting to know each other? Whaddya think? Besides, how am I supposed to survive if I get fired?"

"You could always sell your body."

"You cold, cruel-hearted...!"

Flum fought the urge to throw the same accusation back at her. Though she was a rather disagreeable woman, unlike Dein and his crew, Y'lla could still change. Ever since Dein and the rest of his clique moved on to the church, she'd had less and less to do with them. Flum didn't see much reason to keep pushing the matter.

"I think a pay cut is good enough," she told Gadhio.

"Heh, you're too kind, Flum."

"Oh, thank goodness. Th... Hey! Did you say reduction in pay? Now hold up a second! Why should my pay get cut?!"

"You should be thankful you weren't fired."

"Hmph." Y'lla decided to stop while she was ahead.

"Now that I'm here, I'm not going to tolerate the way you've been slacking off," Gadhio said. "You'd best be ready to actually do your job from now on."

She hung her head at this. "Yes, sir."

Flum restrained herself to just smirking as she watched this play out.

Gadhio mentioned that he had some work to take care of before heading off into the back room. Y'lla glared daggers at Flum the moment he was gone.

"This is all your fault. I'm gonna have to cut back my food budget now because of you!"

"Hey, you reap what you sow."

"Where do you get off with such a high and mighty attitude? While we're at it, if you know Gadhio Lathcutt, does that mean you really are *the* Flum Apricot?"

"Oh, so you finally noticed?"

"I mean, who would figure a legendary hero would be a slave slumming it up in the West District now?"

"Eterna's here too, you know."

"Eterna? Eterna Rinebow? How is the quest to defeat the Demon Lord even gonna succeed without the three of you? I mean, what is the church even thinking?!"

To a normal commoner, the very idea that three members had left the great journey to stay in the capital was cause for great concern. There had been rumors about Eterna being in the capital, of course, but they hadn't gained much traction. She rarely left the house, anyway. Gadhio, however, was a completely different story. It was hard to miss such a massive figure moving about town, and that would only get worse as he took a more active role in running the guild.

"I've been hearing a lot of strange stories lately," Y'lla said, "and I can't help but wonder if the church is somehow involved with those disgusting dead bodies we ran across the other day..."

Apparently, rumors of the church's involvement with the swarm of eyes had spread rapidly through the capital. A major figure like Gadhio abandoning the great journey—tantamount to disregarding the church's orders—only added fuel to the fire.

"Also...can he really just stroll back into the guild like this?"

"What, do you have a problem with Gadhio?"

"I can't really say. I just know that there are some out there who call him 'Gadhio the Coward.'"

Flum snorted at this. "*Gadhio?* The very embodiment of bravery?"

"I mean, he is now, sure. But according to the stories, he left his friends behind and came back alone once."

"So now you're just making up stories 'cause you're bitter about your pay getting docked, huh?"

"No, of course not! Listen, try asking some other adventurer if you don't believe me. Or just ask Gadhio himself."

Flum couldn't imagine even forming the words to ask Gadhio if he really was a coward. All she could do was offer up a noncommittal nod.

A short time later, Gadhio finally returned.

"Starting tomorrow, I'll be here to perform my job as the guild master."

Having thus notified Y'lla of his intentions, Gadhio and Flum left the guild together before turning toward

the East District, where Gadhio's home was located. Flum followed in silence, her face screwed up in a look of concern. Y'lla's story was still fresh on her mind.

"Did something she say get to you?"

"Not something she said exactly, more...a story I heard."

The street grew much wider, cleaner, and busier as they crossed into the Central District.

Eyes quickly fell on Gadhio's imposing figure as they traversed the bustling crowd. Every once in a while, someone would glance at Flum, but only to gawk at the symbol burnt into her cheek.

Finally, Gadhio broke the silence. "Gadhio the coward...yeah?"

"So you know about it?"

"I mean, it's true."

"No it's not! Why, you're the..."

"No, I am a coward. And I must bear the weight of that label."

His tone made it clear that this was the final word on the matter. There had to be more to the story, but Flum dared not push any further. The two walked along in near silence. An uncomfortable tension hung between them as they passed into the East District and wound their way to the gates of a grand manor.

As soon as Gadhio came into view, a soldier standing guard at the entrance bowed his head. "Welcome back, sir."

"Whoa, you live here??"

Beyond the steel-barred entrance lay a sprawling yard—practically a park. Farther on, Flum could make out the shape of a large building.

"Well, it's not all mine exactly."

The two stepped through the gate and onto a stone-paved path. Trees bearing red blossoms twisted overhead, creating a sort of natural archway directing them toward the manor proper up ahead.

Off in one corner of the yard stood a massive tree that lorded over all the greenery around it. In another corner, there was a space set up for children, filled with swings, play equipment, and a sandbox.

Flum heard that S-Rank adventurers could make quite a living for themselves, though she had always imagined this in more mundane terms, like being able to afford to eat steak every day or order whole cakes just for yourself. This was something else entirely. Flum, the little girl from the country, stared around her with great interest as they walked through the lavish yard. The look of excitement and wonder on her face seemed to affect Gadhio, too, as he slowly relaxed his tense expression.

Once they made it to the front of the house, Flum could hear someone running full tilt inside. The door flung open, and a beaming little girl bounded into Gadhio's arms.

"You're back, Daddy!!"

This hit Flum like a thunderclap.

Thinking it over, it shouldn't have been all that surprising. Gadhio was thirty-two, after all. But she'd never once heard him mention a family before, so all she could do was stare at him wide-eyed, her mouth hanging open in shock.

Gadhio put his hand to his head and let out a heavy sigh.

ROLL
OVER
AND
DIE

002

Why We Fight

"**W**HOA, GADHIO, you have a kid??"

"No, I... Listen, Hallom, didn't I tell you to not call me Daddy?" Gadhio gently patted the girl's head as he spoke. He seemed so at ease, so familiar with her that they certainly *looked* like father and daughter, whatever their actual connection was.

"Daddy is my daddy. Besides, Mommy agreed!" Hallom puffed out her cheeks in annoyance.

Gadhio stood there smiling wryly to himself when a red-haired woman in her thirties approached the door. "Welcome home, Gadhio," she said.

"Oh, hi, Kleyna."

Flum figured this must be his wife.

"C'mon, just let her call you Daddy."

"I can't. It wouldn't be right to Sohma."

"Sohma...and Tia too, right? Gah. Sometimes you're too faithful for your own good, you know."

"Can we talk about this later? We have a guest."

"Ah, I see." Kleyna finally took notice of Flum's presence. "Sorry for discussing such heavy matters before you. How rude of me. You wouldn't happen to be Flum, would you? Gadhio's told me so much about you and how talented you are."

Flum blushed at the sudden compliment but accepted it graciously. She'd grown a lot since her days of completely zeroed out stats and no grasp of the Cavalier Arts to speak of.

"Anyway, this is no place to sit around and chat. Please, come inside. Will you take her to the parlor, Gadhio?"

"Right. We've got a lot to discuss, so I'd appreciate it if you could give us some privacy."

"Aaah, that kind of conversation. Gotcha."

Hallom pouted. "Awww, but I wanted to play with Daddy!"

Gadhio hefted the girl up and passed her over to Kleyna. The girl looked to be around six, maybe seven years old. She couldn't have been light, and yet Kleyna handled her with ease. Flum noticed scars on Kleyna's arms—marks of someone who used to live as an adventurer, maybe? Perhaps she and Gadhio were old friends.

"Right, right. Daddy will play with you a bit later, so why don't you play with Mommy for a while."

"I'm bored of playing with Mommy. I want Daddy!!!"

Kleyna lifted the squirming child up and over her shoulder even as she continued to protest. Holding the girl in place seemed easy enough for her as they both disappeared farther into the house. Flum, still in shock over what she'd just witnessed stared blankly at the now-empty doorway.

"C'mon, Flum."

"R-right!"

Flum had to follow at a slow jog just to keep up with Gadhio's impressive stride.

Expensive-looking paintings and a large chandelier adorned the parlor's walls and ceiling. A gasp of surprise escaped Flum's lips as she sat on the perfectly padded sofa. Everywhere she looked were signs of extravagant wealth, verging on excess at some points. Nothing in the room seemed to match the Gadhio she knew.

Gadhio let out a sigh and sat down across from Flum. "I was supposed to just get you up to speed about the church and hand off some gear."

"Gear?"

"There's a lot of gear we've acquired over the years out in the storehouse. Some of it is cursed, so I figured it might be of use to you."

"You're just going to give it to me?"

"It's of no use to me."

"Thank you! I'm more than happy to take it off your hands."

The majority of adventurers tended to simply throw away cursed gear or, in cases where the curse was particularly extreme, auction them off as curiosities. She'd seen some of these items during her market runs, but so far, nothing really caught her eye. Meanwhile, the equipment she was currently wearing had been dug out of a pile of corpses, so she was more than happy to accept Gadhio's offer.

"But that'll have to wait until later. I'm sure you're wondering about who that girl back there was."

"Of course I am."

After all, he was living with a woman who clearly wasn't his wife and a young girl he insisted wasn't his daughter. Flum's head felt like it might burst from all the bizarre explanations running through her mind.

"Kleyna is Sohma's wife. Sohma was a good friend of mine, and Hallom is their child. He died fighting a monster six years ago."

The pieces began to fall into place for Flum. Assuming Hallom was seven years old or so, that'd mean Gadhio was the only father she really knew. That explained why she called him Daddy, but Kleyna...what about her?

"Was Sohma a strong warrior like you?"

"Even stronger. He was our team leader."

"You were on a team?"

"Sohma, Kleyna, Tia, Jaine, Louh, and me. Three S-Rank and three A-Rank adventurers. We prided ourselves on never losing a battle, no matter who we found ourselves up against. Pure arrogance on our part."

That was hardly arrogance. With three S-Rank adventurers on the team, they were stronger than pretty much anyone else around.

"In fact, we built this house for the six of us."

"Wow, you were all so close that you even lived together?"

"We just loved each other's company. Tia and I had just recently gotten married. We were in the prime of our lives." A sad look overtook Gadhio's face as he gazed down at the table in front of him.

"You were married?"

"Well, Sohma and Kleyna got hitched, so I figured I might as well be, too. Tia died only a short while after I vowed to protect her with my heart and soul. I was a

71

feckless coward." His voice was filled with anger and resentment.

"I'm guessing they don't live here anymore... What happened?"

"Six years ago, we took on a mission to slay a dragon. We joked on the way there about how it'd be a cakewalk. We'd be back home in the capital in no time. Hallom was still so young—not even one at the time—so Kleyna stayed home. But the creature we ran into was no ordinary dragon." Gadhio took a deep breath as the memories came flooding back. His voice grew strained. "It was a creature with a helix where its face should have been."

"You fought against a monster possessed by an Origin core six years ago??" Flum couldn't stop herself from blurting out.

Gadhio responded with a grave nod. "We never even saw it strike. Jaine and Louh died instantly, but Sohma fought on even as his body was pulped inside his armor. Tia took the hit that was meant for me. It pierced right through her heart. I was the only one to walk away."

Even six years later, the pain was clearly still fresh. Flum doubted Gadhio would ever forgive himself as long as he lived.

"I ran for my life. My peers called me a coward the moment I set foot in the capital again. They weren't wrong, of course. I was a coward. What else would you call someone who left their friends and wife behind to save themselves?" Gadhio clenched his jaw and squeezed his hand into a tight fist. "I made my way back to the place we were attacked to at least try to make things right with a proper burial, but all I found was Sohma's armor and sword. I never had a chance to bring my wife home."

The regret in his voice was palpable.

"I devoted myself to the sword to ensure I would never again commit such a sin. As long as I wear Sohma's armor and wield his sword, I will remember how low I sank and remember to go *no lower*. It doesn't lessen the pain, but my feelings don't figure into it."

Flum was at a loss for words. She'd only known Gadhio for about six months. What could she even say? Her mind raced.

"No matter what your past may hold, you're still a hero to me, Gadhio. I could never think of you as a coward!"

Her words were harmless but pointless. Flum was annoyed at herself for not being able to come up with anything more meaningful, but even so, Gadhio's expression softened slightly, as if her intent had gotten through just the same. He began to look like his normal self.

"You're really too kind, kiddo."

"No, I just..."

"Anyway, enough of this sob story. We have other things to discuss."

"About the church, right? Is there more than what we already talked about?"

"Correct. There are a few more things I learned back at the Cathedral. I should have told you right after our battle, but I wasn't in the best condition to assemble a coherent sentence at the time. I needed time to collect my thoughts."

Gadhio had been targeted by the eye-swarm because of the intel he gathered on the Children when he snuck into the Cathedral. It was pretty impressive that he still remembered the details of what he found, considering the circumstances.

"I don't have the full story, but apparently there are three research teams working with these cores."

"I heard from Ottilie that there were multiple teams, and only one's responsible for the Spiral Children," Flum said.

Gadhio nodded. "Within the church, that team is referred to as the 'Children,' due to the nature of their work. 'Necromancy' and 'Chimera' are the other two."

"The names alone creep me out." Flum felt a chill run up her spine.

"Team Necromancy has been working on using spiral cores to raise the dead as front-line soldiers. Dafydd Chalmas is their leader."

"I think I remember Ottilie telling me something about researchers named Dafydd and Echidna going in and out of the Cathedral..."

"Echidna oversees team Chimera. Each team also has a cardinal assigned to it."

"Those are the ones who report directly to the pope, right? I remember hearing there were around five of them."

"Cardinal Talchi Kanswolker manages the church land and buildings. He's also in charge of the Necromancy project."

"So he's pulling double duty? I guess they must be running short of hands."

"He's likely just an observer, not a manager. Researchers tend to get carried away—take how Ink was handled, for example. I doubt the church authorized that."

All other evidence of human experiments had been handled with the utmost secrecy. No matter how useless Ink may have been to Mother, if the church was involved, there was no way they would have been as careless about handing her off to Flum as Mother had.

"I guess anyone conducting that kind of research must be a messed-up individual," Flum said.

"I'd say the church is the most messed-up of them all, considering they're the ones commissioning the research

in the first place. Anyway, let's get back on track. Team Chimera is studying the use of cores to transform creatures into monsters."

"Sounds like they're coming at it from a bunch of different directions. Do you know which cardinal's in charge of Chimera?"

"Slowanach Seity. He oversees church personnel."

"So another cardinal playing dual roles. And do you know who's responsible for the Children project?"

"The records mentioned a Mich Smithee and Farmo Fimio. From what I've learned, Farmo is the head of the department that oversees healing."

"Sounds like they're all big players. I wonder if this Mich Smithee person is Mother?"

"It's pretty likely. Besides the utility of taking on an alter-ego for a clandestine operation, it sounds like the person was intent on actually playing the role."

"We only spoke briefly, but he was definitely an odd one. Now we know his name, it'll be easier to track him down."

"Correct. I plan on shadowing Mich Smithee. Losing their base of operations is sure to have stirred up the hornets' nest."

That was definitely true. Though there was still one point that Flum couldn't quite get over. "Do...do you

think that the creature that attacked you six years ago was part of the Chimera project?"

"They're the only ones using monsters like that."

So Chimera had been active outside the capital at least six years ago, if not longer. It was no great leap to infer that the Anichidey complex must have been theirs, too.

"Are you saying we should take Chimera out first?" Gadhio asked.

Flum gave a firm nod. She could only imagine the hatred Gadhio must have felt toward them. They took away not only his friends but his beloved wife as well.

"It's true that I have a personal grudge with Chimera I mean to settle, no matter the cost, but the Children or Necromancy programs are equally guilty in my eyes." Gadhio's voice took on a low and menacing tone. "In the end, we'll crush them all. I've dedicated my entire being to this end."

He was already a skilled adventurer back when he was working with the rest of his teammates, but it was clear Gadhio had improved greatly since then. For six years, he'd poured his blood, sweat, and tears into getting to where he was now.

All for hate.

With no target to focus his anger on, he'd turned that hate into his strength. Now that he'd finally found his

enemy, everything he'd kept bottled up was looking for a way out.

"And what about you, Flum?"

"What do you mean?"

"I'm still not sure about what their endgame is, but it seems likely the church sent you on the great journey because of your unique ability to destroy Origin cores. They probably aren't done with you yet."

"That's what I've been thinking, too."

Not only was the church still after her power, but so was the so-called spirit of Origin...whatever that was. When the facility in Anichidey was abandoned over a decade ago, Flum had been just a little girl living an unremarkable life in her small village. And yet, she'd found her name in the facility's notes. If they'd been fixated on her for that long, it was doubtful they'd give up so easily.

"I see that you're willing to fight them one way or another," Gadhio said. "But are you really prepared to take on such fanatics?"

The look on his face was grave, but the kindness behind his words showed through. Flum had only recently uncovered her true power. Combat took its toll not only on the body but on the spirit itself. Gadhio worried that Flum's new, harsh reality would break her down with time.

"I'm not being reactive here. I have my own motivations."

Flum's voice was steady and firm. She didn't think of herself as "strong," really. Rather, she considered herself capable of fighting as long and hard as she needed to simply because she had someone there to support her and someone to come back to. "I have Milkit, and I plan to live here in this city, together with her. That's why I fight. I may not be as powerful as you, Gadhio, but I'm still prepared to give it my all."

"This Milkit's quite important to you, huh? Maybe even..." Gadhio paused for a moment before cutting himself short. "No, there's no need to put a label on it. I'm just glad to know where you stand."

"Right. So please remember that I'm here for you whenever you need it, Gadhio."

Gadhio's expression softened into a smile to match Flum's. "I'll be taking you up on that."

After finishing their business in the parlor, Gadhio led Flum to the storehouse. The polished stone hallway glimmered beneath their feet, lined with vases, flowers, and busts. Each of the decorative doors she passed looked like works of art in their own right. Each individual item looked more expensive than Flum's entire house.

They took a flight of stairs into the basement, where Gadhio opened a door and led Flum into a room full of wooden mannequins dressed in leather and plate armor, dresses, and robes of all manners and sizes. Up on the shelves were helmets, tiaras, gauntlets, boots, brooches, and other defensive equipment. A glass case was filled with neatly arranged accessories. The wall was covered in a wide variety of weapons, including single- and dual-handed swords, spears, hammers, maces, staffs, and bows.

Flum casually cast Scan and quickly realized that all the equipment was Legendary and Epic tier. The equipment in this room alone was worth more than the entire manor upstairs.

"This is absolutely amazing..."

"I know I should just get rid of it all, since it's not doing me any good, but there are just too many memories for me to let go."

Flum hazarded a guess that some of the equipment in the room had once been used by Gadhio's friends and wife. Alas, the equipment that would really be useful to her wasn't to be found in this room but in the one beyond.

The two moved into a smaller storeroom where all the cursed equipment had been carelessly dumped. The coppery tang of blood stung Flum's nostrils as she knelt to examine the pile, spotting a steel gauntlet covered in blood. There were several other items like it in the heap.

"Louh had a thing for collecting stuff like this. All weird equipment, really."

"He must've been a pretty interesting guy."

Gadhio looked off wistfully into the distance. "We all told him to toss them out. Who would've thought that the day would come where it came in handy?"

Flum reached out toward the pile and cast Scan on each and every piece, feeling the stains that their previous owners left, even hearing the faint echoes of voices from days long past as she went through them.

Finally, she stopped at a helmet.

"Find something you like?"

"Your friend certainly acquired an impressive collection."

"You seem to be conflicted, though."

"I mean, if I'm going to take something, I can't help but think that it should be an Epic tier. It's... You're really okay with me taking something like that, right?"

"The higher the tier, the stronger the curse becomes. And the stronger it is, the less use it is to me."

"Well, that's good, then."

"So, just anything Epic tier?"

"No, not quite. I was thinking about this helmet, but..."

Flum showed the sharp-angled metal helmet to Gadhio. It was pitch-black and marked with purple streaks.

"The bizarre shape of it would really cut down on my peripheral vision. It's not just cursed. There's something else going on with it."

She clanked the face guard open and shut several times.

"That's true. Perhaps it was only meant for use as a decorative piece but wound up cursed anyway. It wouldn't be so bad if you could just sense your enemy's presence, of course."

"I can't really do that quite yet."

If she could increase her Perception, then she could locate her foes without relying on her eyes, like Gadhio could do. But as it was, the helmet was of little use to Flum, so she set it back down. She could practically feel the hate radiating from it, but she ignored it and continued her casual inspection of the equipment.

"Hmm, now this..."

Flum held up a leather belt.

Name: Leather Belt of Wailing Agony
Tier: Epic
[This equipment lowers its wearer's Endurance by 363]

[This equipment lowers its wearer's Agility by 212]

[This equipment lowers its wearer's Perception by 749]

[This equipment removes its wearer's resistance to poison]

[This equipment increases its wearer's sense of pain]

Though it had quite the foreboding name, it looked like a normal dark, double-notched leather belt. Flum wondered for a moment if the color came from the blood of many victims, but it smelled completely normal, which ruled out that theory.

Judging by its thickness and length, it wasn't for holding up pants. It seemed to be a decorative accessory, meant to wrap around your torso. She figured she could probably include it as a part of her daily wear, though she did worry about whether it would start screaming at socially inappropriate moments.

Well, she'd cross that bridge when she came to it.

"Are you sure you're okay with it? The enchantment says it increases your sense of pain." Gadhio watched Flum with a keen eye as she wrapped the belt around her torso.

Suddenly, she punched the stone floor with her fist. Blood pooled in her hand, and she felt the blow travel up through her bones. In seconds, her wounds closed, leaving her looking just as she did at the start.

"Hurts less than it used to. Reversal *rules*."

Gadhio furrowed his brow at the sight of Flum hurting herself so casually. "Pain is meant to tell you when to stop. Don't do anything stupid."

"I know. Besides, it's not like I don't feel *any* pain. In fact, I probably overdid it there."

Gadhio remained concerned. Flum tended to intentionally put herself in harm's way in a fight, an inevitable consequence of her Reversal ability, which required her to make physical contact with her target. Some might even consider that devil-may-care fighting style a tactical asset. Most people went into combat expecting their opponents to treat their bodies like the precious resources they were.

He could only hope this enchantment wouldn't make her already bad tendencies worse.

Name: Cackling Slayer's Damascus Gauntlet
Tier: Epic
[This equipment lowers its wearer's Strength by 1,312]
[This equipment lowers its wearer's Magic by 674]
[This equipment lowers its wearer's Perception by 377]

While Gadhio worried to himself, Flum picked up another piece of equipment: an angular gauntlet with spikes jutting out all the way down to the fingertips. Like most of the others, it was black. She wondered if the metal had gone black out of its deep-seated hatred for humanity, much like her Souleater blade had.

She was currently using a blood-stained steel gauntlet, but there was just no way she could keep it in the face of Epic equipment like this. Flum was a little sad to see it go, considering it was one of the first pieces of equipment she found after meeting Milkit, but it also seemed a bit odd to be sentimental about a blood-stained gauntlet.

As he pondered what to do with her unused equipment, Gadhio chimed in with a recommendation.

"Is that cursed, too? If you don't need it anymore, you can just leave it here."

"I'll take you up on that!"

Flum whispered a word of thanks to the gauntlet that had seen her through so much before placing it on top of the pile of cursed equipment. She then took her two new pieces of Epic gear and looked them over.

The belt and gauntlet disappeared in a burst of light, and the symbol on the back of her hand gave off a gentle glow. Pulling up her shirt, she noticed a similar mark located just underneath her navel.

So now she had four items equipped and altering her stats.

Strength: 2,036
Magic: 1,267
Endurance: 1,572
Agility: 1,164
Perception: 1,315

With a total stat value of 7,354, this put her firmly among the mid-range, A-Rank adventurers. Quite an impressive change compared to where she'd been when Jean first sold her off.

Flum felt lighter on her feet, with more magic coursing through her, and as if all of her senses were finely honed.

"I'll be taking these two then."

"Sure thing. I've gotta admit, it must be pretty handy to be able to reverse negative status effects. Cursed equipment tends to inflict greater penalties than the bonuses offered by their non-cursed equivalents, so that must be a great boon for you."

"It has its pros and cons." Most people could improve their stats with continuous training, but Flum wasn't so lucky. Put another way, this meant that she was so weak that, without the equipment she relied on, even an F-Rank monster could wipe her out. "I guess it's convenient that I don't really need to work at it to become more powerful."

"Alas, the real world isn't quite so simple."

"I wish it were. It's not like it hurts anyone."

Gadhio let out a good-natured snort at this. "You could say that again."

His voice carried a tinge of sadness.

ROLL
OVER
AND
DIE

003

A Meat Puppet Suited for Testing the Blade

THE TWO LEFT the basement and made their way back upstairs. Within seconds, Hallom was diving into Gadhio's arms.

"C'mon, Daddy, let's play!!"

She clearly was tired of waiting; she wasn't going to take no for an answer.

Kleyna came jogging down the hallway, a look of concern on her face. "Don't just leave Mommy waiting like that when we're playing hide and seek, Hallom!"

"You must be losing your touch if a child can get one over on you, Kleyna," Gadhio said.

"It's not so simple, you know. Hallom's been getting much better at the game lately. If I don't do my very best to find a hiding spot, she finds me in no time flat!" Kleyna feigned annoyance to try and cover up her embarrassment.

"You can play now, right, Daddy? You're done with your work, right?"

"I am, but it would be rude to my guest." Gadhio gently patted the girl's head. She looked far from convinced.

"You really like Gadhio, don't you, Hallom?" Flum asked.

"Yup!"

"Well, I'd hate to get in between you two, so I think I'll be on my way and leave you guys to your fun."

"Aww, you're leaving? Why don't you play with us, too?"

Flum had figured she was getting in the way, but apparently, Hallom had taken an interest in her.

"Now, now, Hallom, you can't be bothering other people like that. I'm sorry, Flum. She doesn't always realize what she's saying."

"No, I don't mind at all. Are you sure I'm not a bother?"

"Of course not. In fact, I'd love an extra pair of hands."

As Gadhio said that, Hallom hurriedly reached up and seized Flum's hand. She led her back to her room, where the two played together through the afternoon and into the night.

After turning down an invitation to dinner, Flum left Gadhio's house with an exhausted sigh. "It's terrifying just how much energy kids have..."

Even with her boosted stats from her newly acquired cursed equipment, she felt completely drained. She knew Milkit was waiting for her back at the house, so this was no time to drag her feet. She needed to hurry back to the West District. Just as she started off, Flum heard a familiar yet entirely unexpected voice call out to her.

"Well I'll be, if it isn't Flum."

It was Leitch, the man who sent her off to Anichidey in the first place, dressed in a casual white button-down shirt and a black vest. Since he didn't have any bags with him, Flum assumed he was out on a walk.

"Did you just come from Gadhio's house?" he asked.

"Ah, well, I...umm, I've known Gadhio for some time."

"Ah, yes. I heard that you're also living with the famed Eterna Rinebow as well. To be completely honest, it never once crossed my mind that I was working with the legendary Flum Apricot when I sent you off for medicinal herbs, but it all makes sense now. I can't believe you'd try and pull one over on an old man like me, Flum." Leitch smirked as he teased her gently.

"I'm hardly worthy of being called a hero. I was never of much help."

"I don't know about that, but you were certainly a hero to me when you saved my wife."

"There's no sense in trying to flatter me, you know. Anyway, how is your wife doing?"

"My darling's doing quite well, thanks to you. She was quite thrilled—even said it was just like magic."

"I'm glad to hear she's well enough to be telling jokes now, too."

"I have to say, I had a good chuckle at that."

Leitch and his wife, Foiey, had been concealing the fact that she was healed with ill-gotten medicinal herbs from the church. Though a rather frank and good-natured woman, Foiey had the sharp wit befitting the spouse of such a powerful merchant. Even if Leitch hadn't told her exactly what happened, she'd probably guessed.

"Well, well, fancy meeting you here, Leitch." A woman dressed to the nines stepped up to Flum and Leitch. She wore a glamorous dress tagged with several large corsages, over which she'd layered a red fur-lined coat. Her nails glimmered with prismatic polish, and she wore several rings studded with huge gems. Flum couldn't help but imagine how much it would hurt to be on the receiving end if those ornamented hands ever formed fists. Her hair had an opalescent sheen, and her face was caked in a thick layer of makeup. Her perfume was layered on so heavily that it practically assaulted the senses.

"Ah, Satils. I take it you're out for a walk as well?"

Leitch smiled at the woman and the two massive bodyguards that stood at her side, his demeanor markedly different from when he'd greeted Flum. This was clearly business.

Even Flum, hayseed that she may have been, recognized the woman. Satils Francois ran several stores in the capital, making her a business rival of Leitch's.

"A change of environment never hurts. And look—it even gave me the opportunity to see you, Leitch. Is the slave girl yours?" Satils shot Flum a familiarly icy look.

"Hardly. This here is quite an accomplished adventurer, I'll have you know."

"Well, I'll be—and here I thought she was completely unarmed. I must admit my surprise that such a girl could carry out any task of note."

"Appearances and numbers don't always speak to ability. I trust this young woman entirely."

Flum felt a tingle run up her spine as he said that.

"Hmm." Satils gave Flum a demeaning once-over, though she did seem somewhat more interested from Leitch's reaction. A moment later, she furrowed her brow, and her expression took on a look of bewilderment.

She had probably just cast Scan on Flum. "Well, she must be quite a special girl for you to speak so highly of her."

"That she is."

"And she's cute, too. I thought I might have some use for her if she weren't yours, but I guess I'll have to give up on that little plan."

Flum cocked her head to the side. "Use?"

She had no idea what Satils was talking about or how she intended to use a slave. What she could tell was that there was something deeply twisted about her, and it was best to keep her distance.

"Aaah, it's so hard to find an adorable slave these days. Be a doll and introduce me if you happen across one, eh Leitch?"

"I don't keep slaves."

"Is that so? How bizarre to willingly turn down such a useful tool. Listen, why don't we pop down to the market together sometime. I'm sure you'll have a grand time once you see them in person!" After letting off a devilish cackle, she turned her back on them and walked away.

Flum allowed herself a sigh of relief once she was out of sight.

"So that was Satils Francois?"

"Correct. As I'm sure you noticed, she's a beguiling person with ghastly interests."

Leitch's response knocked the wind out of Flum. "Wow, that's...*open* of you."

"Publicly, she deals in books and apparel. Behind closed doors, she's a fence and a smuggler." Leitch's disdain for the woman was clear. He made no effort to maintain even the pretense of a smile.

"Why don't you report her, then?"

"I've done my due diligence; I have more than enough evidence of her crimes. But her ties to the church are strong. If I move against her, I'll suffer for it. The church has no issue with taking out their rivals."

"Sounds like you know an awful lot about the church."

"The church broke the apothecaries over their knee, and they keep a hand on the open markets. It pays to pay attention."

Despite the negative impact they had on the life of the average citizen, the church continued on its merry way, prioritizing their own needs and benefits. Leitch couldn't be the only merchant who felt his business would be far more profitable and serve his customers better without the church's input. Alas, they were simply too powerful for anyone to openly say so.

"That's why they look the other way, despite Satils' proclivities," he continued. "Until recently, she maintained a working relationship with a dealer in illegal slaves."

"Why wouldn't she just use a legal route?"

"Ever since the regulations around slavery were strengthened, the market's withered. The only way to get responsive slaves—those who were newly enslaved, or haven't already given in to despair—is through illicit channels."

"Responsive... It sounds like they're being tortured."

"That's absolutely correct. Satils takes a perverse pleasure in destroying beautiful things."

Leitch couldn't have learned all this by chance. He must have been actively investigating Satils' activities.

"What's more," he continued, "the illegal trader she did business with was recently murdered. It's not uncommon for such people to be killed by their own slaves, of course, but this was a horrific incident. I hear the scene was like something out of the backroom of a butcher's shop. Of course, nothing about this ever reached the presses."

Slave trader, multiple bodies... This story sounded all too familiar to Flum. In fact, she was nearly certain she was the one who killed that man.

"We've been looking into ways to locate all the illegally traded slaves, and... Are you okay, Flum? You seem tense all of a sudden."

"Huh? Uh, no, it's nothing." Flum tried to brush it off.

She was taken aback to hear sudden mention of the

man she killed, but something else was bothering her. A person buying up slaves from an illegal slave trader to torture them out of a desire to destroy something beautiful…it all came together too perfectly.

Could that Satils lady have been Milkit's previous master?

If Flum's hunch was right, then she was also the one who gave Milkit that poison.

She could feel the anger welling up within her. Flum glared in the direction she watched Satils depart in, suddenly desiring nothing more than to chase her down and lop her head clean off.

She took several long, deep breaths to calm herself down. Though she was able to steady herself some, it did nothing to change the fact that that woman had hurt Milkit. The knowledge set a fire blazing in Flum's chest. She was surprised by her ability to maintain even this much of her composure as the rage in her heart solidified into pure hatred.

"Then we'll just have to kill her." Flum's voice was barely audible as she balled her hands into tight fists. Her nails left bloody half-moons in her palms.

Leitch slowly reached out to put a hand on her shoulder, shocked at Flum's sudden change in demeanor. "Are you okay?"

She felt his fingertips tap on her shoulder.

Flum slowly turned her head to face the older gentleman and smiled. "Ah. I'm sorry. I just kinda got lost in thought for a second."

"Oh, I see. That's fine, then. I was just thinking about how much you'd changed since we last met."

A lot had happened since then. It hadn't actually been that long at all, but it felt like a lifetime ago to Flum.

"I just finally found a purpose, is all. Back when we last met, I still wasn't sure what I should do with my life." Flum flexed her hand, gazing at her palm. What would she have to do to ensure she and Milkit could live here in peace?

All she wanted was a normal life. She didn't *want* to have to kill people, or to be constantly wounded and dismembered herself. But there was no other way for her to hold her own against the church, an organization that treated people as if they were disposable. If she didn't put herself at risk, then she'd never stand a chance against Origin, the source of all her problems.

"You can cry about how unfair the world is, but that won't make your problems disappear," she said. "All you can do is fight back."

"That's true. You need to be strong if you want to protect the weak. People can't help but want to push their own will on others, after all. If the roles were reversed, I imagine those who were previously weak would quickly become the strong."

"Having one of them disappear is the only solution."

"Flum, I am forever in your debt. If there's anything I can do, anything at all, just say the word."

"No, it's fine. I already have someone who supports me unconditionally...and besides, I really don't want to get you involved."

Leitch offered up a knowing smile. It was already too late for that. "The church has already been watching me for some time, you know. I have a reporter who's been doing some digging."

"Reporter...you mean, like from a newspaper?"

The capital had several different newspapers—ones that merely reported recent events, newsletters sent out by the adventurers' guild, and yet other publications which served as the church's mouthpieces. The one thing they all had in common was that they never dared paint the church in a bad light. To do so would be career suicide.

And yet, somehow Leitch had a reporter working for him?

"Well, since you're already here, why don't I introduce you? Welcy!!"

A moment later, a woman wearing a hunting cap rounded the corner and waved before jogging over, her form-fitting pants hugging close to her body.

"This here is Welcy Mancathy."

She smiled brightly and offered out a hand. "Nice to meet ya, Flum."

"Mancathy...so that must make her your younger sister?"

"Unfortunately, yes."

"And what's that supposed to mean, Leitch? Huh?" Welcy demanded.

Leitch mumbled to himself about how this was self-evident even under the oppressive pressure of her gaze. "Anyway, my sister is quite a gifted reporter."

"Hey, I was the one who found out Satils was supplying medicinal herbs to the church, ya know."

"To the church?" Flum said. "But why...?"

"Well, even people in the highest echelons of the church can come down with illnesses that magic can't cure. But they're trading in considerable amounts of the herbs, so that can't be all there is to it," Welcy said.

"We're still getting all the facts lined up, so we're not ready to publish just yet. However, this should help win some room to negotiate with the church." Though Leitch's tone remained calm and composed, the conversation had taken a rather serious turn.

"Anyway, aren't you running late, Brother?"

"Hm? Ah, yes, right. You see, the previous owners of the house I gave you came by to visit, Flum."

"Do they want the house back?"

"No, no, the house is yours now. Actually, I was quite surprised to see them. Rude as this may sound, I was surprised to learn they're still alive."

Flum was intrigued about the previous owners, but Leitch appeared to be in a hurry, and she didn't want to stop him.

"Well, I should be going then. Welcy, please give her your card."

"Right, gotcha. I spend most of my time chasing after Satils right now, so if you happen on any dirt, be sure to stop by my office, okay?" Welcy pulled out a palm-sized card and handed it over to Flum.

Flum looked down at the card, which was completely blank.

Welcy looked at her confused expression before shooting her a grin and casting a spell. "Burn Projection."

A flame licked across the front of the card, leaving her company name, address, job title, full name, and even a small caricature of her. Actually, that didn't quite do it justice. It was a full-blown portrait.

"I use words and pictures to accurately depict the

world on paper. Welcy Mancathy, world revealer and newswoman extraordinaire at your service." She ended her clearly practiced catchphrase with a satisfied grin before turning to follow after her older brother.

Flum held the card up against the darkening sky and read the contents once more. "Newspaper reporter, huh..."

Just how much damage could the power of the pen do to the church? She didn't know the answer, but she was happy to have made a new ally.

Flum stuffed the card into her pocket and turned toward home.

Milkit angled the watering can ever so slightly as she drizzled water over the planters lining the front of the house. Once she was finished, she knelt down and leaned in close to gaze at several pink flowers that they received from an older woman in the neighborhood. Despite her bandaged appearance, the older woman was kind to Milkit and had started stopping by recently to pass along dishes she'd made.

The seedlings weren't even beginning to show signs of budding when she first received them. With care, though, they'd grown, and just a day ago, begun to flower.

Milkit felt proud of the achievement, however small it was—a feeling she never experienced before meeting Flum. She was, simply put, comfortable. It wasn't an earth-shaking feeling, just a warmth that calmed and soothed her heart.

Sniffing the air, she caught a whiff of dinner cooking in the kitchen. Tonight, she was making mushroom and tomato stew with basilisk meat, a thick pop bean soup, and a Caesar salad. For dessert, she purchased some tagore, a type of citrus fruit common in the capital. The fruit was about the size of an orange, but it came apart in large chunks and had a notoriously potent fragrance whose sweetness bombarded the senses as you ate it. It was far less tart than most citrus, which made it massively popular in the capital.

She wasn't done making dinner and had no intention of finishing it until Flum got home. It wasn't like she'd found an excuse to come outside because she'd been wondering where Flum was and why she hadn't come home—of course not. Or, at least, so Milkit told herself.

She brought a hand to her chest.

Ever since she met Flum, something had fallen into place where she'd never even known there was a gap to fill. As they began living together in this house and Milkit was able to eat properly, she could feel her body filling out more. Her master seemed to approve of this development, so she continued to push herself to eat, perhaps to excess. She would need to start cutting back eventually, but that was hardly important to her right now.

A gentle warmth seemed to emanate against the palm of her hand, coming from deep within her chest. Maybe that sensation was what pushed her outside, impatiently waiting for Flum's return.

She had no idea what it was called, though it grew stronger and stronger by the day. Flum had told her that the feeling was called "trust," though something inside told her it had grown far beyond that. It wasn't the relationship between master and slave—after all, this was unlike anything she ever felt for a previous master.

So just what was it? Milkit stared off into space and mulled it over, but no answer came.

"Heya, Milkit." She felt warm hands rest on her cheeks. Looking up, she was delighted to see Flum's smiling face.

There were still some things she wanted to think about, but right now, just offering up a warm smile and greeting her master took priority.

"Sorry I'm so late. Do you need help with dinner?"

"I just need to get a few things ready, but I'd appreciate the help."

"Gotcha. We'll knock it out and chow down on some of your world-famous cooking."

Milkit giggled. "Well, I hope I don't disappoint."

The two walked hand in hand, taking the warmth and happiness surrounding them over the threshold. As the door closed, the world outside returned to being cold and unassuming, made of brick and stone.

A lone, burly figure stopped briefly in front of Flum's house before snorting and continuing on his way through the empty streets.

**ROLL
OVER
AND
DIE**

004

The Fools Who Desecrate Sacred Grounds

"**E**TERNA, YOU BETTER wake up! It's almost dinner time, ya know!"

Eterna opened up her eyes at the sound of Ink's voice from where she was sprawled out over her desk. She rubbed at her eyes and glanced over toward her bed, where Ink greeted her with a bright smile.

"G'morning!"

Even though she couldn't see, she somehow could gauge the movements of those around her. Ink was dressed in a far-too-large shirt she'd borrowed from Flum, and her black hair stuck up at odd angles due to a severe case of bed head.

"Darn, looks like I fell asleep."

"Yep! You were completely zonked out. Like, snoring

away. You even started mumbling things about your mom and dad while you were asleep."

"Huh..." Eterna nodded in cool acknowledgment and let out a small sigh.

"That's a pretty somber sigh. So you had parents too, huh?" Ink never knew her own parents. The question was posed in innocent curiosity.

"Well, I'm human. Of course I had parents. Granted, I don't even know what they looked like."

"Oh, really? I guess we're similar that way."

"In that respect, yes, our situations aren't all that different. I had surrogate parents, too."

"Were those the people in your dream?"

"Ever since I came here, I've dreamed about those days quite often. I used to live here decades ago, you know."

"Now that you mention it, I heard you were squatting here when Flum first showed up."

"I just came here to use this room. It was...familiar to me."

"...Wait a second. Did you just say several decades ago?"

"That's right."

"Whoa! How old are you, Eterna?! Judging by your voice, I figured you were pretty close to Flum's age!"

Ink wasn't able to see what she looked like, though even if she could, that likely would have only compounded her confusion; Eterna both looked and sounded like she was in her mid- to late teens.

"I dunno. Honestly, I don't know when I was born, but I figure I must be around sixty or so, give or take a few."

"You're an old lady!"

"Don't say stuff like that, you'll hurt my feelings." Eterna might have come to terms with her long life span, but that didn't mean she was keen on being called old.

"But if you're that old, that must mean your parents already passed, right?"

"Well, one of the reasons I accepted the task of slaying the Demon Lord was to learn that for myself, actually. Before I set off, I stopped by the town where they last lived and paid my respects at their graves."

"Well, I'm sure they'd be happy to know you're doing well."

"One can hope."

Eterna closed her eyes. She could practically see Kindah and Claudia standing before her. It was unfortunate that she couldn't see them in person, but the knowledge that they'd lived fulfilling lives brought her comfort.

"I still can't believe you're that old," Ink marveled. "I wonder if I would've noticed if I could see you."

"I doubt it. I only look a little older than you."

"Really?? How can a normal human..."

Suddenly Flum's voice called out from the first floor, cutting Ink off.

"Eteeeeerna! Dinnertime!"

"Aah, Flum's calling."

"I'll be back with your dinner shortly, Ink."

"Okay! Looking forward to it!" Ink grinned broadly as Eterna left.

The young girl was almost back to her normal self now, though Eterna still wanted to keep an eye on her a while longer. She left a small school of fish she'd sculpted from tap water floating in her wake as she headed downstairs. If anything happened to Ink, they would relay the message down the chain to Eterna.

The smell of tomato stew struck Eterna with hunger pangs that intensified as she stepped out into the hallway. She placed her hands on her sides to soothe her growling stomach as she started downstairs.

◇ ◇ ◇

"That was great!" Flum beamed as she put her hands together in appreciation. Milkit and Eterna followed suit before Eterna headed upstairs with Ink's plate, leaving Flum and Milkit behind to clean up.

The two worked perfectly in sync and made quick

work of the dishes, Flum washing and Milkit drying, before stowing everything neatly. Flum thought absent-mindedly about just how great it would be if she could draw out this carefree feeling forever, which invited her little voice of self-sabotage to crack open the reserve of gloom she'd built up, reminding her it wasn't to be.

Milkit mumbled to herself. "Wouldn't it be great if every day could be like today..."

The knowledge that they were both thinking the same thing at the exact same time warmed Flum's heart. "I'll do my best to make it happen."

"Ah, I'm sorry. I didn't mean it like that."

"Nope, you and I were on the same page, so that pretty much seals the deal. After I take care of this whole thing with the church, we can just live out our lives in comfort."

The question of when that would be was another story entirely. Just thinking about the challenges she was up against made Flum's head spin. But as long as a peaceful life lay on the other side, she knew she could push through.

"Will we still live in the capital when it's all over?" Milkit asked.

"Well, I've gotten pretty used to this house. Though I *would* like to go visit my hometown sometime and make sure my friends and family know I'm alive."

"It'd probably be best if I don't accompany you, then. It'd be a bit awkward to have a slave with you."

"Huh? I'm gonna introduce you to my *parents*. This wonderful girl here is an important partner of mine...or something like that."

"Partner?" Milkit's heart skipped a beat. The word carried *nuances* she had to unpack.

"I mean, you're not my slave, and I feel like *friend* hardly cuts it. I guess I don't really have the right word for what you are to me. I'm gonna have to think it over before I actually introduce you to them."

"I...I think partner is a bit of an overstatement."

"Maybe. Maybe not. But things change, ya know? You just have to get used to it, I guess."

"I suppose so. But speaking of meeting your parents, do...do you think I'll have to take off my bandages?" Milkit set down a plate and absentmindedly tugged at them.

"I never really thought about that, actually."

It would probably be best to show Milkit's uncovered face to her parents, though Flum felt deeply bothered by the mere thought of anyone other than herself seeing Milkit's face. She was happy to have it all to herself. The nighttime ritual carried a special meaning for them.

In the beginning, Flum intended to help Milkit get used

to the feeling of having her face exposed and then bring her out into the open. But in reality, things had only gotten worse...or, rather, more complex. Now Flum had no desire to share the right to see Milkit's face with anyone else.

But it did seem a bit impolite to keep her face covered up when Milkit met her parents. Flum's mind ran around and around in circles over this problem.

"Well, I guess we'll just deal with it when the time comes."

She decided to put it off for another time. Milkit looked relieved to hear it.

"Yes, I suppose we still have time."

"That's right! Quite a long time, probably..."

The two girls laughed in an attempt to lighten the mood. Flum couldn't help but be sheepishly aware how likely it was that her possessiveness would only have increased by the time the battle was finally over.

I'll probably end up introducing her with the bandages on, at this rate...

It's thanks to you that I can have dreams again.

This was the first time Milkit ever had such a vivid dream. In fact, it was more than just a dream—it was a

113

memory, drawn up from her dark, grimy past. A past that her recent happiness had helped her forget.

That very happiness, however, made the darkness lying ahead of her all the more somber.

"Hey, don't you forget. You were born to be sold, remember? You better give it your best and make me some money."

Those were the first words Milkit could remember being spoken to her. She couldn't have been more than three.

Her parents were deadbeats who'd sold Milkit off at the first opportunity. Shortly thereafter, she was purchased by a wealthy noblewoman who had lost her daughter to illness, and with her, her grip on reality. She'd purchased over a dozen children from the slave trader and treated them like servants while simultaneously showering them in love and affection as if they were her own. All of the children were given names and kept well fed. It was a glamorous lifestyle. Of course, the purchase and sale of children was already illegal at that time, so she acquired all of them through black-market channels.

This was when Milkit was first given her name.

Once the slaves the woman purchased reached the age of three—the same age her late daughter had died—she immediately lost all affection for them and sold them back to the slave trader. Babies were generally of little use as slaves; having someone who would raise the children to the age of three was quite convenient for the slaver. Shortly after Milkit was sold back, the woman's activities reached the presses, and she was run out of the capital.

It was then that the slave trader said those words to her. She didn't have a markedly strong response to them, other than the casual observation that this must be her lot in life.

After that, Milkit bounced back and forth between the slaver and several wealthy buyers.

"I hate it... This is all so scary..."

The words ran over and over in her head as she dreamed. The events of her past came back to her, playing back before her eyes.

"Please, no, I don't want to go back there..."

She could not make the nightmare end.

Milkit survived the way insects did, wriggling out from underfoot and finding shelter in the dark. This became normal to her. She didn't even consider her life particularly unfortunate, though the concept of happiness was also lost on her. Now that she did know about all these things, the memory of her old "normal" brought a scream of terror to her lips.

No matter how hard she fought it, the nightmare continued into the next chapter.

"Aah, yesss. Look at your delightful ribs, your collar-bone. You don't get it, though, do you? You're still so small, I guess. But you know, you only really get 'em thin like this when they're young."

This was a man who derived pleasure from seeing his slaves gaunt and excessively thin.

"Yes, yes, just like that. Look at me with those cold, empty eyes. I love it! Glare at me, hate me for the pain I'm causing you!! Curse me, I love it!!"

Then the woman who got off on having lowly slaves talk down to her.

"God teaches us that we cannot put a price on human life! Thus, slaves who are bought and sold for money must not be human and are not granted His protection. Thus, I am unblemished by any pain I cause you, even if it results in your death!"

Then there was the church official fixated on harming children. Time and again, her buyers had possessed some manner of perverse ideology.

Milkit figured that her life was over after being purchased by the church official. However, due to her good fortune—or misfortune, depending on how one looked at it—the man's misdeeds caught the press's attention, so he tearfully sold off his slaves out of fear of being discovered before he laid a hand on her. She was around ten when she ended up back with the slave trader.

Alas, it wasn't long before she found herself purchased by a new master—a woman named Satils Francois.

In Satils' eyes, everything more beautiful than herself deserved to be destroyed. Milkit was almost certainly purchased for just that purpose.

"Just looking at your face fills me with such rage, you know. What's a pathetic slave like you doing with a face like that, anyway?"

In the beginning she was satisfied with just belittling and whipping the girl—a fate far better than the ones suffered by the other slaves, if only because she didn't actually intend to kill her. But then three other slaves living with Milkit all died in quick succession, and suddenly, Satils' brutality came to an end. In fact, she started to treat Milkit with kindness. She lavished her with food which, unknown to her, had been laced with the mustardo toxin that scarred her face.

"What a pitiful creature, having to live with such a hideous face. And you were once so pretty, too! Kyahahaha!"

She laid it on heavily and often, cackling wildly with each repetition. However, this seemed to do wonders for Satils' mood. Milkit remained fed, and in time, even received a bed of her own.

Meanwhile, Satils continued her brutal torture of the other slaves. She liked to lash them, lacerate their thighs, and kick them in the stomach while wearing high-heeled shoes. Many died vomiting blood and were disposed with the household trash. However, Satils treated Milkit like little more than a curiosity, a tool to be used to boost her own twisted ego.

"My, my, my. How awful it must be to have such a disgusting face, you poor thing. I wonder what could have caused this to happen?"

Despite the pleasure she took in torturing her slaves, the number she'd done on Milkit sated her urge to hurt her further...for a while. Around three years after she first bought Milkit, Satils finally tired of her and sold her back to the slave trader. Deprived of her good looks—her only selling point—Milkit was thrown into the cell to die.

"Aah, it's finally over now."

Milkit sensed, somehow, that the dark cell smelling of rotting flesh was a suitable place for her life to reach its end. Her heart barren, she waited for the appointed day.

Yet that day never came. All because she reached out and took that outstretched hand.

The dream should have ended there, but the nightmare seeded doubt and uncertainty in her mind. No matter how long she waited, her master never came. Instead, the slave trader finally arrived to begin his show. With no one there to save her, Milkit was left to the ravenous ghouls that fell from the ceiling, much like the other slaves had been.

"Why...why won't it end? It didn't happen like this! I...I didn't... Stoooop!!"

Even with her memories of living a happy, peaceful life together with Flum firmly in place, the nightmare dragged her through every detail of being eaten alive. The slave trader sat there, enjoying the show from his front-row seat. When Milkit turned to look back, she spotted Satils sitting next to him, laughing raucously at the sight.

"I don't want to die! I don't want it all to end here! I...I have a reason to live!!"

Milkit's eyes shot open.

"Was that all...a dream?"

The room was still dark, only faintly illuminated by the light of the moon. She rolled over onto her side and watched Flum's chest rise and fall a short distance away in her own bed.

Not so long ago, she'd been numb to her lot in life. Now, even thinking about it was excruciating. The slave trader would never try to kill her again, nor would Satils ever be able to raise a hand against her or feed her poison. But knowing what she knew now, her past—regardless of whether any of it could happen again—was terrifying.

Milkit longed for the warm embrace of her master to help soothe her fears. If she just asked, she was certain that Flum would let her sleep in her bed. If she was just in Flum's arms, she knew the nightmares would never come back.

"That's...that's a little too much." Milkit chided herself for her spoiled attitude.

Her master might be incredibly generous and kind, but Milkit couldn't take advantage of her like that. Flum was almost certainly exhausted from the battles she had to fight. It was Milkit's job to try and ease her burden.

"Good night, Master." Milkit shut her eyes once again, struggling to stay strong as the darkness came over her. In time, she settled into a dreamless sleep.

After an uneventful night, morning came as it usually did. Flum woke to faint birdsong in the distance. She was still half-asleep when sounds from downstairs broke into

her awareness: the chopping of a knife against a cutting board and the sizzling of something in the frying pan.

These were the sounds of a normal life. Of tranquility. Of *her*. Now that she actually gave it some thought, these were the same sounds Flum heard her mother making every morning when she woke up back in her hometown.

She felt a wave of nostalgia wash over her as she propped herself up, stretched, and then hopped out of bed and made her way downstairs with a dramatic yawn.

"Good morning." Milkit greeted her with a warm smile the moment she came into view.

"Mornin.'" This was the best Flum could manage at this hour, though it still elicited a laugh from Milkit.

Right as Flum was about to duck into the washroom, she turned and stepped in close to Milkit, their faces mere centimeters apart as she inspected her.

"I-Is there something on my face?"

"Did you have a hard time sleeping? You look exhausted."

Flum was right. After waking up in the middle of the night, Milkit had a hard time getting a proper rest. She felt like her body was made of lead. But she wasn't going to let it impact her daily routine.

"No, it's fine."

Flum eyed her suspiciously for a moment before deciding to accept her answer at face value. She turned and went back to the washroom. After scrubbing her face and fixing her hair, she returned to Milkit's side.

"You're up early today. Do you have a job lined up?"

"Nah, I just kinda woke up is all. Hey, you want me to cut this?"

"Yes, please. Oh, Master..."

"Yeah?"

Milkit reached out and pressed down some stray hairs that stuck up from the top of Flum's head. "There we go."

"Heh, I was still a little out of it when I did up my hair. Eterna would've had a field day with it if she saw me."

"She's always perfectly groomed."

Every day, first thing in the morning, Eterna's hair was immaculately done—probably thanks to the water magic that she used to set it all in place. Flum felt it gave her morning routine an unfair advantage.

"Once this is done cooking, I'm going to head outside to water the flowers," Milkit said.

"Got it. You know, those flowers you've been growing really are beautiful."

"They certainly are. Now that I'm a bit more comfortable with gardening, I was thinking about planting some other varieties next time."

"I think that's a great idea. Can I come along when you pick them out?"

"Of course!"

Flum continued helping out with breakfast as she settled on their next plan. "Great, we'll go shopping on my next day off, then."

Milkit's face lit up as she began to think about where they would go next.

After finishing the fried eggs, Milkit slid them onto a plate and stepped out of the kitchen, leaving Flum to work on the salad alone. After chopping the vegetables and setting up four servings, Flum paused for a moment and listened.

She didn't hear anything coming from outside.

She jogged to the door to have a look.

"Milkit?"

Milkit was nowhere in sight. Her watering can lay discarded on the ground. Maybe she was out getting water, or perhaps the neighbor had called her over to chat?

No, that definitely wasn't it. Flum's heightened senses picked up on an ominous sound.

"There are two people on the roof..."

She was enraged by her own carelessness.

"Dammit! I can't believe I let this happen again!!"

Waiting for Milkit to come outside before kidnapping

her was hardly the work of a novice. This could only mean that Milkit was the intended target, not Flum. She didn't know who could have ordered this, but it'd only been a few days since Nekt abducted Milkit. She really should have been more aware of this possibility.

She bit her lip in frustration until it began to bleed.

Flum kicked hard off the ground, rocketing up onto the roof and landing on her knee. She jerked her head back and forth, spotting two shadowy figures escaping to the east.

She clenched her jaw and took off after the men, not even stopping to spare a moment's hesitation when she reached the edge and sprang to the next roof. She bounded from rooftop to rooftop in pursuit of Milkit's captors.

"Scan!"

The burly man holding the unconscious Milkit was named Tryte Ransila. His strength and endurance were both over 2,000, and he had a combined stat value of around 8,000. The second man, Demiceliko Radius, was much lankier than his comrade and looked like he was enjoying bounding across rooftops. His agility was in the upper 2,000s, and he had high perception, which all made sense based on his movements. He, too, had a total stat value of around 8,000, though his endurance was only in the triple-digit range.

This put them both around A-Rank. They would be no pushovers, but Flum knew she was more than a match for them. The only problem she faced was in closing the distance.

Focusing her prana into her right foot, she leapt off the roof high into the air and clear over an entire house.

"Hey, I think she's gettin' closer!"

"Whoa, someone's after us?? No one told me about that! This was s'posed to be a simple job!"

The two men began to worry as they saw the small girl gaining on them. If they cast Scan on her, they would find that all of her stats were at zero. They had heard the name Flum Apricot before, of course, but that didn't explain why the girl pursuing them had the mark of a slave on her cheek. And if she wasn't the legendary warrior, then why was this girl able to keep up with A-Rank adventurers like themselves?

"Heh, guess we don't have any other choice. I'll deal with her. You go on ahead, Tryte."

"You sure you got this?"

"She's just a little punk. Remember that chick Susy? She may have been an A-Rank too, but when push came to shove, she was begging for mercy. Girls ain't no match for a real man when ya get down and dirty. Not in the streets anyway, if ya follow me. Gyahaha!"

"That was a long time ago. Didn't we poison her?"

"Aah, yeah, her eyes were bloodshot and spasming. Good times, good times. Beats the hell out of runnin' for the hag. Gah, I need a little excitement in my life! I got an itch in my soul! I need the *hard* shit!"

Demiceliko ran his hands erratically through his hair. "Is it really time for that right now? Anyway, just leave the girl to me. If you get into too much trouble, just run."

They were working a job outside the guild's oversight. Though the returns were higher, so was the risk.

"First, I'm gonna give her a quick warm-up test." Demiceliko popped open the case hanging from his belt and pulled out two daggers coated with a thin liquid. "Hah!"

He spun around and threw the first before leaping backward and throwing the other. He still managed to maintain his original speed, even running in reverse.

The two daggers traced an arc through the air as they flew at Flum.

Demiceliko drew another dagger from the case. Even if she was able to dodge his initial attack, he planned to keep up the pressure. Flum made no attempt to alter her course. He sneered at her.

"Just gonna take it, huh? Once you're paralyzed, I'm gonna use you like a doll, girly!"

Just as the tip of a dagger made contact with her side, Flum cast Reversion. The dagger flipped around and flew back at Demiceliko.

The second dagger found its mark and plunged deep into Flum's right hand with a sickening squish. Despite having plowed straight through her hand, she felt little more than a faint pang run through her arm. Thanks to the belt's enchantment nullifying poison, the liquid coating the dagger had no effect.

"So that's what reversal does?? I knew it was a rare affinity, but I've never seen the like!"

Demiceliko dodged and dove to a nearby roof. Still in midair, he tossed another dagger her way.

Flum somersaulted through the air to dodge the incoming attack while yanking the dagger out from her hand and hurling it where she anticipated Demiceliko would land.

Her form left something to be desired, and she had little practice with such a maneuver, so she wasn't able to get enough speed on the knife. It *did* catch him off guard by coming right toward his feet, stopping him in his tracks and forcing him to go on the defense. Demiceliko drew a fifty-centimeter blade and knocked the dagger out of the air.

Now that he'd stopped moving, though, Flum had

almost closed the gap between them. Demiceliko reached back and drew a short sword from its sheath at the small of his back as he prepared to take Flum on in close-quarters.

"I know most A-Rank adventurers out there, but I gotta say you're a new one for me. And just a little girl, too..."

Flum wasn't sure what he was trying to say, but he seemed to have a rather dim view of women. Ultimately, she really didn't much care what he thought. All she was worried about was saving Milkit.

"This is for Milkit!!"

Flum summoned forth a pair of black gauntlets before drawing her Souleater from its pocket dimension. She had no real plan or strategy beyond cutting him down.

Demiceliko was taken by surprise at her impressive speed and leapt backward, barely evading Flum's slash, which left only a deep cut in his shirt.

"You're a waste of time. Totally lacking in all the places where it counts for a little love hole like yerself. Guess I'll do ya a favor and teach you a little respect!" He leapt forward and chopped at her thigh with his longsword, leaving a light gash. Blood stained her torn pants. Demiceliko then sprang back just out of range again before Flum could take another swing. "Shadow Mist!"

A deep, black mist gathered in the air, blocking out much of Flum's vision. She tried to fall back, but Demiceliko came lunging out of the darkness and chopped into her arm. He followed up with quick slashes to her side, cheek, leg, shoulder, and back, leaving shallow cuts in their wake.

"Whaddya think, huh? How does it feel to be lost in the darkness and surrounded by nothing but pain? Me, I love it! I'm having a great time! Feels almost as good as having my way with a corpse! Gyahahaha!!"

His fighting style involved blinding his victim and gradually piling up damage until they grew too slow and weak to avoid his coup de grace.

"You're an idiot."

Flum was unimpressed. Her injuries healed quickly, and she felt little in the way of pain. Even the mist was something she could deal with easily by letting loose her stored up prana.

"Hyaaaaaaaaaaaaaah!!"

The shock wave unleashed by Prana Sphere, a Cavalier Arts technique, blew the mist away with ease.

"Wh-what the hell was that?!"

Looking over, she saw Demiceliko trying to escape to a nearby roof. Flum swung her sword and unleashed a Prana Shaker.

Demiceliko dropped on his stomach to avoid the arc of cutting force before springing back to his feet and preparing to throw another dagger. However, Flum wasn't done with her assault quite yet.

"Come back...Reversion!"

Flum had used her reversal magic on her prana blade. Demiceliko turned around just in time to watch in horror as the force blade he'd just dodged reversed course and flew back toward him, lopping his legs off at the thigh.

"Wh-whaugh?!"

His legs remained on the roof while his torso tumbled to the ground below, where his head smacked into the pavement with a wet thud and a gasp. He thrashed his arms about in a desperate attempt to flee as Flum landed on the ground next to him, scraping her sword along the ground as she closed in. His panic did nothing to quiet her bloodlust.

"Hyah...haaah...gah, it hurts! I...don't want it to hurt! I...need pleasure! Run...must run...!!"

He mouthed more garbled nonsense as he tried to drag himself along. Unfortunately, he was far too slow to outpace Flum's casual walk. The world grew dark as he mustered what little energy he had and looked up at the young girl with the ice-cold stare.

"Where's Milkit?"

The other man had long since disappeared, so Demiceliko was her last hope of getting the information she needed about where to find her.

"Please, let me live! I beg of you! There are so many women I haven't violated, I can't die yet!"

Flum simply repeated her question over and over until it became apparent he wasn't willing to talk. Then she hacked his left arm off.

"Ngyaaaaaaaaaaaaaaugh!!" Demiceliko let out an ear-piercing scream.

She shook the blood off her blade and asked again. "Where is Milkit?"

"Please spare me! I didn't mean no harm. I just needed money, ya see! You misunderstand, I wasn't actually havin' fun or nothin'! I'm sorry, okay? I'm sorry, lady! I was just doin' what I was told—I'm really a good adventurer, ya know. Really, I am!"

He may have been the scum of the earth, but someone who climbed their way up to A-Rank was unlikely to give up any information about their employer.

"I really don't want to do this, you know."

It was true, she didn't. She hated the pain, the suffering, and she hated inflicting the same on others. But if that's what it took to save Milkit, then so be it. If she didn't take action, there was no way this cruel and unfair world would come to her aid. Of that much Flum was certain.

She pressed the tip of her sword against the back of Demiceliko's hand and pressed down until the blade cut cleanly through, bone and all.

"Gyaaaaaaaaaaaaaaaugh!!"

If he had enough energy to scream like that, Flum figured he wasn't going to die any time soon, but it was starting to look doubtful he was going to give in, no matter what she did to him.

She focused on the hilt of her blade, running the power of her reversal magic through it and into his flesh.

"Rending Reversion!"

SNAP!

Demiceliko's finger snapped as his thumbnail reversed in on itself, eliciting an ear-piercing scream from the man.

"Where did you take Milkit?"

He shook his head aggressively.

If he was going to die anyway, he might as well spit it out as far as Flum was concerned. Unless she was still going way too soft on him. He was an A-Rank, after all.

She reversed the rest of his fingernails as well, though that didn't get her any closer to getting the information out of him. She'd need to use her power on another body part, then.

"Demolition Reversion!"

His thumb tore right off his hand with a stomach-churning squelch, and his mouth opened wide in agony. "Hnngg...gaaaaaaugh!!" Demiceliko tensed his muscles in an attempt to bear the pain.

"Where did you take Milkit?"

He shook his head again. This time, Flum blasted the rest of his fingers off as well.

"Waaaaaaauuuuugh!!"

She blew his hand apart for good measure. His screams were little more than an annoyance for Flum at this point. "Where did you take Milkit? Unless you tell me, you're facing a fate worse than death."

Flum knelt down in front of Demiceliko and began running her hand over his face. Eyes? Maybe his brain?

"You want me to do that?"

"N...nooooaaaaaaugh!!" Tears, mucus, and saliva poured out of his face. "Okay, okay. Fine, I'll...I'll tell you, just stop!"

He had no idea what she planned on doing if he kept silent, but it was clear she would make good on her threat. "It...it was Satils! She told...t-told us to bring her the bandaged slave!"

"That old hag? Hasn't she done enough to Milkit?" The words came flying out of Flum's mouth before she even had a chance to think. "So where did you take her?"

"A basement! There's a place with a hidden room in the basement. You have to take a tunnel from a building with a green roof off to the southeast. The outside looks like a house, but it's a fake. It's just an entrance."

"So that's where I'll find Milkit." Flum stood up and took off toward the East District.

Demiceliko raised his hand and began to summon up all of his remaining magic. "Heh...heh, you dare turn your back on me, little girl? I'll show you, wench! Shadow Cannon!"

A fist-sized ball of black energy launched toward Flum's back.

"You just never learn..." Flum spun on her heel and slashed right through the ball of energy before continuing on into the man behind it, chopping him in two. Demiceliko died instantly.

With a wave of her hand, Flum's blade disappeared, and she immediately took off running toward the East District.

005

I Hate It, But What Choice Do I Have?

WELCY HAD SET UP in a three-story apartment across the street from Satils' manor early that morning in the hopes of getting the information she needed to blow the story wide open.

"If I could just figure out where she's hidden her den, I could start putting together a plan to get inside..."

After Welcy ran into one of Satils' valets "by chance" and got him thoroughly drunk, he let slip that there was a hidden room located within the manor. However, he didn't know exactly where it was. She also couldn't find any definite proof of a connection between Satils and the church.

Welcy rested her elbows on the windowsill and casually gazed out at the scene before her.

BAM!

She jolted back at the sudden noise that came from up above.

It was followed by a series of loud thuds. It almost sounded like someone was moving across the roof. They then jumped off the roof, falling right in front of her window, and landed several meters below on the hard pavement.

Welcy lunged forward in excitement, her entire upper body hanging out the window as she looked down.

She could hardly believe her eyes—she knew this girl.

"Flum?! What are you doing??"

Flum's clothes were soaked with blood. She looked back up at Welcy, her gaze intense, though her lips turned upward in a gentle smile when she recognized the figure standing in the window. Her eyes, however, retained the same burning intensity as before.

"Oh, Welcy. This is great timing, actually. I'm about to break into Satils' hidden chamber. Do you want to come along?"

"Wait, really?! Hold on, I'm coming down!"

How Flum had gotten her information, Welcy couldn't say, but she wasn't about to turn down a scoop like this. She raced down the stairs and dove into the street, following Flum as she headed in the opposite direction from the manor.

"We're talking about the same chamber, right? In the manor?"

"Yes. Apparently, the entrance is elsewhere."

"Huh. So how'd you find out? Or are you going to keep your source secret?"

"I heard about it from an adventurer Satils hired shortly before I killed him." Flum made no effort to conceal any part of the story.

"Killed?"

"They kidnapped my partner."

"Oh, wow, I guess that explains it." That seemed like a good enough explanation to Welcy for Flum's strange behavior.

"Here it is."

Flum stopped in front of a single-story house with a green roof. She grabbed the knob and twisted, only to find it was locked.

"Wait, really? The secret entrance is just in some normal house? I guess that makes it a pretty good escape tunnel in an emergency, too."

Flum pressed her ear against the door as Welcy droned on. She could hear something just inside. She decided to simply knock on the door, like she would at any normal house, and moments later, a man in his thirties opened the door and peered outside. He smiled down at her warmly.

"What can I do for you, little lady?"

Flum made no attempt to conceal her murderous glare. "I'm looking for a young girl with a bandaged face and the man who kidnapped her."

"Kidnapping? Oh my, crime like that is rare here in the East District. Do you mean to say such a criminal is lurking here in our neighborhood? You know, now that you mention it, I recall seeing some strange figures hanging around here lately."

"Could you tell me more about them?"

There was something suspicious about the way the man smiled, though he readily agreed. "I'd hate to keep you standing here in the door all day. Why don't you come on inside?"

"Thank you."

Flum quickly stepped inside.

"Wait, no!" Welcy tried to stop Flum from going in, but it was no use. She hurried after the younger woman. The moment they were through the threshold, the door slammed shut behind them.

Welcy glanced back instinctively.

"Die!"

She was stunned to find a second man wielding an axe rushing straight toward her. Yet another man stepped into the small space as well. The three armed men lunged in almost simultaneously.

"Eyaaaaaaak!!" Welcy let out a shriek of terror and dropped to the ground, throwing her hands up over her head. Much to her surprise, the outcry stopped abruptly.

She slowly opened her eyes as she heard a wet thud. Turning to look in the direction of the noise, she saw the top half of the man lying on the floor. She scanned the room for the other men, finding that they had also been cut in two.

Flum gave her Souleater a shake to knock the blood free before the sword disappeared in a flash of light.

The room was now completely silent but for the groans of the first man, who had been cut at the waist. He was still alive but just barely. Welcy could see his organs spilling out of the gaping wound and blood pooling underneath him. She quickly threw a hand over her mouth at the stench.

"You okay?"

Welcy let out a shriek in surprise at how calm Flum sounded. "D-did you just k-kill them?"

Flum offered a hand to Welcy. "Yeah. If I didn't, they would've done the same to us."

She had a point. Even so, Welcy hesitated, dwelling on

how simply Flum could make the decision to kill. Flum, reading the terror on her face, withdrew her hand and turned away.

"No, I mean…it's not like that!"

"I understand how precious life is. But not everyone feels that way."

After all the fighting Flum had done, she encountered more than her fair share of people like that.

"There are a lot of people out there who are more than willing to take another's life if it profits them. These men certainly wouldn't have listened to reason." Milkit's life and her own were the two most important things to Flum. As long as she held to those clear and simple values, she could act without hesitation before her opponents had a chance. "Is it really so wrong to kill such people before they can kill me?"

Welcy understood that Flum lived in a world that regularly forced her to choose between life and death—and that she was fighting to get out of that world. "I'm really sorry about that."

"Don't be. You were right to feel that way, Welcy. Anyway, let's go find that room."

Flum sounded cheerful, but it was clearly forced. Welcy gently slapped herself on the cheek in admonishment for having put Flum on the spot like that.

The air was damp and musty, though it also brought up a long-forgotten, uncomfortable memory in the recesses of Milkit's mind.

"Hnnng..."

She was lying atop something soft.

"I was making breakfast with Master. Then I went outside to water the flowers, and..."

She put her hand down on the ground to steady herself and pressed the other to her head as she slowly sat up. No matter how hard she tried, she couldn't remember anything after watering the flowers.

"Everything just went black all of a sudden. How did I get here?"

She slowly turned her head and took in the room. There was a desk on the right side covered with papers. Next to it was a glass cabinet filled with sinister-looking medicines and metal instruments. The room was made of a dull, grey stone that seemed to sap all warmth out of the air.

She slowly turned to take in the left side of the room.

"Good morning, Milkit." A woman in gaudy makeup appeared before her. She was grinning so broadly that her gums were showing.

Milkit was temporarily taken aback at how close the figure was, though she recognized the face instantly. Satils Francois, her previous master.

"B-but...why? How??" She was so terrified she could barely speak. Milkit shook her head violently, mumbling to herself as she scooted backward. "No...it can't be...no..."

Satils laughed at the sight.

"My, my, we've been apart for just a short time, and now here you are, back to acting like you were human! How splendid! I take it you found a nice master?"

"Hah...hah...no! Nooo!" Milkit began crawling on all fours into the corner.

This brought another delighted laugh from Satils before she stood up and closed in on the retreating Milkit. Milkit clawed at the wall with her bare hands in a desperate attempt to find a way out.

"You don't need to be so scared, you know. Besides, it's not like anyone is going to come and save you."

"Master! Masteeeeer!!"

"Is your master so kind that they would go out of their way to rescue a disgusting little slave like yourself? I must say there are much better slaves out there to use for your own satisfaction, if that's the case."

"M-m-masssssster...! Waaaugh!"

Satils reached out for the back of Milkit's head and grabbed a fistful of hair before pulling the girl's face close to her own. She had a crazed look in her eyes.

"Unfortunately for you, you will never see your master again!"

"That's not true! That's... It's not...!"

"Oh, and when did you get bold enough to talk back to me? Now listen here, you'd best not get too full of yourself."

"You're...you're not my master!"

Satils was practically hysterical now. "Slaves like you don't have the right to choose their master!!"

With her hand locked firmly in Milkit's silver hair, she slammed the younger girl's face into the ground. She plucked one of Milkit's hairs from her head and gave it a lick, a look of pure rapture on her face.

Milkit began to crawl toward another corner of the room, though no matter where she looked, she couldn't identify anything that looked like a door. She was surrounded by four blank walls, and any direction she ran would ultimately lead to another dead end.

Knowing her prey had no means of escape, Satils walked over toward a bookshelf, her extravagant gown sashaying as she went. She pulled a dagger off the shelf, the blade glinting under the light cascading off the chandelier overhead.

"Aaaaaaaaaaaaaaaah!!"

Satils slowly approached the terrified girl. "This room was made to meet my unique specifications. A hidden room deep within a hidden room, you could say. I'm the only one who knows this place exists. How can I be so sure, you may ask? I killed everyone who worked on it!"

"Masteeeeeeeeeeeeeeeeeer!!"

Satils chuckled. "You can scream as much as you like. No one will come and save you, or rather, no one can. This place is my escape, my private paradise! The only ones who may set foot in here are myself and my playthings! Now dance! Move like a butterfly with its wings plucked off! Dance I say, like a child in agony from a thousand cuts!"

She spread her arms and spun in a slow circle.

This room was a particular favorite of hers, tailor-made for the toys she meant to torture most exquisitely. She could spend hours, days even, starting at the fingertips and slowly cutting down their entire bodies, salving the wounds to inflict even more pain. By removing their eyelids, she robbed her playthings of even the brief reprieve of sleep. Once they died, she'd dispose of the body, clean the room, and move on to the next. As she cleaned up her previous victim, she would fantasize about how the next scenario would play out.

"You know, I kept hearing these strange rumors about a girl with a bandaged face, and I couldn't help but think you were the only one that fit that description. What's more, rumor had it you were cured of the poison that afflicted you! Did your master do that for you? How kind of them to fix your face so I could enjoy breaking it all over again. And it looks like you've even rediscovered your emotions! The last time we were together, you wouldn't react to anything, no matter what I did. Not really a desirable trait in a toy. I mean, I spent so much money on you, and I was so disappointed when I didn't get to hear your ear-piercing screams. I'm sure you feel bad about that, don't you?"

Milkit shook her head over and over.

"What an attitude! I guess someone will just have to put you back in your rightful place. I certainly don't mind the job. First off, the bandages have to go. I want to see what your delicate face looks like before I break it, so I can really savor the contrast! Now, hurry up and take them off!"

Milkit absolutely wouldn't let that happen. Only Flum was allowed to see her face. She curled up into herself against the wall and tried to cover her face.

"Oh, you don't want to show me? Still trying to be true to your master, is that it? Kyahaha! Now that I think about it, I must say your outfit's rather garish. Are those from your master as well? Such fancy clothing is hardly practical, you know. It must be fulfilling some sort of fetish for your master! You know the relationship the two of you share you isn't love, don't you? It's nothing but a sexual perversion!"

"You're wrong! Master isn't like that!!"

"Kyahahaha!! What an amusing turn of events! Who knew I'd be so wonderfully entertained today? I really, truly, want to...rip you to shreds!!"

Satils lunged toward Milkit.

Her heavy breathing felt like pinpricks on Milkit's pale skin, causing her teeth to chatter.

"This knife is an appetizer. Or perhaps a pre-dinner drink to whet your appetite. I have whips, pins, and poisons just waiting for their turn. Aren't you excited? Say the words, just try them out. What, cat got your tongue? Say it. C'mon, say it. I told you to say it!!"

"Hnnnn..."

"Oh, look, the little knife is getting ever so closer to your body. It's coming now."

Milkit gasped.

"The cold sensation of metal on flesh is quite terrifying, isn't it? Go ahead, be afraid! Show me your face, I've been waiting to see it for so long!! I'm going to destroy it for good this time! Can you think of a greater ecstasy?!"

Milkit tensed up as the knife began to slice away her clothing. Though her flesh was spared, the sight of seeing her collar cut apart brought her even more pain than a cut would have. Her master bought her these clothes, and she treasured them—and the memories she'd made in them—more than her own body.

The woman above her would sully those memories.

"Next up, the skiiirt!! Watch as I cut your precious clothes away! You're trembling now, aren't you? Your body and mind are reacting as one as sadness consumes you. Aaaah, I love it!"

As promised, Satils cut through the frill-lined skirt, exposing Milkit's thighs and underwear.

"Oh, my, what a vulgar sight! If your master does show up to save you, I'm sure it'll only be to join the fun! Not that it matters—I'll have killed you long before that happens. I wonder if your corpse will still get them hot and bothered?"

Satils let out another cackle.

"Waaugh... M-master!!"

A knife thrust in front of Milkit's face cut her cries short. Satils raised and lowered the knife as she laughed, enjoying Milkit's response. But it was only a matter of

time until she grew tired of it, took hold of Milkit's head with her left hand, and slammed her face against the wall.

"Hyauungh!"

Satils seemed to enjoy the sound. She continued to bash Milkit's head against the wall.

"Haugh...auauh...st-st-stooop!"

Blood poured down Milkit's forehead and from her nose before pooling at her collarbone.

"You know, the more you tell me to stop, the more I want to do it, right? You know what they say when you're in school—you always want to tease the person you like the most! Love is pain. You'd better learn to endure it so I can enjoy myself!!"

Satils began to slam her head even harder against the wall. Even giving it her all, however, she didn't quite have the strength to hit Milkit hard enough to knock her out. Finally, she let Milkit collapse to the floor, where the young girl groaned absently to herself.

"M-master..."

She fully believed Flum would come. She had to. But if what Satils said was true, her wish would go unfulfilled. Milkit knew there were many people in the world stronger than Flum, and countless challenges out there that even her master couldn't overcome. But even then, she chose to have faith.

149

"H...help..."

"What's that? Forgot your place as a slave, did you? Are you asking your master to pick up the slack?"

Milkit groaned. She knew Flum would come and save her, but also that Flum would have to make sacrifices of her own in the process. As a slave, she knew she should never ask her master to risk herself in such a way, and yet, she couldn't help it.

"You're quite entertaining, Milkit! It's almost like you were born for me to kill you!" Satils stood up and delivered a fierce kick to the prostrate girl's stomach.

"Hngh!"

"I could almost..."

"Aungh!"

"...kill you now..."

"Uyaugh!"

"...before I've finished having my fun!"

"Nuuhaaaagh uunnngh..."

In addition to the dull pain throbbing in her head, she felt a sense of nausea wash over her. She could lose consciousness at any moment. A thin line of saliva trailed out of the corner of her mouth.

"This wonderful girl here is an important partner of mine..." Flum's words from just a day ago echoed in her mind, re-anchoring her to reality.

She wasn't a slave. She stood side by side with Flum, as equals. Even Milkit didn't quite understand what that said about the nature of their relationship, because she'd never been this close to another human before.

"Keep hoping for salvation! You forget who you are, slave. Beg to be saved all you want. All you'll do is make me enjoy this even more!"

Milkit whimpered. Even so, she knew she and Flum had chosen to support each other. Wasn't it only natural that they should seek each other's help?

Wasn't it only natural for her to have hopes and dreams?

"P-please save me, Master...!"

This wasn't like casting a spell or reciting a prayer. The mere act of saying these words would do little to change her situation, but something was changing within Milkit regardless. A change which brought great joy to Satils.

The older woman broke out in laughter. "You really think someone's going to help you? What a worthless slave. I'm certain your master's done with you by now! Gahaha—"

A loud crash cut her laughter short. The whole room shook, and a moment later, a cloud of dust and debris filled the room as a hole opened in the wall.

"Haha...ha..."

A small figure stepped through the newly created entrance.

"...ha?"

Satils stared blankly at the hole in the wall. When the dust cleared, the identity of the shadowy figure became apparent.

"You're that Flu...bwaugh!"

Flum's punch caught Satils square in the face, sending her flying back into the opposite wall.

"Waaaaaaah!" Milkit sobbed openly, so happy she couldn't begin to form words. "You...you came! I...I thought...hic...I thought I'd never see you again, Master!!"

"Milkit!! I'm so sorry I let you get so hurt... If only I'd paid more attention to you, this never would've happened!"

Milkit clung tightly to Flum. The mere warmth of her body eased Milkit's worries and took away all of the pain in an instant.

"No, please don't say that! You came to save me, Master! You've nothing to apologize for." She pressed her tear-drenched face hard into Flum's shoulder, quickly soaking her shirt.

Flum's eyes also began to well up with tears. Not from sadness, but out of relief to see Milkit safe and sound.

Welcy walked casually into the room and stopped

152

to inspect the desk. "Hmm, correspondence with the church, orders—ooohh, receipts. Is that an *intact church seal* on some of these? Yep, there's no denying this one."

The notes documenting Satils' under-the-table dealings with the church would prove to be incredibly useful to her research.

"Hey, Flum, what should..."

Welcy turned back to inquire about what they should do with the documents and froze. She'd figured that they would head back out once they found Milkit, but the look on Flum's face told another story. It had taken on the same cold, brutal look Welcy had seen before.

She was holding the Souleater in one hand and staring daggers at the quivering Satils.

"Why? H-how did...but you..." Satils blabbered. There was no way they should have been able to find their way here through her labyrinth, even with Flum and Welcy putting their heads together.

Except...

"I made a straight line through," Flum said.

No need to find a door if she just destroyed everything in her path with her prana and reversal magic.

"But what about...those two A-Rank...and B-Rank adventurers??"

"They're dead."

Satils' eyes went wide. There was no one left to protect her.

"And you'll be joining them."

"N-now wait just a moment. You won't get away with that, you know..."

Satils' face fell as her own words came back to haunt her: no one knew where this room was but for her. Even with the walls torn down and a clear path to the room, the entrance was still well hidden. She'd done so well keeping this room secret that, shy of Flum letting it slip, her body would never be found.

"M-money, do you want money? I'll pay whatever you ask. Anything you want, it's yours as long as you let me live!"

"Hm, all right then. I guess I'll just let you pay for the injuries you caused Milkit. How much will that be?"

"About...five thousand gold pieces or so. Or maybe ten...ngauh!!"

Flum grabbed Satils by the collar and pulled her in until their faces were practically touching.

"You think money can make us even? Get it through your thick skull: your life isn't worth what you did to her."

Satils trembled. "I... No... Please, I don't want to die..."

Flum pressed her palm against Satils' ear and cast Reversion, causing her flesh to rupture before dropping her to the floor. Satils' piercing scream echoed in the small room. She threw her hand up over the side of her head as blood gushed out, panting in fear.

"Did you get what you need, Welcy?"

"I, uh...yeah, pretty much."

"Good. Can you take Milkit out with you?"

Milkit looked worried. "You're not coming with us, Master?"

Flum offered up a gentle smile. "I don't want you to see what's about to happen here. You might hate me."

"I would never hate you, Master! No matter what happens!"

Flum laughed and shyly placed a finger to her own cheek. "I'm really happy to hear that."

She paused for a moment.

"Anyway, this is going to be pretty gruesome, so I really think it's better that you don't see it. So can you do me a favor and go with Welcy?"

"I...I understand." After what she just endured, Milkit didn't want to be away from Flum's side for even a second. But if Flum was about to kill this cruel and abusive woman, it was probably best that she not see it.

Flum maintained her smile until Welcy and Milkit were out of sight. Then her expression changed immediately, as if a switch had been flipped,

She picked the discarded knife from the floor and looked down at the cowering woman. Flum absently wondered what this woman, who mere moments ago had cackled at Milkit's suffering, calling slaves as her playthings, thought of the switch in their positions.

"Are you ready? I guess it doesn't matter, because I'm going to do it anyway."

"W-wait a minute! You don't need to... My money, it's yours!! Just don't...!"

"I don't care about money. You know, I don't even really want to do this. But I just can't let you live after what you've done."

Not for her past sins, nor for the new ones. Flum was filled with rage over how this old hag could do such awful things to someone as weak and helpless as Milkit.

This woman would suffer the greatest punishment Flum could conceive.

"Please...someone...heeeeeeelp! Gyaaaaugh!! My aaaaaaaaaaaaaaaarm! My...face, it... gyaugh?! Hyyaaaaah... haaah...ngayaaaauh! My nose, it...nnngaaaaaaaah!!"

Satils would suffer a greater pain and fear than what she subjected Milkit to.

"No, please... I don't wanna die...eaaauuuugh!! Stop... no...please...gaaaaaaugh!"

Flum would offer her no quarter.

"I...aaaaugh...nnngggggfff......hyauuugh...no... faaaaaugh...ki...ill...m-meeeeeee...!"

Muscles contorted and twisted in on themselves, blood spattered everywhere, and bones snapped as Satils crumpled in on herself with a final, bestial scream. Her cries were so loud that Milkit and Welcy could hear them from where they waited outside the room.

"You're...Milkit, was it? Is Flum always like that?" Welcy asked shakily.

"No, she's an amazingly caring master. She's only acting like this because she cares so much for me. More than anyone else ever has." Milkit blushed as she spoke.

"I see. You must be something really special to her then."

Soon after, the sounds in the room finally ceased. Her execution complete, Flum came running out of the room and into Milkit's arms. The smaller girl smiled and pressed her cheek against her master.

Welcy let out a sigh as she watched the two girls hold each other in a tight embrace.

"I think I'm starting to understand what my brother meant when he said you were trustworthy... Maybe..."

ROLL
OVER
AND
DIE

006

Re

AFTER LEAVING SATILS' hidden room, the group made their way to Leitch's manor to let Milkit get some rest. She was asleep within minutes of lying down in one of his many guest rooms. Flum, freshly dressed in some borrowed clothes, lay next to Milkit and gently stroked her hair as she slept.

A short time later, Leitch burst into the room. "Did you really kill Satils?!"

He must have heard about it from Welcy. Flum nodded, going on to explain everything that happened, from Milkit's past to the day's events.

"I'd heard stories about her...eclectic hobbies, but I never imagined she was Milkit's master," Leitch marveled. "Don't you think the church might suspect your involvement, especially considering their connections with her?"

"Her body is in a place where no one will find it, so I think we'll be fine for now."

"Well, we've got plenty of evidence of her crimes now, at least. If we're careful about how we leak it, I shouldn't suffer any blowback."

Suspicion would quickly fall on Flum and Welcy if they went public with that information so soon after Satils went missing. If they doled it out discreetly over time, though, people would probably come to believe Satils had met an entirely fitting end. The same applied to her relationship with the church. Getting the truth out there was all a matter of timing.

"We'll just have to trust Welcy's judgment," Flum said.

Leitch nodded. It seemed he and Flum were of a similar opinion on the matter. He stepped out to discuss the situation with his sister.

Alone once again, Flum gazed at Milkit's angelic face and gently stroked her cheek through the gaps in the bandages until she, too, grew tired. Despite the fact that it was still before noon, she'd already experienced more than most did in an entire day. She was exhausted.

Without any real reason to fight it, she decided she may as well get some sleep and rested her head on the bed.

Three hours later, the two woke up to learn that Leitch

had called over a nun he trusted to come heal Milkit's injuries.

Flum tentatively stepped into the house, trying not to make too much noise, as she could imagine the mood Eterna was in. She only made it a few steps inside when she was confronted by her, leaning up against the wall. Sure enough, she looked cranky.

Their eyes met for a tense moment before Eterna let out a breath, relieved to see Flum and Milkit were back and in one piece.

She closed the distance with Flum and poked her forehead.

"Ow!"

Eterna stuck out her lower lip. "I was worried, you know. You were both gone by the time I woke up." She leaned close and sniffed at Flum's neck. "I smell blood. One of Leitch's messengers stopped by and gave me an overview, but I want the full story."

Flum had had her clothes washed, but apparently, the smell still clung to her skin. "Milkit was abducted by her previous owner, and I went to get her back."

"You say that so casually. That's huge!"

"I don't disagree. But as you can see, I got her back safe and sound."

Milkit bowed her head apologetically. Eterna harrumphed and crossed her arms. "Was the church involved?"

"I don't think they had anything to do with Milkit's abduction. At least, not directly."

"Well, that's good. It looks like you guys made it out none the worse for wear, so I guess there's nothing left for me to say. But next time something like this happens, I hope you at least let me help."

Flum had been too fixated on chasing down the culprits to think about anything else at the time. If she hadn't given chase right then and there, she might never have been able to save Milkit. Besides, Eterna was still asleep at the time, and they couldn't have left Ink alone, since she might easily be a target for kidnapping, too.

Still, Eterna was right. Had Flum only called out for help, they might have handled the ordeal much faster.

"I'll do better next time."

"Well, I certainly hope so. Anyway, why don't we all get something to eat? I made lunch already."

An enticing aroma wafted out from the living room, eliciting a round of groans from Flum and Milkit's empty stomachs.

◇◇◇

They decided to stay indoors the rest of the day, choosing instead to make dinner with whatever they had on hand. Though Eterna's lunch was delicious in its own right, she seemed saddened to be outdone once again by Milkit at dinnertime—a fact Milkit appeared quite proud of. It wasn't every day you could beat a hero, after all.

After dinner, Flum insisted that she join Milkit for her bath. Milkit appeared embarrassed by the thought, but Flum persisted. Milkit eventually caved, though her embarrassment only skyrocketed upon entering the room.

Flum stared longingly at Milkit's back.

"Whoa, look at your skin, Milkit! It's absolutely flawless! I'm jealous." She reached up to stroke the other girl's hair. "I just love the color of your hair. Sometimes I have to wonder to myself if maybe you're really some kind of angel or fairy, ya know..."

Milkit's cheeks flushed red.

The two young women pressed close together as they slid into the narrow tub, their body temperatures rising far above that of the water.

After they finished with their bath, it was finally time for bed.

Flum and Milkit sat on the bed in pajamas matching in all but color. They undid Milkit's bandages, bantered back and forth for some time, and then finally headed to their respective beds. The lights went out, and the room was bathed in darkness.

Flum shut her eyes the moment her head hit the pillow. Milkit was left staring blankly ahead until her eyes adjusted to the darkness, and the ceiling began to take shape in front of her.

I'm...scared to sleep.

It was true. After her encounter with Satils, she was certain the nightmares waiting for her would be more graphic than before. She started to consider if it would be better to just wait the night out, rather than sleep.

"Hey, Milkit...why don't you come over here and sleep with me?" Flum lifted up her covers and waved Milkit over.

The sight of her master's smiling face in the dim moonlight sent Milkit's heart racing.

"I...I couldn't. It's a single bed, after all. There's no room for the two of us."

"It'll be fine if you squeeze in close."

As with earlier in the bath, there was little room in Flum's tone for debate.

"But...why now? It's so sudden..."

"I saw that sad look on your face right before we went to bed. You looked terrified to sleep alone."

"...You could tell?"

"Not so much tell as...more that I felt the same way."

"You did?"

"I kept thinking about what I'd do if you just disappeared again while I was asleep. But if you're here in my arms, I don't need to worry about that, right?"

A moment was all it took for someone to be snatched from you—Flum had experienced this twice already. The fear that coursed through her was hard to define but very real.

"Are...are you sure it's okay?"

"I want you to come over."

"Then—then I suppose I'll take you up on the offer." Milkit grabbed her pillow and climbed under the covers with Flum.

Her body warmed up quickly as she lay there in Flum's arms. She could feel herself calming down immediately, which made her simultaneously overjoyed and mortified. Though she felt far more at ease, her heart pounded, which in turn made it difficult to sleep.

"Why don't you scoot in?"

Milkit was trying to respect Flum's space by staying on the far end of the bed, but Flum pulled her in close.

165

"Hah..." Flum snickered. "Whoa, your heart is pounding, Milkit. I'm just hugging you, ya know!"

"I...I know, but...you're just so amazing, Master."

"Maybe, maybe not. But that's got nothin' to do with sleeping together while holding each other, right?"

Milkit laughed lightly. "It's all the same to me, Master."

Gazing upon Milkit's smiling face up so close, Flum corrected herself: she outshone an angel. She was a straight-up goddess. She forced back her instinctive desire to worship such a beautiful being, though her ears rung with her own pulse at the thought. Still, the hammering in her chest was hardly a bad feeling. She quite enjoyed it, actually.

Only the warm embrace of her master could set Milkit free of her nightmares. The warmth of her body, the beat of her heart, the smell of her skin... These were all the gentle assurances that Milkit needed to know that Flum was still nearby, even when her eyes were closed.

"M-master?"

"Yes?"

In Satils' dungeon, Flum had answered Milkit's prayers. But in that moment, she began to worry she had destroyed the relationship between a slave and her master. To be fair, Flum had never treated Milkit like a slave. Milkit just defaulted to thinking in terms of slave-master

relationships because it was the only kind she'd ever known.

Now that their relationship had taken a turn into something else entirely, Milkit wasn't sure how to handle it. She'd tried being reserved, practicing self-control, and limiting herself to what she knew best. As long as she followed her scripts, she'd be okay. But she couldn't keep the walls up any longer. She was ready to step outside the world she knew all too well.

"Well, I...umm...if it's all right with you..." She was so nervous that she fumbled to find the right words. "I... I would like to begin sleeping in your bed from now on, if it's okay with you."

She was ready to make her own, selfish desires known.

Flum leaned in close to Milkit until their foreheads were touching and smirked. "I was just about to say the same thing."

Flum's words resonated deep within Milkit's heart. She knew Flum would never lie to her, and it filled her with rapture to know the person dearest to her returned her feelings.

"Hey, why don't we go buy you some new clothes tomorrow? Your other ones are all cut up."

"Let's. And maybe we can get you some new clothes too, Master."

"Only if you pick them out for me."

"I'm not so confident about that, but I'll give it my best."

Flum chuckled. "I'm looking forward to it. Is there anywhere else you want to go?"

"Hmm...well, I'd like to try some delicious new dishes, if we could."

"Delicious, huh? Well, why don't we just go all out and go to a fancy restaurant?"

"A fancy restaurant?"

"Hey, no need to be so modest. You don't need to worry about money, okay?"

"It's not about money. I worry my cooking won't compare to the food at a really fancy place."

"Ahh, is that so?"

"I want you to think that my cooking is the best there is and prefer it to going out."

"I mean, I already do, sooo..."

The two continued to talk well into the night about their plans for the following day as they lay in the small bed. This, in turn, kept them up far later than they anticipated, and it took at least another hour before they finally fell asleep.

The next day, Eterna eyed the unusually cheerful girls with suspicion. She took a bite of sausage and swallowed before finally speaking up. "You guys going on a date today?"

A spoonful of soup went down Flum's windpipe in surprise, sending her immediately into a coughing fit. Milkit ran to her side and started to rub Flum's back as she handed her a cup of water.

Flum drained the glass and took a deep breath before shooting a glare back at Eterna.

"It's not like that!!"

"Sure seems that way."

"What're you talkin' about?! We're just going out to replace Milkit's clothes from yesterday and do some window shopping along the way!"

"Most people would call that a da..."

"Shopping!! I mean, isn't it a little weird that you'd be saying Milkit and I just heading out someplace together is a date?? You agree, don't you, Milkit?"

"That's right. Master and I are just going shopping."

Eterna remained unconvinced. "I mean, that's what a date is..."

But that wasn't how Flum and Milkit intended it, despite the ambiguous nature of their relationship. They weren't friends, exactly. More like partners. No—if

anything, they were family at this point, though they were intent on not labeling it in any more detail.

Eterna shrugged in defeat. "I don't get it."

◇ ◇ ◇

A short time later, Flum and Milkit went out into town. Walking hand in hand, Milkit kept glancing over at the side of Flum's head.

"Is there something on my head?"

"I just noticed that you were using the hairpin I made for you."

"Oh, this? Of course I am. It was a present from you, after all."

Milkit had made the hairpin and given it to Flum just a few days back. Seeing it woven neatly in Flum's hair, she couldn't help but start to worry it might get in Flum's way in a fight, or that it was a little too flashy for Flum's usual style.

"It's really pretty. I love it." Regardless, Flum seemed taken with it. Milkit tried to push her negative thoughts away and be happy her master was so pleased with her gift.

Finally, the two reached their destination: the same shop where they'd purchased Milkit's maid uniforms

before. The employees all knew them at this point, probably in no small part because of the sums Flum spent there, and no longer seemed to pay their slave markings any mind. Flum and Milkit bounced around the shop looking over the selection before taking a few that really stood out to try on.

"Hmm, this might be good for special occasions."

"Are you sure? I think it's a little bland."

"I wouldn't call it bland, just...normal, maybe? But everything looks great on you, Milkit. I'm always so jealous."

"That's not true at all. But if you keep saying that, I might accidentally start to believe it."

Milkit was wearing a markedly simple maid outfit consisting of a beige dress with a thick, white apron. This was all topped off with a small cap sitting atop her head that kept her hair out of her eyes. The dress was built for pure functionality, lacking glamour. Still, it seemed too handy not to have around for housecleaning.

"Do you really think it suits me?" Milkit shifted about uncomfortably under Flum's intense gaze.

"I dunno, I'm always worried that you're so beautiful someone might just try to steal you from right under my nose, but with this, I kinda feel...at ease? It's good for home, I think."

Milkit turned back to face the mirror. She tugged at the skirt and adjusted the hat a few times.

"If you think so, then this is my first choice."

"Sounds good!"

With that decided, Milkit began changing into the next dress.

"You know," Flum said. "I just noticed that you wear a lot of frilly clothes. Do you like that style?"

"I've always thought dresses like that were really cute."

"Huh, so does that mean you don't really like the other one we just looked at?"

"No, not at all. I always choose the same types of clothes. I think it's refreshing to wear something new." Milkit finally finished changing and opened the curtain but only enough to stick her head out. Her face and neck were a bright pink. "Y-you chose this one, didn't you, Master?"

"Right, like I mentioned earlier, I like all the frilly dresses you wear. Is there a problem?"

"N-not exactly, just...look." She finally opened the curtain up, showing off the dress.

"Whoa." Flum was at a loss for words.

The top was covered in frills and just as adorable as she'd expected. The bottom, however, was another story. The skirt was short. Extremely so. It left Milkit's thighs

entirely exposed and was only long enough to—barely—hide her underwear.

Milkit's face burnt red as she tugged repeatedly at the hem. The way she moved was enough to send Flum's heart racing. "Whoa, I'm so sorry...I had no idea the skirt was so short."

"I-If this is what you're looking for, Master...I...I'll wear it around the house..."

Flum shook her head, resisting the temptation. A voice in the back of her mind cried foul; she tamped it down.

"N-no, it's okay. Let's try the next one. Next!"

"Okay..."

Milkit shut the curtain, let out a deep breath, and put her hand to her chest. Her heart was pounding in embarrassment. She thought back to Flum's bright red face.

"But maybe it couldn't hurt to have something like that around to wear from time to time..."

Several minutes later, she opened the curtain again wearing a new dress. In stark contrast to her usual maid uniforms, this one was a sheer white dress.

"You chose this one as well, right, Master?"

"Oh...yes." Flum was completely entranced. Milkit always seemed like such a pure, beautiful creature to her that she figured a white dress would suit her perfectly.

173

But she'd had no idea just how stunning it would look on her. "You look like a noble's daughter."

"You exaggerate, Master. No noble's daughter would walk around with bandages like this."

The bandages only added to Milkit's charm, as far as Flum was concerned. Besides, if she were to walk around town in a dress like this with her face exposed, Flum was convinced everyone would fall in love with her at first sight.

"You're stunning." The words came out of her mouth before her brain had a chance to catch up. She only wished she could capture the image in ink on paper or paint and canvas, so she could keep it forever.

"Well, I guess I'll...I'll change."

Beginning to feel embarrassed under Flum's intense stare, Milkit disappeared back behind the curtain. When she emerged, she was back in the maid uniform she was wearing when they left the house that morning.

"So what do you think? Did you decide?"

"I think I'd like to go with the first maid uniform. It was also quite reasonably priced."

"Compared to the others, yeah." The second one she tried on, the one with the miniskirt, had been the most expensive. "Well, that's settled then, I think you could still pick out another two or so, though."

"You're not buying anything, Master?"

"I don't think anything in this store really suits me."

"I, for one, would like to see you try out a different style once in a while."

"Oh? All right then, I'll let you pick out something you think would look good on me."

"Are you sure?" Milkit took off with a slight skip in her step to go pick out some clothes. It was rare to see her so excited.

Flum watched, faintly worried at how quickly Milkit had jumped at the chance. "Did she really wanna to dress me up that bad?"

Milkit handed her an outfit and, before Flum even had a chance to look it over, pushed her into the changing room. She beamed as she watched the curtain, waiting patiently for her master to step out.

Flum hesitated for a moment when she saw the clothes but pressed on and changed into them. After several moments, she opened the curtain, revealing a frill-covered maid uniform that closely resembled something Milkit would usually have picked for herself.

"Woooow!"

Milkit put her hands to her cheeks and gazed at her master. Flum blushed heavily and tugged at the dress.

Though Milkit had worn maid uniforms all this time,

Flum had never considered just how embarrassing it was to wear one.

"This really...isn't...me."

Milkit replied excitedly. "Hardly! I think you look absolutely stunning, Master!"

This only caused Flum to blush even more furiously. She wanted nothing more than to shut the curtain but resisted the urge for Milkit's sake. "This hardly feels like wearing clothes."

"I think you wear it well."

"I really don't see how someone could clean in this."

"That dissonance makes it all the better!"

"You sure are excited right now."

Milkit hesitated at this. "I...I'm sorry. I guess I got a little too worked up."

It wasn't every day she had the chance to get her master to wear something just for her...though that wasn't exactly true. She knew all she had to do was ask, and Flum would wear anything she wanted, though Milkit couldn't bring herself to find the words. If Flum didn't offer, she knew she wouldn't have another opportunity for quite some time.

"We'll...we'll try some other clothes out some other time. I'm glad you're so happy, but I think this is about my limit."

"No, please don't worry about me. Please go ahead and change!"

Flum slammed the curtain shut and changed back into her usual shirt and shorts in record time. This was much easier to move around in. After cinching her belt closed, she looked herself over in the mirror.

"I really want to see Milkit smile like that, but I just don't think I can relax in those kinda clothes. What a tough spot to be in."

After stepping out of the changing room, the pair picked out another two maid outfits for Milkit before leaving the shop in search of a high-end restaurant.

The thoroughfare running through the Central District was just as busy as ever. Flum kept a tight, protective grip on Milkit's hand as she led her companion through the mass of people.

"I can't believe how many people are out today. It feels like the crowds get bigger every time we're out here."

"It certainly seems like tourist and merchant traffic is on the rise, and there are more carriages, too. Look, the crowd is parting up ahead just to make way for the

carriage over there, and everyone's kind of bunching up together."

There had apparently been talks about making a road exclusively for carriage travel, but the kingdom had its energies focused elsewhere, and the plan fell by the wayside. It wasn't just roads, either. The capital continued to grow in size and population while infrastructure, repairs, and public safety remained neglected. These shortcomings didn't go unnoticed. The public was increasingly unhappy with the lack of any resolution.

"You okay with crowds?"

"I'm fine."

"Good. I'm going to force my way through, so don't let go of my hand no matter what."

Flum pushed on, parting the crowds ahead of her as needed, as she bore down on the renowned restaurant they had decided on.

Though it was on the high end, the restaurant didn't have any sort of dress code that would prevent them from entering. Moreover, the waitstaff didn't even bat an eyelash at the slave mark on Flum's cheek, alleviating her fears that they would be turned away at the door. She could count on progressive attitudes to prevail in the capital to a certain extent, though they still suffered some blatant sidelong stares from other diners and even a few that tried to trip them as they walked past. Not like a normal person could trip Flum, of course. In the end, the bad actors were the ones more likely to get hurt.

After enjoying a few minutes of quiet at their table, a waitress stopped by with a menu. Milkit's eyes went wide as saucers when she peeked inside the menu. She looked back and forth between Flum and the numbers written inside.

"Order whatever you want."

"B-but I..."

Even with the offer on the table, Milkit still couldn't fathom going so far as to order something so expensive for herself. On the other hand, it also seemed rude to Flum to have her master take her to such a place and order something cheap. She ended up choosing something she had really wanted to eat.

Flum followed up by ordering something even more expensive for herself.

The dishes that came out looked like works of art. Flum smiled as she watched the look of bliss cross Milkit's face whenever she took a bite, her eyes closing and forehead wrinkling while sighing with joy. In a matter of no time, both of their plates were cleared.

Though the bill was ghastly, the satisfaction they derived from it was more than worth it.

"Man, that was amazing."

"It really was delicious. I'm not sure I could even make that at home."

"I'd be the luckiest girl alive if I could have an amazing meal like that and then enjoy it again and again thanks to you."

"Please don't get your hopes up quite yet. I still can't really cook as well as the professionals, you know."

"What're you talkin' about, Milky? I've told you countless times—no one cooks better than you."

"Milk...y?"

Flum had been caught up in the moment, and the name had just come out naturally. She laughed it off and moved on. "So where do you wanna go next? Maybe go see some flowers?"

Her mind raced as she tried to come up with more ideas for their lovely date. They could go to an accessory shop so she could buy a gift for Milkit to return her kindness or perhaps visit a different shop to try on more clothes. Or they could look through the market and search for more cursed equipment, check out some new cooking utensils for the kitchen, and then pick out something for dinner.

Ultimately, she just wanted to have as much fun as possible to get Milkit's mind off the whole Satils ordeal.

"Anywhere is fine, as long as I'm with you, Master. I always have a great time with you!"

Milkit rarely expressed herself as openly as Flum did, so this was quite a showing for her. For once, she'd decided to take Flum up on her kindness and just let herself enjoy life to the fullest without worrying about the small things. Or at least that was the plan for the time being.

"Hm?" Milkit turned to the side and stopped suddenly. This, in turn, tugged Flum to a stop as well.

"What is it? Why'd you stop all of a sudden?" Flum turned to glance in the direction Milkit was looking.

There was a tightly packed crowd moving together like a massive, undulating wave. Through the gaps between people, Flum spied a figure that stood out from the rest.

The woman was wearing a gaudy dress decorated with corsages, and a fur-lined red coat was draped over her shoulders. Above her brightly painted nails she wore rings outfitted with massive gemstones. Her hair practically shone like an opal.

The face...the face caked in makeup was one that Flum would never forget.

"B-but how?"

"You, you killed her, Master!"

As much as they wanted to deny it, that changed nothing about the sight that confronted them.

That was no ghost standing up ahead. It was her in the flesh, laughing, walking, and talking as if nothing were wrong.

"Satils Francois...!"

As soon as the name came out of Flum's mouth, the woman glanced their way and locked eyes with Flum before bursting out into a broad, toothy grin.

Flum felt a chill run up her spine.

ROLL
OVER
AND
DIE

007

Dreams Are a Blissful Insanity Known Only to You

SATILS MOVED AWAY so quickly, it was like she'd never seen Flum and Milkit at all. They stood there in stunned silence for a few moments before Flum finally came to her senses. She couldn't let Satils just get away like that.

"We're heading after her!"

"O-okay!"

Shortly after they picked up the trail, it quickly became evident that Satils was making the rounds of the shops she operated within the Central District. After dropping in on several stores, she walked straight past the church and made her way back to her home in the East District.

Flum wanted to confront her then and there, and figure out what was going on, but she was all too aware it could be a trap. She stopped at the street corner and eyed the entrance.

"I should probably talk to Eterna about this." She turned back to Milkit, who was white as a sheet, and patted her head. What awful timing, considering she just helped Milkit get over her nightmares... "This is a real head-scratcher. Wealth alone shouldn't be able to bring you back from the dead."

"That's...really her, isn't it? I wanted to think that it's just an impostor, but it doesn't seem so."

"Well, we don't have any proof yet, but she looked like the real thing to me. What did you think, Milkit?"

"She seemed real to me, too. Everything about her, even the way her skin clung to her body, gave me the same awful feeling she did."

They only had that gut instinct to go off of, but that was exactly what was the hardest to duplicate about a person. It was nearly impossible for an imposter to give off the very same vibe as the real deal.

"There's no way she could've survived after what I did to her."

"Do you think an Origin core might be involved?"

There were three research teams operated by the church. Assuming they were involved, the most likely one would be...

"Necromancy."

"Bingo, lady."

Just as Flum reached her conclusion, the two heard a young voice speak up from behind them. She spun around with the Souleater drawn and swiped at her target.

"Whoa, that's quite an aggressive greeting!"

Milkit let out a small gasp as soon as she saw the boy's face. "Nekt!!"

"Heh, so you remember my name. How sweet of you."

The preteen boy standing before them, dressed in a white shirt, was named Nekt Lyncage. He was one of the Spiral Children.

Nekt chuckled to himself, unfazed by Flum's attempt to murder him.

"You sure are confident, aren't you?" Flum snarled. "Showing up out here in the open like this, even while Gadhio is fast on your trail."

"Fast on my trail? Gimme a break. Mother's research is carrying on just fine, thank you very much. I'm helping! Everything's easier now that we don't gotta haul Ink's dead weight around, actually."

"You little punk!" Flum stepped between Nekt and Milkit and prepared to face off.

However, he showed no sign of preparing to attack. "Whoa, hey, don't bark at me like a rabid dog. I'm just here to talk, so chill out. Seriously, I'm not here to fight today."

"You don't strike me as someone who's going to be swayed by words."

"Don't lump me together with the other teams' creatures, okay? We Children became one with our cores from our earliest days. We're used to them. I'm my own person, not a mere puppet of Papa Origin."

That much was true. He even talked like a bratty little kid. What's more, Flum knew that even with all her equipment, she would be no match for Nekt, who had nearly killed Gadhio in their last encounter. Even less so while trying to protect Milkit. Now was no time to let her emotions get the best of her.

Flum slowly lowered her blade.

"Glad to see you're willing to listen to reason."

"Cut the fluff and get to the point."

"All right, we'll keep it simple then. I want to join forces."

Flum hesitated. That was completely unexpected.

"I'm just going to tell you right now, I'm totally serious about this," Nekt continued. "Everything I'm about to say is under the assumption that you already know about the Chimera and Necromancy projects."

Flum glared, unblinking. "Well, I'll at least hear you out."

Nekt shrugged. "I guess that's a start. So anyway, you know that there are three teams within the church performing research on Origin cores, right? But do you know why they aren't all a part of the same team?"

"To make them compete?"

"Bingo! Wow, you're smarter than I thought. I had you pegged for the type who tries to solve all her problems with force. Anyway, we don't really get along with the other teams. I guess that makes sense, but it means that two of the teams are destined to be cut off in the future."

"So you want to join forces to crush the Necromancy team."

"Wow, you're on fire today. So, what do you think? Pretty tempting, huh?"

Flum launched straight into her refusal as soon as he was done talking. "No thanks. There's no way I'd team up with the people who kidnapped Milkit!"

She would never forget the terror of losing Milkit. Flum could only imagine that Milkit was even more afraid of Nekt than she was. The idea of working together with him was absolutely ludicrous.

"Well, you sure don't seem to like me all that much. Y'know, I only did it because that Dein guy asked me to. I had no interest in that bandaged lady over there."

"And I hate that. Call it Origin's voice, or your own will—you still don't have a moral bone in your body!"

"Huh, I guess I can't argue with you there. I haven't really talked to a lotta people outside of the research team, so I can't really say whether I'm immoral or not."

"Well, I'm glad you agree! Anyway, I'm out of here." Flum cut the conversation off there and clasped her hand around Milkit's to make her exit.

Nekt watched as they turned to go and raised his voice just a tad louder than necessary as he called out to them. "I don't suppose you're going to ask Eterna Rinebow for advice, are you? I'd recommend against that."

"What are you going on about?"

"Now remember, we didn't actually do anything. But think this through. That Satils lady was given a core and brought back to life, yeah? Obviously, Necromancy is involved. They worked hard for years to keep their work under wraps, and now they throw it all right in your face. What d'you reckon are the chances they'd try something similar with the other heroes, too?"

"Hnng...! Hold on tight, Milkit!"

"Okay!"

Flum wrapped an arm around Milkit and took off toward their house at full speed.

Nekt waved to them as they ran off until they were out of sight. The smile immediately disappeared from his face as he let out a heavy sigh.

"Haaah... I guess this is how it's gonna be for now. Or maybe they saw through my little ruse. Maybe I *am* missing my moral compass." He turned in the opposite direction and grinned. "But nothing I said was untrue. They've gotta be going after the other heroes as well."

He didn't need to lie to Flum to sow the seeds that would bring her over to his side.

Gadhio finished up his administrative work at the guild earlier than he anticipated, so he decided to head home. He'd taken over his role as guild master in the hopes of finding out more about the church from his guildmates, but thus far, his efforts proved fruitless. The group he was looking into had its fingers in every pie in the kingdom, and even though he knew it would be difficult to unearth any meaningful information about them, he still felt like he was fighting an uphill battle.

He decided to go home early and spend the rest of the evening with Kleyna and Hallom.

"I'm really not good at stuff like this..." Gadhio muttered

under his breath as he gently swung a boxed cake back and forth in his hand.

Just the thought of their excited faces made him tense up. The last time he'd been so overcome with shyness over giving someone a present was with Tia.

"Well, I certainly hope Kleyna and Hallom enjoy this."

He knew he couldn't hang on to his lost wife and best friend forever. Gadhio had loved Tia and Sohma more than anything, and as long as he continued to blame himself for their deaths, he would never be able to move forward. At the same time, a part of him wanted to live up to Kleyna and Hallom's expectations. Buying this cake for them was his first step in that direction.

The cake shop Gadhio chose was one Flum recommended to him.

"Cyrill and I went there once. Their cakes are so good!" Despite all the hardships she suffered, her eyes still shone brightly as she spoke. He could only wonder what had possessed her to recommend a cake shop to the last person you'd expect to see in line at such an establishment.

As these thoughts ran through his mind, he finally found himself standing at the manor entrance. Before he had a chance to grab the doorknob, the door came flying open in front of him.

"Haah…haah… G-Gadhio! You're finally back!" Kleyna panted.

"Oh, hi, Kleyna. I was out picking up a cake for Hallom."

"Th-thanks. But, but…now's not the time for that!"

She looked fine. Did that mean something happened to Hallom?

Kleyna took Gadhio's arm and started to drag him before stopping in her tracks. Gadhio's eyes fixed on the figure that appeared in front of them, and he froze up as well.

"Welcome back. Or, hang on, shouldn't you be saying that to me?" The woman spoke in a warm, cheerful tone. "I'm home, Gaddy."

The bright smile gracing her face was no different than it was six years ago.

"T-tia…?"

Standing before him was the woman who had given her life for him. The woman he loved more than anything else. The woman who had once been his wife.

"In the flesh! It's me, your adoring wife, Tia Lathcutt!"

He should have been filled with pure bliss, but instead his mind was completely blank.

"That's… There's no way in hell…"

He'd seen her die with his own two eyes. And yet here she was, standing right in front of him, very much alive.

Alarm bells were ringing in his head, warning the well-trained adventurer to keep his distance, but the feeling of exhilaration quickly took hold and blew those thoughts away, filling every crevice of his mind.

The cake box fell from his hand and dropped unceremoniously to the floor as he stepped forward to pull Tia into a tight embrace.

ROLL
OVER
AND
DIE

008

Drowning in Indulgence

"**H**EY, THAT'S a little tight there, Gaddy." Tia smiled as his massive arms wrapped firmly around her.

"Tia..." Practically every possible emotion was running through Gadhio as her name escaped his lips.

"Don't look so blue. I'm right here." Her love and affection was clear in her voice as she slid her own arms around his waist.

"Tia..."

"Getting such a warm hug from a shy guy like you, Gaddy, really makes coming back totally worth it."

He could feel her in his arms, warm and alive. She was too real to be a dream.

"But I'm serious, you're really hugging me a little tight there. I give, I give!" Tia playfully punched her fist into his back.

Gadhio finally came to his senses and loosened his grip, instead moving his hands to her shoulders and looking her in the eyes.

"You've gotten a lot stronger, Gaddy. Those six years passed like nothing for me, but I can tell you changed just looking at your face."

"And you haven't changed at all, Tia." He brought his hand to her pink cheek, but his finger shook before making contact. He was afraid he'd send this illusion crumbling down like a statue made of sand. When his index finger finally made contact, he was greeted with the feeling of silky soft skin.

No matter how many ways he reconfirmed it, he still had a hard time believing it.

"But your warmth hasn't changed one bit." Tia placed her hand over his as he stroked her cheek. She smiled warmly and looked up at him, almost as if she, too, were confirming that he was there. Kleyna watched from a distance, a complicated look on her face, as the two remained lost in their own private world.

After a short while, Tia slowly, reluctantly drew her hand away.

"There's a lot to discuss, so why don't you come inside?" She turned to Kleyna. "So, whatever happened to my room?"

"Um, well...we left it just as it was. I've kept it clean, too."

"Oh, thank you. I guess we'll continue the discussion there, then?" Tia took Gadhio's hand and led him inside as Kleyna watched on.

She couldn't believe it. Without any knowledge of what was going on behind the scenes at the church, she couldn't even begin to assemble an explanation for what happened. All she could do was stand there, alone, and watch Gadhio and Tia disappear into the house.

Off in the countryside, there was a grove of trees that grew the most beautiful fruit. The fruit, however, would slowly consume the body of anyone who ate it. This was common knowledge to all who lived in the region.

One man, in an attempt to prove his mettle to his friends, decided to eat one of these fruits. He managed to get one down, showing them what he was made of, but strangely enough, he began to eat the same fruit day after day. Everyone he knew pleaded with him to stop, but he continued until the poison got to him, and he vomited blood and died.

Now, why did he continue to eat the fruit, knowing what would happen to him?

The answer was surprisingly simple: the fruit was unbelievably delicious. The man simply couldn't resist.

Louh had told Gadhio this story many years prior. At the time, Gadhio laughed it off and thought the man was an idiot, but considering where he was now, he wondered if he was in any place to judge.

"Hmm, you've certainly gotten wild, Gaddy." Tia sat atop Gadhio's lap on the sofa in her bedroom and ran her hands across his face.

This was the way they always sat whenever she wanted to be doted on. In truth, they'd only really been that close for a year or so prior to her death. Not very long at all.

"I liked how clean-cut you were back in the day, but I think you look pretty good now, too. You still have the same face, but you look so strong and rugged. I've got a pretty amazing husband."

"Oh?"

"Yep, without a doubt. At least I think so." She dragged her finger across his well-toned chest. Gadhio unconsciously slid an arm around her waist. "Six whole years, and yet it feels like it all happened just a month ago to me."

"I guess the house hasn't really changed much."

"Yeah, I was surprised to see my room was pretty much as it was. But the layout of the capital and the people around town are all so different. Kleyna and...Hallom,

was it? Them too. It's hard to imagine Sohma's kid is so big now." A twinge of sadness hung in Tia's voice. It was no simple matter to overcome a six-year gap.

Gadhio's guard slowly began to drop the more time he spent with her. She had emotions, and her body was warm. If this wasn't Tia, then he didn't know what to believe anymore.

"I guess that means I'm changing too, huh?"

"You mentioned coming back to life. What happened?"

It was the one question he didn't want to ask, but the whole situation was so beyond the realm of what was normal that he had to believe that the church was somehow involved. He had to ask.

Depending on her answer, he might have to kill her.

"Honestly, I don't really know, but apparently something called an Origin core was put into me that brought me back to life."

And there was that name, just as he predicted.

Gadhio clenched his hands into fists and spoke in a terse voice. "Hmm... I see."

"You sound like you know what an Origin core is, Gaddy. I guess I don't really need to explain then, huh? Anyway, they managed to rein it in to the point it wouldn't turn me into a monster, and then they gave me permission to leave."

Her explanation took him by surprise. If the church was trying to lay a trap for him, why reveal such information so freely? Or maybe they were hoping to get him to let his guard down by feeding him lies.

Gadhio frowned and knitted his eyebrows over his inability to figure out their plan.

Tia watched his face for a long moment before slowly extending her finger and tracing the wrinkles in his forehead. "You've got your serious thinking face on again. We're finally back together, you know. You should smile a bit more."

"It's not that simple. Origin cores are incredibly dangerous. The monster that killed our team was transformed and powered by a core."

"Dafydd said as much. Apparently, they couldn't really control the cores as well back then. I doubt I can really convince you of much beyond that, but all I can say is that I'm alive again."

"Dafydd Chalmas... So it *is* the Necromancy project."

"So you know about that, too. He's a rather calm, reserved man with glasses who's always in a lab coat. Apparently, he brought his own wife back from the dead."

The more he asked, the deeper the story became. Gadhio was starting to wonder if all he needed to do was ask to find out where they kept their lab.

"You're looking at me like you're not sure why I'm telling you all this. I have nothing to hide from you, Gaddy. Besides, Dafydd told me I didn't need to keep anything secret."

Gadhio started to become annoyed.

"I just don't get it. Just what does the church want here? What do they hope to achieve by bringing you back to life and sending you here to meet me?"

Tia smiled gently back at Gadhio before continuing on. "I don't know what's going on with the other research teams, but at the very least, the Necromancy team just wants to bring back the dead. They want to help anyone out there suffering over the loss of a loved one. Dafydd knows the feeling all too well. I think that's all there is to it."

She didn't seem to be lying. At the very least, not to him, judging by everything he knew about her before she died.

It was true that an Origin core could perform miracles unlike anything man had ever seen—assuming its power was contained and bound. In fact, one such miracle was sitting right here in front of him.

"...No. I just can't believe it." Gadhio shook his head.

Tia looked at him sadly for a moment before a smile sprung to her lips. "Dafydd said it was tough to get people to accept it in the beginning. After all, I've been dead for six long years—not just to you, but Kleyna, too. Of course it's a shock for me to show up all of a sudden like this."

"I'm sorry. I wish I could just be happy about it."

"There's nothing to apologize for. Will you meet with me again?"

"Again? Do you have to go somewhere?"

"They still need to make some small adjustments to my body. If I let my guard down too much, Origin may take over, apparently. I need to head back to the lab in another two hours or so."

"I see..." The disappointment was clear in Gadhio's voice.

No matter how much he suspected it was some trap of the church's, this was still his long-lost wife sitting in front of him. There was no denying the joy he felt.

"Aww, I'm touched you're so sad to see me go, Gaddy. Listen, I've been told that once the adjustments are done with, we'll finally be able to live together again, so just hang in there for a while longer, okay? Can we at least stay in each other's arms like this until I have to go?"

"I have no complaints."

Tia giggled. "Good. You've always been a sweetheart."

The time passed peacefully, almost like a dream. Though the feeling of uncertainty still reigned within

Gadhio's heart, it grew weaker and weaker the longer he felt her warm body resting against him. It was dangerous; he knew that. But the reward was massive compared to the risk.

Slowly but surely, Gadhio felt himself sinking deeper and deeper into a warm, comfortable mire from which he could not escape.

Kleyna took the box Gadhio dropped back to the kitchen and opened it, only to find two slices of cake. Obviously, he hadn't bought them for himself.

She bit down on her lower lip as a host of feelings she couldn't identify washed over her.

Suddenly, Hallom was at her side. "Hey, Mommy, who was that lady?"

"That's Gadhio's wife."

"Daddy's wife? Isn't that supposed to be you, Mommy?"

She'd never said the words, but she always felt that was the direction things were going. Hallom, and even Kleyna, held out hope that the day would come. Maybe not now, maybe not even in a year, but she figured that in another two years or so she and Gadhio might finally marry.

"His real wife came back. There's no place for me anymore."

"Real wife? So you were a fake, Mommy?" Hallom meant no harm with her words, but they stung deep. After all, Kleyna's feelings were all too real. "So does that mean that Daddy won't be my daddy anymore if she's around? If that's how it's going to be, I don't want her!"

"Come now, Hallom, you can't say that..."

"But she's scary! You're a lot better that she'll ever be, Mommy!"

"Well, I guess I can't be mad when you're flattering me like that, kiddo." Kleyna knelt down and patted Hallom's head. "Tia's a good person. I'm sure you'll take a liking to her once you guys have a chance to talk."

"Not a chance!"

"You know it's not right to make up your mind before trying something."

"No, I don't mean it like that, Mommy! She's just really scary!"

Hallom didn't seem to hate her. Rather, she just seemed afraid. The look on her face said it all. Kleyna looked worriedly at her daughter and began to stroke her hair when Hallom leaned in to whisper in her ear.

"That lady is empty, Mommy."

Kleyna tilted her head at this odd statement. "Empty?"

"She laughs, but she isn't really laughing. She looks like she's having fun, but she really isn't."

"Hmm? I'm sorry, honey, but Mommy doesn't understand what you're saying. Can you put it another way?"

"I can't really explain it. I don't really understand it either. But that's how I felt!"

The way children saw the world was sometimes incomprehensible to adults. Kleyna figured Tia had just rubbed Hallom the wrong way, but once they actually had a chance to talk, they'd get along. After all, Tia had always won children over, no matter where they went. If anything, Kleyna had been the one they were afraid of.

Dismissing what her daughter had said, Kleyna went back to stroking her hair. She shot Hallom a smile. "Do you want to eat some cake? Gadhio bought it for you."

The look of worry stayed plastered to Hallom's face even as she nodded stiffly. She was in no position to turn down cake.

After parting ways with Nekt, Flum dashed through crowds at full speed with her arms still tightly wrapped around Milkit. Her only concern was getting back to her house in the shortest time possible.

Even when it came into sight, she ran full steam ahead straight into the house, shouting for Eterna as she went. "Eterna, are you okay??"

"What's gotten into you all of a sudden?"

Flum was instantly relieved to find Eterna relaxing at the dining table. "Haah...haah...it's good to see you. We ran into Nekt just a bit ago, and he made it sound like you could be in danger. But I'm glad to see you're okay."

She slumped down in exhaustion. Even with her massively buffed endurance, it still took a lot out of her to run through the city at top speed, carrying another person the whole while.

Milkit hurried to the kitchen to get a towel and handed it to Flum to wipe away her sweat.

"The Children? What're they up to now?"

"That's just it—he actually came to propose that we work together to crush the Necromancy team. Apparently, team Children doesn't get along with the others. Obviously, I turned him down, but...I dunno, it looks like Nekt must've tricked me."

She took a look around the room and couldn't identify anything out of place. But why would Nekt lie to her about Eterna being in some kind of danger?

"Where did you run into him?"

"In the East District near Satils' mansion."

"What were you doing out there? I thought you and Milkit were out on a date today."

"Well, it wasn't exactly a date, you know, and..." Milkit's cheeks flushed a pale pink as she rejected Eterna's assumption.

"We ran into Satils on the main thoroughfare, just as alive as she'd ever been!" Flum cried. "I figured it had to have something to do with that Necromancy group Gadhio mentioned before."

"Hmm, so Necromancy brought Satils back...?"

A dark look came over Eterna's face, and she averted her gaze. Flum was confused.

"Umm, well, so I kind of came back here as soon as I could to talk it over with you. What do you think? I was thinking maybe we could keep an eye on her, take her out again if we have to, but it's pretty clear the church brought her back for some purpose. That could only mean we're already being watched."

"That sounds about right."

Even Milkit was confused now at Eterna's uncharacteristic response. The room fell into silence for a few moments before Milkit finally spoke up. "Eterna, are you...?"

"I want to go think...alone. I'll be away for a bit."

"Oh, umm...okay. Be safe!"

A gloomy look clouded Eterna's face as she left the house. Flum and Milkit turned to each other as they heard the front door clatter shut and cocked their heads to the side in unison.

"Eterna certainly was acting strange."

"I don't know why she would've been so taken aback by the story about Nekt and Satils. Unless maybe something else happened that I didn't notice?"

"You know, it's been bothering me for a while, but the glasses up on the shelves are out of place."

Flum looked over at the shelf, though she was unable to notice any real difference. "So maybe Eterna and Ink used them?"

"Three have been moved, so it wouldn't make sense if it were just the two of them."

"Hmm, maybe someone came over, and Eterna made tea for her guests? It's probably best to just ask Ink. She should've been able to hear whatever it was from the second floor."

The two made their way upstairs. Unfortunately, Ink was still unable to leave her room, so they had little choice but to talk through the door. Flum's knock was met with a bored greeting from the other side.

"Hey, Ink," she said. "We're home."

"Oh, hey, welcome back! How was your date??"

Flum's shoulders slumped. So Ink was in on it, too. "I'm tellin' ya, it's not a date..."

Ink giggled. "Oh yeah?"

Judging by the energy in Ink's voice, it was hard to imagine she was still in recovery at this point. It seemed like her convalescence was progressing perfectly.

"Listen, that's not important right now. There's something I want to ask you about."

"Oh, you mean about the guests? I don't know anything about the people who came over."

Milkit mumbled under her breath. "I knew it..."

"I guess that makes sense," Flum muttered. "You can probably only hear people moving around from up here, anyway."

"No, I can hear conversations just fine, I've got great hearing. I was asleep. I only woke up in time to hear them getting ready to leave."

"Do you know how many people there were? How old?"

"One man and two older people, a man and a woman."

"Three people..."

"That matches the number of glasses."

"The old man and woman seemed to be pretty close with Eterna." There was a certain sadness to Ink's voice as she said this.

Flum had never heard of Eterna having any acquaintances in the capital. Then again, she knew very little about the circumstances that brought Eterna to the capital in the first place or even what kind of life she led. Eterna appeared to be around Flum's age, but from how she spoke, she seemed older than that. Her mastery over magic was far beyond what someone in their teens could achieve. She was well versed in the use of medicinal herbs and long-lost healing arts. One could devote their entire adult career to these studies and still never hold a candle to Eterna's knowledge.

"I'm guessing she didn't tell you anything about the visit if you're here asking me."

"Did she keep it a secret from you, too?"

"I wish she'd just keep it all under wraps, but Eterna isn't really good at hiding things and just kinda gets into a bad mood instead."

That pretty much matched Flum's experience. Something big had happened, and Eterna must have been sorely conflicted over whether she should discuss it.

"Maybe you should ask her yourself?" Ink suggested.

"No, Eterna's probably decided this is something she doesn't need to discuss with us right now. All we can do is wait until she decides it's the right time."

"You're really thoughtful, Flum."

"Not really. I just know Eterna is a whole lot smarter than I am. I figure she must be doing the right thing."

"Well, I'd still say that's thoughtful."

"Me too."

"You know you guys aren't getting anything special from me no matter how much you compliment me, right?"

Though Flum might not be giving anything away, Milkit was more than satisfied by the look of embarrassment on her master's face.

Shortly after leaving the house, Eterna found herself roaming the streets of the East District. The words of the man who visited her only a short time ago echoed through her head.

"True strength lies in overcoming the death of one's body. There is no act more powerful in this world than cheating death...or at least, that's what I think."

The man, Dafydd Chalmas, had brought her surrogate parents, Kindah and Claudia, with him.

As she mentioned to Ink just a short time ago, they died many years ago; she had already made a pilgrimage to honor their graves. That could only mean they'd been brought back just like Satils was—through the power of an Origin core.

"I have a dear friend named Susy who is my polar opposite," Dafydd had said. "She's incredibly active and hates being cooped up in the house, but despite our differences, just being together helps us bring out the best in one another. When we were very young, we promised we would get married someday. As the years went by and we grew, matured, and settled into our own jobs, we stayed as close as ever, and finally, we decided to make good on that promise. At the time, I felt like nothing in the world could come between us and the bright future that awaited us."

As Dafydd spoke, Claudia gently stroked Eterna's hair, as a mother would her daughter's, while Kindah watched affectionately.

The touch stirred up distant memories and soothed the ache of wounds Eterna forgot existed. But as the happiness flooded back, so did her fear of loss.

"Susy was an adventurer, you see. Gifted in the art of the spear, she rose through the ranks quickly and reached A-Rank at a young age, much to the astonishment and admiration of her peers. I was immensely proud of her, but there were others who were jealous of her achievements."

Dafydd's face grew dark as an uncomfortable memory sprang to the forefront. His gaze dropped to his hands, fixed on his wedding ring.

"One day, she was betrayed by her colleagues. They hacked her to bits and left her behind. It was only thanks to an adventurer who happened across her body that I even knew of her fate."

He went on to describe the gruesome details of her death. Susy's face had been distorted with agony, what remained of her hand clutched tightly around her treasured pendant. Her body was beginning to rot by the time it was returned to him, but somehow, even her grave-stench exerted a powerful pull on him.

"From there, I hit rock bottom. All I looked forward to was the day I could die and be together with Susy. It wasn't until I found the church of Origin that I felt hope again. I was drawn into their ranks until I found myself studying the Origin cores."

There was something Eterna found deeply annoying about Dafydd. The church was her enemy, but she didn't believe he was lying. Everything from his words to his expression and tone of voice carried the weight of truth.

"While I was conducting my research, I reached a revelation: I should be able use this power to bring back the dead. I wrote up my thesis and submitted it to a cardinal.

Much to my surprise, I learned my proposal would join the Children and Chimera projects as one of the church's highest priorities. With that, the Necromancy team was born to begin our research into how to completely raise the dead—not as bizarre monsters twisted by the power of Origin, but returned to their original forms, with the same personalities and spirit. I'm sure it sounds strange for a person so heavily involved in their affairs to say this, but frankly, I didn't really give a damn about God or the church. All I wanted was to bring my Susy back."

Perhaps the fact that she felt honesty radiating so strongly from him said more about Eterna's mental state than his. Surrounded by the warmth and affection of her parents, she wasn't quite at the top of her game. Part of her wished to let down her guard completely and just embrace their return, though she was aware of the danger that posed.

"I imagine there must be many people out there who suffered losses like mine, and I want nothing more than to offer them salvation. You and the church are enemies, but I came here in the hopes that you would see my side. I apologize for the long introduction, but I came here to invite you along on my journey."

Eterna wasn't wandering the East District without a destination in mind. She knew exactly where she was

heading. She stepped off the main thoroughfare onto a smaller street, just wide enough for a single carriage to pass. She found herself in a run-down residential part of the East District full of decrepit houses and derelict storefronts. Few people walked these streets, which made it a perfect place for a carriage to slip in undetected.

Dafydd had spoken of his dream with a great deal of excitement.

"I'll be waiting here, at the location marked on this map, tomorrow morning. I'd like to show you our research facility. There you will find people who have been saved from the living hell of losing the ones who mattered to them most. I'd like you to see those people and, hopefully, understand what we hope to achieve."

If he hadn't already proved his ability to raise the dead, she would have written him off as a crackpot waxing on about impossible fantasies. But Kindah and Claudia were no different than they'd been when still alive, their affection for her just the same. She knew there was truth to his words, and that shook her to her core.

"Tomorrow morning, I'll..."

Eterna stopped at the place where they were to meet and closed her eyes. She couldn't help but feel taking Dafydd up on his offer would be betraying Ink, Flum, and Milkit. But she would also be able to see her parents again. Maybe this time around, she could live with them like a normal family—a dream she'd held close to her heart for over fifty years.

What's more, meeting with Dafydd would give her the location of their lab. If she deemed the place too dangerous, she could always destroy it. She could still protect Ink and the rest of her friends.

"But that's just an excuse." Eterna shook her head in self-reproach. "No more sugarcoating it. I need to make a decision and take responsibility for my own actions."

There would be no one to blame but her.

Eterna turned to look at the sky as the bright amber of the setting sun began to give way to the deep purples of dusk.

A carriage arrived at Gadhio's house shortly after nightfall. It was time for Tia to return. Gadhio held her hand firmly all the way to the gate, intent on seeing her off.

Standing next to the carriage, he came face to face with Dafydd.

"Good evening, Gadhio. I'm..."

"Dafydd Chalmas, right?"

"I should never underestimate a hero. Much like Eterna,

it seems you already know of me. Yes, I am Dafydd, the chief researcher for the Necromancy project. Pleased to meet you."

He offered his hand, though Gadhio initially ignored the gesture. Feeling Tia's gaze resting upon him, he slowly reached out and gave it a terse shake.

"Sorry for surprising you like this, but I was in a rush, you see."

"Why?"

"I was worried the top brass in the church might do something rash after your run-in with the Children. They want nothing more than to weaponize Necromancy's work."

It made a degree of sense, though Gadhio doubted he'd been promoted by pure altruism. Some of his suspicion was alleviated by the fact that Tia was here with him again. Slowly but surely, she was finding her way back into his heart.

"Let me just get this out of the way: are you setting some kind of trap for me?"

"I can say with absolute conviction that no, we are doing nothing of the sort. I, too, lost a wife. I figured you would understand the pain of losing the one that you love the most. It's a pain that can only be relieved by having that person return to your side."

Dafydd's words struck home. At the same time, Gadhio resented this newly exposed weakness. He hated the church more than anything else, had sworn that he would get his revenge against them, and yet, the sight of Tia's face shook his resolve.

Considering losing her had given rise to that hatred in the first place, perhaps it wasn't so surprising it would weaken once she was restored to him.

"I'm fully aware you consider yourself an enemy of the church," Dafydd said. "You're correct in your understanding that the top members of the church have already weaponized the Children and Chimera projects and intend to use them to sinister ends."

"So you're telling me you're different, and I should look the other way?"

"Basically, yes. Besides, this allows you and Tia to live on and continue your lives together."

"So you're using her as a hostage?"

"If you wish to think ill of me, then sure. But I believe this research can do wonders for a great many people. I only want to sustain the project that brought my own dearly departed Susy back to me."

That much, at least, Gadhio believed, and the force behind Dafydd's words lent him a great deal of credence. Looking him in the eye, Gadhio understood how he felt.

"Anyway, I only came to introduce myself today, but I was hoping you would consider visiting my lab to see for yourself."

"You want to take me to your research facility?"

"I won't force you, of course. I'll bring Tia back tomorrow, so I hope you'll think it over and have a decision ready by then." Dafydd turned and climbed into the carriage with Tia.

"Tomorrow?"

"See you, Gaddy."

"Tia, wait...you can't just leave so suddenly!" Gadhio reached out to take Tia's hand, but she swiftly drew it back.

A sad look washed across her face. "It's already past my deadline. I don't want you to see what happens to me, Gaddy."

Her resurrection wasn't entirely complete yet. Even Gadhio had to admit that he didn't want to see his beloved wife with a spiral for a face. He clenched his jaw and let his hand fall to his side.

"I wish for you two to spend as much time together as possible, which is precisely why I invite you to come visit," Dafydd said, "I hope for good news when we next meet."

The carriage took off with Tia and Dafydd on board. All Gadhio could do was stand there and watch as it grew smaller and smaller in the distance.

"Good news? What does he think...?!" He punched the nearby wall with all his might. "Dammit!"

How cruel of the man to burden Gadhio with a decision like this. Could he really reject him outright now that Tia had been returned to him? On the other hand, it was undeniable that Dafydd was part of the very same organization that Gadhio loathed. His capacity for love and his long-held hatred warred within him, each struggling for supremacy.

Gadhio returned to the house, anger and despair etched plainly across his face. Kleyna was waiting for him inside.

"So I guess...Tia left?"

"Right. She'll be back again tomorrow."

"That's...great, isn't it?" Kleyna did her best to say the words with a smile. But the jealousy she felt sat just beneath the surface, despite her best efforts to squash the feeling.

009

Slipping Gears

ETERNA EXPLAINED very little when she finally returned home. The next morning, long before anyone else woke up, Milkit found a note on the dining room table.

"I have some things to do. Don't worry, I'll be back soon."

She ran back upstairs and woke Flum. After reading the note, Flum put a hand to her head in shock.

"I can't believe she'd just leave us behind and not even tell us anything." Sitting on the edge of the bed, her mind raced over what to do next, but she was still far too shaken by Satils' return to form a meaningful plan of action.

"Do you think this has something to do with the Necromancy project, too?" Milkit asked.

"Considering the strange visitors who stopped by yesterday, I'd say the timing is way too good to be a coincidence."

Just as Nekt said, the church was already putting its plans into motion. They were using the dead to try and split Flum and her friends apart.

Flum's thoughts were suddenly interrupted by a knock at her bedroom door.

"Can I come in?"

"Ink? Of course you can."

The door opened and the small girl stepped into the room.

"Are you sure it's okay for you to leave your room?"

Ink shook her head. "Eterna said I need to stay for a little while longer, but it doesn't seem to matter with her gone all of a sudden."

"So I've heard."

"Speaking of that, Eterna left before the sun came up."

"She left that early?" Milkit was already an early riser, but this took her by surprise.

"I just don't get why she'd go so far to keep where she was going a secret from us..." Ink trailed off.

"Listen, why don't we all get some breakfast in us before we continue this conversation? You won't be able to think straight on an empty stomach."

Milkit was concerned about Ink needing to be fed, but she also figured breakfast would help get her mind off Eterna.

The three made their way downstairs. An unexpected voice interjected before they reached the dining room.

"Hope I'm not interrupting anything." Nekt was lounging in one of the chairs at the dining table.

"What in the hell are you...?!" Flum took several steps forward and drew her sword.

"Whoa, whoa, calm down. I knew you guys were in a bind and figured I'd offer you a helping hand. Oh, hey, Ink. How've you been?"

Ink responded through clenched teeth. "I'm doing well."

Nekt seemed to pick up on her unfriendly demeanor but dismissed it with a cheerful laugh. "Anyway, it's just like I said, isn't it? Eterna Rinebow is in trouble."

"Did you know this would happen?"

"I figured as much, but the decision was left up to her. That's just the kind of guy Dafydd Chalmas is, and that's exactly why things worked out this way."

Dafydd's sincerity was his most powerful tool in shaking Gadhio and Eterna to their core. It wasn't just the care with which he chose his words, but the earnestness with which he spoke, winning him the trust of whoever listened.

"Do you know who Eterna went to go meet?" Flum demanded.

"That I don't know. Like I said before, the Children and Necromancy groups don't get along. My best guess would be she was off to meet her grandparents or something, considering those were the ones Dafydd brought over yesterday."

His description matched perfectly with the group of visitors Ink mentioned the night before. As far as Flum could gather, the older couple had some kind of connection with Eterna, and the younger man was a researcher on the Necromancy project.

"Looks like even heroes are just human at the end of the day. But that's neither here nor there. Honestly, I thought the Necromancy group's work was just plain stupid. Dying's a natural part of life, so spending Papa's power on something as useless as raising the dead seemed like a waste to me. But maybe I was wrong. Humans would rather fixate on the past over preparing for what's coming in the future. I think the members of this household prove that quite well, really."

"I already told you, I won't be joining you." Flum grew even firmer in her stance on the subject.

Nekt shot a confident grin back at her, almost as if he sensed that there was still a weakness in her facade for him to break through. "Because you have Gadhio Lathcutt by your side, I suppose?"

"Y...no, not Gadhio, too??" Flum couldn't conceal her surprise.

A wide grin broke out across Nekt's face at her reaction. He let out another condescending laugh before continuing on. "It looks like he left behind his precious woman and child to head out as well—probably for the same place as Eterna."

"No way!"

"Now, now, calm down, lady. I didn't do this, y'know. Being mad at me won't get you anywhere. I don't know the details, but I did see he was in the company of a woman in her twenties. A lover or a sister or something?"

Flum was sure it was Tia. If she was alive again, it would completely undermine his resolution to avenge her. It didn't seem out of the realm of possibility that he would leave Kleyna and Hallom behind in favor of his wife.

Many people spoke of Gadhio as a dry, emotionless man, but Flum understood how he felt all too well.

"So, what'll it be, Flum? It looks like you're all alone now, and your two would-be allies are of no use to you anymore. Can you really carry the fight all on your own? Remember your battle with that thug Dein? He didn't even have Papa's power to help him out. Do you think you can keep pulling victories out of your hat against all odds?"

Flum knew the limits to her power all too well. Eterna and Gadhio were being taken to a place that might be developing even more powerful Origin cores than what she'd dealt with thus far. There was no way she could win on her own—not just against the Necromancy group but Nekt as well. He'd already taken Milkit away once before. What choice did she have but to take him up on the offer?

"Hmm. You still hesitate, even with your back up against the wall." Nekt crossed his arms and watched her with great interest.

"It's hardly an easy decision!!"

"This isn't such a bad offer, is it? I mean, if you don't want to, sure. We can just pretend this whole conversation never happened. It makes no difference to me. I was just thinking it'd be helpful if you were on our side, is all."

"Is this part of Mother's plan?"

"Nope, I'm acting on my own."

"So you're here all by yourself without Mother's blessing? No connection to the Children team?"

"Now, now, you're twisting my words. I never said I wanted you to ally with the Children. I suggested you join forces with *me*. Neither Mother nor Papa have said anything about this, and none of the other Children are involved. Does that alleviate some of your concern? Just nod your head, and you'll have gained a powerful, if temporary, ally. All with zero risk to you."

Zero risk was clearly an overstatement. There was no such thing in the church's power games. Nekt wouldn't be seeking Flum's help if it didn't benefit him in some way, and any benefit to Nekt would benefit the church.

Milkit nervously tugged at the hem of her dress as she watched Flum cogitate. Meanwhile, Ink stood facing straight ahead, looking gloomy. She was far more hurt by the fact that Eterna left her behind without saying anything than she was concerned by Nekt's appearance.

"I guess I'll interpret your silence as a no, then. If you still haven't made up your mind, then I guess I'll just have to take matters into my own hands."

"Wait!" Though she was annoyed at Nekt forcing her hand like this, Flum had no choice. "You really just want to destroy the Necromancy group, right? You won't do anything to Milkit or Ink?"

"Listen, I've nothing to gain from killing you, much less from those two. I have better things to do with my time."

She was reasonably sure Nekt had no intention of harming either Milkit or Ink. Besides, he could have already done so if that was his plan. He had more than enough chances when they were trying to save Ink. This didn't mean she trusted him as far as she could throw him, but...

She'd have to compromise. She just wasn't strong enough to go it alone.

"All right then, what's your answer, lady? Are you going to work with me or not?" Nekt gave Flum a scornful look as he stood there, clearly confident in his position.

"I..."

Just as she was about to choke out her reluctant response, she heard a sound that changed everything.

"I'm home." A lethargic voice echoed from the doorway.

A figure made its way through the entrance hall before sticking its head into the dining room. All eyes in the room fell on Eterna.

Everyone suddenly froze. Nekt's unquestionable superiority began to crumble around him.

"Huh, one of the Children? Just what's going on here?" Eterna sounded surprisingly calm in spite of the circumstances. Flum was beside herself.

Flum and Nekt both launched into their own line of questioning.

"I'd love to ask you the same! Did you go somewhere with Dafydd?!"

"Right! He brought an older couple here yesterday to meet with you, didn't he?!"

"Huh. So I guess you guys figured it out. Sorry for not saying anything about that. Anyway, I decided not to pursue it any further. I've already visited my parents' graves and made my peace with their deaths, after all. Right now, Flum, Milkit, and Ink here are far more important to me."

"Oh, Eternaaaa…!" Ink's voice quivered as she dove head first into the older woman's arms. Eterna held her tight and began to stroke her hair.

"Huh, judging by her reaction, I'm guessing you guys thought I just left her to finish recovering all alone?"

"With a note like that, I think anyone would be concerned!" Milkit's voice was uncharacteristically harsh.

"Wow, even you, Milkit? Listen, I'm really sorry, you guys. I really did plan on being right back, so I figured a brief note would be enough."

"Where did you go?"

"I went to visit the graves of Kindah and Claudia Rinebow, my adoptive parents."

"But you just saw them back in the flesh. So you must've already known their bodies were gone, right?"

"That's correct. I found traces of the digging. The work looked recent." Her face tensed. "In other words, the church robbed their graves and pointlessly disturbed their endless slumber to win me over and sustain their research. Dafydd Chalmas and his crew are a bunch of grave robbers."

"Huh, you guys...you really do your homework. Wow." It was Nekt's turn to be at a loss for words.

"Maybe," Eterna said. "Or maybe I'm just more of a romantic than I'd like to admit."

Nekt smirked, shrugging in defeat. "I mean, whatever. Wish I could be as chill as you."

Flum shot him a suspicious glance. "So I guess you're giving up now that Eterna's back?"

"Yup."

"So why are you still here?"

"I might've stood a chance with you on your own, but the odds don't really look too good for me with her here, too."

Yet he still didn't disappear, even though he almost certainly could have whisked himself off with Connection anywhere he liked.

Finally, an answer to his odd behavior came to Ink. Knowing his personality, it was unlikely that he would ever admit to it even if she were right, but she still needed to ask.

"Nekt came to visit me, not convince Flum... Didn't you?"

"What?? No way! Why would I want to have anything to do with a reject like you??"

"I dunno. You're acting kinda weird, Nekt. You were getting really annoyed with Flum earlier."

"Who wouldn't get annoyed watching someone waffle around?"

"No, I don't mean like that. I don't think it had anything to do with Flum at all, actually. If anything, you sounded kind of sad just now."

"Heh, and when did you become my counselor, Ink? The only reason I came off that way was 'cause I had everything all tied up before that witch ruined it all!"

Eterna cut straight to the chase. "Or maybe you're just afraid you'll be discarded, too."

Nekt shot a furious gaze in her direction. "What a baseless accusation..."

"Well, Mother discarded Ink. Frankly, I was surprised by how cold he was to Ink the moment she was no longer of use."

Mother had acted like a real mother to Ink, right until it became more convenient to leave her for dead. Though Eterna hadn't seen the event play out herself, she heard about the sudden change from Ink.

"The reason Mother abandoned Ink so easily is because their relationship *wasn't* that of a mother and daughter. Ink was a specimen, one that was no longer needed," Eterna said. Even as the words came out of her mouth, she clutched Ink even tighter to reassure the younger girl that that wasn't what *she* believed.

"What're you trying to say?" Nekt demanded.

"The Necromancy group has actually brought the dead back to life—their goals are within reach. The Chimera group is also likely making steady progress. That leaves the Children group. The team has to implant cores into their subjects and then wait eight to ten years for results. It's hardly efficient, is it?"

"And yet here I am. I'd say I'm a pretty significant result, no?"

"But there are only four of you, and you're not much stronger than Gadhio or myself. I can't imagine you're capable of wiping out all the demons."

"So?" Nekt was getting more and more incensed as Eterna continued, maybe because he felt insulted, or because she hit closer to home than he wanted to admit.

"I think the ultimate goal of the Spiral Children project is something far different. They call you the second generation; well, what's stopping them from creating a third or even a fourth generation? Once those children exist, Mother will lose interest in you and discard you just like Ink."

Nekt sighed and went silent. After a few tense moments, he let out a hollow laugh and threw his hands in the air as if in surrender. "Well, this definitely puts me in a tough spot. You've got quite an imagination on you, but that still doesn't explain why I should be afraid. Unlike this failed experiment, my powers are proven, and Papa still loves me!"

"Sounds like denial to me."

"What the hell do you know??"

"A lot, in fact. I was experimented on by the kingdom, too."

"Wha...?!"

This left Nekt at a loss for words; Flum and Milkit stared wide-eyed at the sudden confession. The only one who didn't react strongly was Ink, who already knew Eterna's true age, though she was still taken aback.

"You were experimented on, too?" Nekt demanded.

"It was around fifty years ago, now. I was a prime guinea pig—young, orphaned, slum-dwelling. That was what led to me living here."

"They performed experiments here?"

"Not *here*, per se, but this is where the test subjects lived. The heads of the research group—our caretakers— were the Rinebows. They must've been in their twenties at the time."

Eterna went on to explain what had happened to her. The experiments had been carried out with the goal of creating humans that could fight toe-to-toe with demons. No one in the kingdom knew much about human experimentation at the time, so they threw everything they had at the wall to see what stuck. The results were predictably lethal.

Claudia had given Eterna her name in the hope that perhaps she would live just a bit longer than the others had. As it turned out, it worked. Eterna was the project's sole success: her life span extended and her magic deepened.

Word came down that the pipeline project was to be canceled early due to its low success rate, and Eterna would be disposed of. Kindah and Claudia helped her escape from the capital before that happened, and she spent the next fifty years of her life living in the mountains as a witch.

Nekt stood entranced, absorbing every word of Eterna's story.

"In the beginning," Eterna said, "we were on our best behavior because we were scared we'd be kicked to the curb. But Kindah and Claudia were far too kind to do that. They never turned anyone away. If they'd been anything like Mother...well, I'd be terrified. Just like you, Nekt. If there was anyone out there who could help me—friend or foe—I'd be desperate to make contact with them."

He remained silent and stared off into the distance, lost in thought.

Flum spoke up next. "You know, Nekt, there was a thing you said earlier I keep coming back to. You said neither Mother nor Papa said anything about this. Going by what Eterna said, I understand about Mother. But the fact that Papa...err...Origin isn't talking to you must mean..."

Nekt was dismissive. "Papa's been busy. But...you're right, he's been quiet lately, since before I came to see you."

In other words, not just Mother, but Origin, too, had already lost interest in the second-generation Children.

"I understand the fear of being abandoned by the people who matter most to you."

"Oh, c'mon. I don't need a slave's sympathy."

"I'm not trying to offer my sympathy."

"Let me guess, you're going to say Ink and I are both pitiful rejects? Hah! Gimme a break, lady. I came here to get you to do my bidding, and now here I am, seconds from a big mushy group hug. How bizarre."

It was clear to everyone in the room he was putting on a show of false bravado—including Nekt himself. All he could do was double down.

Ink turned to Nekt and spoke to him in a solemn, even tone. "You want to destroy the Necromancy team to change Mother's mind, don't you?"

"Ink, you're assuming this third generation even exists. It's pure speculation."

"I'm just saying if that were the case, maybe Flum and Eterna would help you."

Nekt brought his hands to his face and burst out laughing.

"You must be joking!" He cackled like it was the funniest thing he'd ever heard. "How is that any different? Besides, Mother is obviously your enemy, so why would you offer your assistance?"

"I'm in," Flum said.

Nekt's eyes went wide. He gawked at her from between his fingers.

"What do you mean?"

"I'll join you."

"You're weirder than I thought, lady. Are you really that softhearted?!"

Flum was dead serious. "Compassion has nothing to do with it. I believe the Children and Necromancy groups are at odds with each other, and now I understand what you're really after. I wasn't interested in joining up with you before because I didn't know what you wanted. If we can achieve your goal, then Mother will reconsider the second-generation project, and nothing bad will happen to us."

"But...!"

"More importantly, I don't know where the Necromancy group is or where Gadhio's been taken. You have any ideas?"

"I have a hunch."

"In that case, there's something for us to gain, and our goals are aligned. Obviously, we're not allies by any stretch, and we might try to kill each other again at some point, but for now, at least, we can lay down our arms and work together." Flum offered her hand to Nekt. "I'm serious about this."

All she was looking for was a handshake. No words were needed; that much was clear to Nekt.

"This is crazy, you know that? Ever since everything went down with Ink, I'd been thinking about how weird this all is..." His teeth ground audibly as he clenched his jaw. Whether it was out of annoyance, anger, or envy was anyone's guess; there was so much going on in his head at the moment that even Nekt didn't know what he was feeling.

No way...

Nekt's pride was too strong to let him admit to such weakness.

No...no, no, no! I...I've come so far to be able to use Papa's power like this; I must be special! So why am I out here begging for help like some snot-nosed little kid??

Nekt was still a child. He wasn't quite mature enough to put his pride aside to get what he wanted.

"So, Nekt, why don't we..."

"That's not gonna happen!! Connection!"

A vortex appeared in the center of his face as he clenched his fist, focusing on unleashing Origin's power to connect his current location to another elsewhere.

"Nekt??"

"He's gone."

"I guess we pushed him just a bit too far."

"That's too bad. He seemed like he was about to actually open up."

"By the way, you mentioned Gadhio earlier..." Eterna knew nothing about Gadhio's wife or of his connection with Kleyna and Hallom. Flum didn't like the idea of sharing the details of his personal life without him around, but it seemed necessary, considering the circumstances.

"Well, you see..."

Flum told her everything she knew; Eterna nodded along and soaked it all in, occasionally speaking up in a hushed tone to prompt her to continue.

"I think part of the reason I decided to turn down Dafydd's offer is because I'm pretty cold, emotionally."

"That's not true!"

Eterna shook her head at Flum's instinctive denial and took a seat. "Heh. I only really spent a few years together with my parents, and then I had fifty on my own to process things and visit their graves. I already made my peace. Gadhio is different. He vowed to get revenge for his lost love."

"You have a point. I had a gut feeling Gadhio would succumb... He loved Tia more than anything."

"That said, we can't just leave this be."

"If only we could have gotten Nekt to tell us where the lab is," Flum fumed,

"Too late for that. There's no sense crying over spilled milk. We'll just have to figure it out on our own."

"You're right. I'll head over to Gadhio's and see what I can find out."

"Anywhere in particular you want me to check?" Eterna asked.

"I'd like you to stay here and keep an eye on Ink. She still can't leave the house." She'd already broken Eterna's strict guidelines about staying in her room.

"I've been thinking about how to deal with any health issues that may come up since we finished the heart transplant," Eterna said. "As long as you stick close to my side, you'll be fine."

"Really??" said Ink.

Eterna's voice suddenly took on a stern tone. "However! Don't do anything rash like running around. That's completely off limits."

Ink nodded, though it was debatable whether she really understood what she was agreeing to.

"Now that we've gotten that out of the way, we can help, too," Eterna said.

"Oh? Well then, I guess I could have you guys go talk to Welcy and see what she knows. She might have gotten some new information in the meantime. I'm pretty sure she should be at her office in the Central District right about now."

"Leitch Mancathy's sister? Got it."

With that settled, the four left the house in their respective directions.

Far beneath the capital's streets and beyond the mazelike waterways was a modern-looking facility that stood out from its modest surroundings. This place, marked by the signs of the bygone civilizations from whom humanity's modern conveniences were copied, was the new center of operations for the Children project.

"Listen, Mother... Mother! If I did something bad, I'm sorry, okay?? Please just talk to me!"

Fwiss banged on a door, practically in tears.

Though each blow was relatively light, he'd been at it for over two hours by now, and his hands were covered in blood.

"Are you mad we couldn't kill those girls? But you know, we worked really hard when we had to move bases! Come on, Mother...I did so much to help!!"

Fwiss was the most dependent on Mother out of all the Children. Ever since Gadhio destroyed their last base and they were forced to move here, Mother paid little attention to the second-generation Children. There was explanation for this sudden change.

This only served to make Fwiss all the more anxious. Were they going to be rudely discarded like Ink was?

"I'm back."

Nekt teleported back to the room, having finished his conversation with Flum mere moments ago. He sat down and leaned casually up against the wall, inviting an angry glare from Fwiss.

"Where the hell were you off to, Nekt?"

"What's it matter to you?"

A white-haired girl holding an old, shabby doll that had seen better days spoke up. "Well, it does. M-mother's going to get rid of us. I'm scared, Nekt. We need to apologize."

"If all we needed to do was to apologize, Mute, Fwiss would've taken care of that a long time ago."

"Well, you broke Mother's rules and left the facility. Don't you think that's a problem?"

"I think you're mixing up cause and effect here. I left because of where we are now."

"What for? You didn't try to talk to Ink, did you?"

"Heh, like it's even worth trying to talk to a dimwit like her that can't even hear Papa's voice. We're just too different, really."

"I certainly hope so."

Neither Mute, who still wasn't sure what Nekt was really thinking, nor Luke, the most mean-spirited of the four, knew anything about the outside world. Mother was everything to them. They saw nothing wrong with being so dependent on him...and why should they? They'd been raised that way.

"Mother, please!! I'm so lonely, I feel like I could die if I can't see your face, Mother! I'll drink whatever nasty medicine you want! You can even poke me full of needles if it pleases you! Please, please, Mother...! Mother!!" Fwiss began to grow hoarse.

Finally, after all that time, it seemed as if his pleas had

made it through. The doorknob turned with a creak, and Mother emerged from the doorway.

"Moth...euangff!!"

Mother grabbed the back of Fwiss's head and kneed him in the face, the power of the blow lifting Fwiss's body clear off the ground. Blood poured freely from his nose and mouth.

"M-mother, why??"

"I can't take your incessant pounding anymore, you little mongrel!!"

Another blow to Fwiss's face, this time with a clenched fist.

"Hnnggf! M-mother, no, I...!"

"Didn't I already tell you?! I'm busy, and I don't have time to deal with you miscreants!"

"I know, but I was lonely, and..."

"You think that's a good enough reason to interrupt my precious research?!"

Mother gripped a fistful of Fwiss's hair and slammed the young boy face-first into the wall over and over again.

"Finally! Finally, I'm about to make some progress!! How is it you don't understand that you only exist to further my research? Huh? Huh?!?!"

"Auugh...hnnngh!"

Fwiss had nearly lost consciousness; a damp spot began to form in his pants as his bladder relaxed. It failed to give Mother pause.

Nekt shuddered.

I...I want to help him, but I...I can't stand up to Mother.

All of the Children knew they would only invite hell on themselves if they stepped in. All they could do was seek help from someone on the outside, but at present, there was no one there but them.

Nekt, Luke, and Mute were all helpless to stop Mother.

"Stimulation, yes! Those *heroes* gave me the shock to my system I needed! Eyahaha! And, and you know what? It's still going strong! My brain crackles with insight—intellectual ecstasy, handed down from on high like divine lightning! And you intend to interrupt this?! Really??"

"Hyauugh... I'm...s-sorry...hngh...gyaugh."

Mother gasped for breath.

"You...you little good-for-nothing lowlifes just can't get it through your thick skulls why I love you, do you?"

"I love... I... Mother..."

"Then just keep quiet. You got that, Fwiss? If you don't, I fear I may begin to hate you."

"I'm...sorry! I'm so sorry! Please, I'll be good from now on, so please don't hate me, Mother!!"

Fwiss clung desperately to Mother's leg. Mother kicked him away like a piece of trash and slammed the door shut.

Fwiss curled up on the floor in a ball and sobbed.

"Fwiss..." Nekt reached out to try and comfort him, when suddenly he stopped.

Those sounds coming from his mouth weren't sobs at all—Fwiss was laughing.

"Ha...haha! See? Mother really doesn't hate me. Hahaha! This pain is a sign of love."

Fwiss was overjoyed.

"Glad to hear it, Fwiss."

"It's fine, Mother's just busy is all. He'll be back soon. It's fine, really. I'm just glad Mother is so kind and caring, to pay attention to me like this. Besides, I'm the one who broke the rules in the first place! Hahahaha!"

No one thought this was the least bit strange. Violence was one of Mother's ways of showing affection—though he'd never gone out of the way to harm the second-generation Children before. Not until they were cooped up in this new lab.

Regardless of the reasons behind this sudden change, Mother was the absolute and final force in their lives. And yet Nekt, alone, was beginning to feel there was something wrong with the whole situation.

Maybe it's because I'm so smart? More mature than the other Children?

He shook his head.

No... I'm no different from the rest of them. Mother's got as much of a hold on me as the rest. The only difference is that when we saw how Ink was so easily discarded, I actually ventured into the outside world.

Not that he had much choice in the matter. None of this came about entirely of his own will, as much as he would have liked to take the credit for it. Ultimately, Mother played their strings and they danced to his tune.

"You're the older brother now, which puts you in charge. You're a smart kid, so I'm sure everyone else will listen to you."

Mother's words echoed in Nekt's mind. Assuming everything was going according to plan, he almost certainly knew of Nekt's attempt to bring Flum to their side.

So is it all for nothing? No...maybe I'm just overthinking it. But am I really doing the right thing? Or is Fwiss actually on to something here?

Flum had said he lacked "morals," but to the Children, that was all they knew. Within their narrow little world, these corrupted morals were right and true.

I...I really want to trust Mother. But this situation is very different from what happened with Ink. She left Mother's side in high spirits.

This was the world as these eight-year-olds saw it. They were doing the best they could within their limited understanding.

Nekt clenched his jaw as he fought to untangle these two disparate points of view.

ROLL
OVER
AND
DIE

010

Past Memories

"HE WENT OFF with his dead wife. That's all I know."
There was a venom to Kleyna's words when Flum
stopped by to ask about Gadhio. Hallom peered out
at Flum from behind her mother, a look of worry on
her face.

"He wouldn't say anything to me about it. All he did
was leave a letter saying that he was going to be with Tia.
What is that, some kind of last will and testament?"

"So, Tia was here yesterday, too. Did you meet her?"

"Yeah, it was Tia, all right. I knew her for a long time;
I can vouch for that. Gadhio believes it's her, too. I think
we can say that much is true."

According to Eterna, there wasn't anything out of the
ordinary with the people brought back with Origin cores
using Necromancy's techniques.

251

"Gadhio's spent the past six years mourning Tia and blaming himself for what happened," Kleyna continued. "I guess I should be happy something good finally came of it."

"Hey, lady..."

Flum knelt down to look Hallom in the eyes. "What is it, Hallom?"

Tears threatened to pour out of the young girl's pleading eyes. "I-Is Daddy not coming back? Ever? Did he just forget about me n' Mommy?"

Flum reached out and stroked the young girl's hair. "No, honey, he didn't forget about you at all. He'll come back soon, I know it."

"Come now, Hallom. Don't bother Flum like that."

"But...but...Daddy's gone! He's my daddy, so why's he with that lady??"

"Oh, Hallom..."

Tears cascaded down Hallom's cheeks. Her father had died before she was old enough to remember him; calling Gadhio her "father figure" would be an understatement. He was the only father she'd ever known.

"Gadhio is a sweet man, Hallom. I know he thinks the world of you."

"...I know."

"So it'll all be okay. I promise he'll be back."

"If you see Daddy and he says he won't come back, you'll tell him he's gonna make me cry and yell at him, right?"

Flum chuckled. "You've got it, kid. I'll be sure to give him a stern talking to and drag him back home if that happens."

Those words seemed to have a soothing effect on Hallom, whose tears began to dry.

After saying goodbye to Kleyna, Flum and Milkit left the mansion behind.

"I'm glad to see Hallom cheered back up."

"She really gets attached to people fast." Even though Milkit hardly knew her, Hallom had waved cheerfully and said goodbye to "the bandage lady" as they left.

"I take it you'll come play with her the next time we're over, Milkit?"

"Of course, though we'll need to find Gadhio first. What do you think we should do now? It's still a bit early, but maybe we should meet back up with Eterna?"

"Nah, there's still one other place I want to check out."

Flum and Milkit made their way to the Central District and turned to the barracks. The guard standing watch bowed his head at the sight of Flum.

"I'm here to see Ottilie. May I come in?"

"Of course, Miss Flum. You can find Miss Ottilie in her chambers."

Flum laughed, despite herself, at just how different the man's reaction was from the other day as they stepped inside. Immediately after crossing the threshold, she nearly ran into a slender man. He was dressed in a uniform similar to Ottilie's—the uniform of the top brass.

"Well, I'll be, if it isn't Flum Apricot. I've heard all about you from Ottilie."

"And you are...?"

"Huh, you mean you don't know who I am? I'm Lieutenant General Werner of the royal army."

"Sorry. I'm not well informed on these matters."

"No worries, no worries. I guess I'm not quite as unmissable as Ottilie and Herrmann, so my name doesn't really get around." Lieutenant General Werner Apeirun preferred to resolve his duties quickly and discreetly. He allowed himself a single indulgence of martial theater—a set of custom-built steel claws. "I guess you're here to see Ottilie? I can show you the way. There's actually something quite interesting that you might want to see."

"Something interesting?" Flum had no idea what he was talking about but decided to follow him all the same.

Much to her surprise, he stopped not at Ottilie's chambers but in front of a linen room.

Werner spoke in a hushed voice and gestured for them to look inside. "Here."

Flum and Milkit peeked inside, only to spy Ottilie with her face buried in the sheets.

"Aaaaah, this smells just like Sis. How glorious it is to be completely surrounded in her scent! I just love this smell! It's so sweet, like the scent of love. Why, why do you smell so wonderful, Sis, and why can I just not get enough of it?? Why must you taunt me?!"

"W-wow..."

Even Milkit was at a complete loss.

"Pretty amazing, huh?"

"I mean, I knew that Ottilie was really smitten with Henriette, but this is something else. Is she always like this?"

Werner shot Flum a thumbs up. "Yup."

She felt her cheek twitch.

"Mmmmph! You're nothing short of absolute perfection, Sis! Aaaah, being wrapped up in her sheets feels just like being tied up in her warm embrace, but better, because now I'm the one deep within her now. Like a child! Like I'm her child. Ugyaaah! Gyah!"

"This is...definitely not the image I had of Ottilie."

Milkit reached over and patted Flum's shoulder to cheer her up.

"I guess you didn't know? Well, this is who she really is, so I recommend you get used to it." Werner's cackling laugh finally tipped Ottilie off to their presence.

"Oh, uh, why if it isn't Flum and Milkit. You, uh, look to be doing well..." Ottilie stood up, sheets still in her arms, and walked over.

"You're...you're not even going to try and hide it?"

"You already saw me, so what's there to hide? Besides, my love for my sister is wholly pure. There's no need to hide something as beautiful as that!"

"Huh..." Flum had no response to that. She decided to bury what she'd just seen in a deep, dark hole in her memory and quickly changed the subject. "Actually, I had some things to discuss with you about the church."

"Oh?"

"You brought them all the way here for that, Werner??"

"Well, I heard you were close with them, so I figured they were here to enjoy your company."

Judging by their attitudes, it was clear to Flum that Ottilie and Werner knew nothing of what the Necromancy group was up to.

"In that case, I guess it'd be better to send them along to Henriette?"

"Perhaps, but she's in a meeting with Satuhkie right now."

"Satuhkie, the cardinal?"

"Right, Satuhkie Ranagalki. Apparently he's been meeting with high-up officials in the royal army to improve relations with the church knights of late."

Now why would a cardinal be trying to ally themselves with the royal army? Flum felt a sense of foreboding creep up on her. If they didn't have any information about the Necromancy effort, then she should probably make an early exit.

"Well, look at that—Sis's door is open. I guess they must be done talking, then. Let's head on in."

Ottilie practically jogged over, eager to see her sister's face.

◇ ◇ ◇

A man and woman were deep in conversation in front of Henriette's office. One of the figures was obviously Henriette; the other was a large, powerfully built man sporting a well-groomed mustache.

"So that's Cardinal Satuhkie Ranagalki..."

Satuhkie turned toward Flum, evidently overhearing her approach, and shot a confident smile her way. Flum felt a chill run up her spine.

"Well, well, if it isn't the famous hero. I heard you'd given up on the great journey, but I never would have expected to run into you here."

"P-pleased to meet you."

Though he was of roughly equivalent rank to Henriette, his hulking frame made him much more intimidating.

"No need to be so scared of me. We have a lot of expectations resting on you, you know."

"Expectations?"

Satuhkie stepped forward and rested a heavy hand on Flum's shoulder. "It may seem like nothing special to you, but that changes nothing about how future generations will look back on your actions. History is written by results, not intentions."

"Umm..."

"My apologies; you probably have no idea what I'm going on about. This is just something I want to get off my chest, but I hope you'll agree with me. You see, I was also among the saved."

"I'm sorry, what is this about?" Flum's confusion was written clearly across her face.

It seemed Satuhkie was being intentionally vague. He went on.

"It's thanks to you that Project Reversion was a complete success. You're proof of that. That's why I'm so glad to have had the opportunity to meet you. I'll need to tell Chatani the good news."

"Project? Chata...ni?"

Shaaaaaaaaaaaaa...

Suddenly, all Flum could hear was a loud hiss in her head. It felt like her memories were being forcefully torn from her, leaving her grasping at nothing. Somewhere in the depths of her mind, she saw an unfamiliar face.

"Project Reversion...research...created..."

Shaaaaaaaaaaaaa...

The tendrils of an awful migraine spread through her brain as the noise intensified. This was necessary for reversion, but it was also quite volatile. Caution was of the utmost importance. The agony was simply a growing pain.

"What...what is this?"

Shaaaaaaaaaaaaaaaaaaaaaaa...

She felt like she was in the middle of a sandstorm, robbed of her sight and hearing and other senses. Who was this Flum Apricot person standing here? She no longer knew the answer. She knew she was "Flum" but couldn't say who—or what—a "Flum" was.

"Well, it looks like my life is about to come to an end."

SHAAAAAAAAAAAAAAA...

The pain was almost too much to bear. It felt like a typhoon was blasting through her skull, like she was

trying and failing to desperately claw her way back from an irreversible change. The fact that she could still fight at all was proof of what made her special.

In a sense, the world needed this person known as Flum Apricot, but she was still a work in progress. Once she was complete, there was no guarantee she would be allowed to keep the happiness she'd found for herself so far.

"Haaauh...nng...!"

Words, phrases, images, and voices of unknown origin bounced around the inside of her skull, filling it to the brim. They tried to force themselves to the forefront all at once, destroying any possibility of extracting meaning from the cacophony.

"Master?!"

Even with the enchantment working to dull her pain, it was still so excruciating Flum could no longer stand. If it wasn't for Milkit holding her up, she would likely have collapsed long ago.

"Hmm, are you having a flashback? I guess some of it still remains with you. Now that's quite a surprise! Gwahaha!" Satuhkie laughed. With that, he turned and left.

There were so many things she wanted to ask about what just happened to her and what he knew, but Flum's mind still couldn't form words. She was barely conscious.

Ottilie looked over at Flum with concern and wrapped an arm around her to help her stand. "What did Satuhkie say to you? Listen, if you're not feeling well, you'd better go to the infirmary to rest."

Flum was white as a ghost. A rivulet of sweat ran down her face, collecting at her chin and dripping to the floor.

"N-no, I'm fine. I'm just a bit lightheaded, is all. I guess I've just been through a lot lately. Haven't quite recovered from it all." She offered up a weak smile, but her voice was still shaky and her expression deathly pale. It was hardly convincing.

"Are you sure you're okay?" Henriette gazed straight into Flum's face.

There was force behind her words, almost like she was asking about something else entirely. Flum had no clue what that question was supposed to be.

She shook her head. "I...I don't know. None of this makes any sense."

"What the hell? A girl collapses right in front of you, and you just walk away like it's no big deal? Those cardinals really do look down on the common people, don't they?" Werner groused.

"Come now, Werner. Just because he isn't here anymore doesn't mean you can just speak your mind."

"I mean, give me a break! Having to work with the church knights is a hassle nobody wants."

He wasn't exactly right. Satuhkie hadn't been looking down on her. He hadn't been laughing out of ridicule or derision.

That had been a mirthful laugh.

What the hell was that? As soon as he brought up Project Reversion and the Chatani, all these images flashed right before my eyes. Seeing isn't even the right word, I felt them.

Flum put a hand to her forehead and glanced over at Milkit.

Milkit was in there, too...or at least I think she was? I...I don't know anymore. It's all gone blank. Screw it all, I just want to forget about the whole ordeal. Right now, I need to talk to Henriette.

Flum took a deep breath, refocused herself, and pushed any wayward thoughts from her mind. She stepped into the office with Henriette to get down to the subject at hand.

Just as she had before, Henriette sat on a sofa across from Flum and Milkit. Ottilie sat next to Henriette, pressing her cheek against her shoulder.

"I understand that you would like to ask me something about the church, but unfortunately there's not much on the subject I can discuss with you right now," Henriette said.

"I figured as much. Did something happen?"

"Well, there are talks of the church knights absorbing the royal army."

"What?? But in that case, the royal family would no longer hold any power. The Pope would effectively be in charge of the entire kingdom!"

"That seems to be the plan. The King is already a dedicated follower of Origin, so in truth, this changes little."

"So the church is just giving up on all pretense to openly seize power?! Once that happens, everyone will suffer as the cost of healing shoots up!"

Henriette wore a pained look on her face. "Pretty much. Unfortunately, I'm fully occupied stalling for time with the church knights. I can't be of much help to you right now."

"Not at all, pushing back against the church is help enough as it is."

"Now, would you mind telling me what's been going on within the capital? I might know something that could be of some help."

Flum figured she could trust Henriette. She decided to tell her everything she knew about the Necromancy project.

Once Flum was finished, Henriette nodded and fixed her with a grim look. "Tia Lathcutt... Now that's a name I haven't heard in some time."

"You knew her?"

"We worked together several times in joint operations with the guild. I'd heard that all of her crew but Gadhio had died, but I had no idea the church was behind it."

"Do you know anything about Satils?"

"Just that she's a disturbed woman who makes her money through illicit means. She loans out money to other nobles at incredibly high interest rates. If they can't pay it back, she repossesses their holdings to pay off their debts."

"That sounds like her."

"The fact that she could build Shoppe Francois to its current extent speaks to her skill."

Flum tried asking Henriette several more questions on the subject, but ultimately, they came up empty-handed with regard to the Necromancy project. They could only hope Eterna had better success with Welcy.

She and Milkit said their goodbyes and left the barracks.

Henriette watched the two slowly disappear into the distance from her window. Once they were out of sight, she issued orders to her subordinates.

"Ottilie, Werner, I want you to keep an eye on them. If you see them in danger, give them a hand. I'll assign a group of ten soldiers to each of you; that should be small enough to avoid suspicion."

This was all the assistance she could spare Flum in her battle against the church. Thanks to Satuhkie's efforts, there was a temporary lull in conflict with the church knights, and she could afford to spare the manpower.

"Yes ma'am! I will do my best to not betray my sister's love!"

"Y'know, I'm not really interested, so I think I'll pass... but you're not gonna let me, are you? Can't you assign Herrmann to this?"

"He's not the best at covert action. You, on the other hand, are perfectly suited for the job."

"Henriette's word is final. Now hurry up and get ready, Werner."

"Fine, fine, I got it..."

Ottilie dashed out of the room with renewed purpose. Werner shuffled after her.

When she could no longer hear their footsteps in the distance, Henriette spoke aloud to no one in particular.

"Ancient legacies, copies of people, counter-spirals... and something about an ark capital? This is all well and truly beyond me."

She still struggled to believe all the things Satuhkie discussed with her, but she also knew that unbelievable happenings were everyday reality in the capital now. Henriette hadn't join the military out of a lust for power

or money. She wanted to protect the kingdom and all the people she loved who lived within it. That motivation now seemed sadly at odds with the position she found herself in.

"And yet, I still need to resist. There are still people I need to protect."

She slipped her coat on and stepped out of her office. She had a meeting with the fanatics who inhabited that demonic cathedral of theirs.

When Flum and Milkit arrived at the predetermined meeting spot in the East District park, they found Eterna, Ink, and Welcy already there waiting for them.

"Sorry to keep you waiting."

"No worries. We only just got here ourselves."

"That's good, then. You came along too, Welcy?"

Welcy flashed a charming grin in response to Milkit's question before handing a sheaf of papers to Flum. "Do you know what this is?"

"It's a list of nobles who borrowed money from Satils!" Ink piped up.

"Hey, don't spoil the surprise, Ink!!" Welcy tugged playfully on Ink's ear, and the two burst into a fit of

267

giggles. It seemed the two had hit it off in the time they were waiting. "Anyway, one of our employees got hold of this ledger earlier today."

The employee in question had brought it in while Eterna was talking to Welcy at the newspaper's office, actually. The timing couldn't have been any better.

"We just got back from speaking with Henriette at the barracks," Flum said.

"Wow, you know the general?"

"You could say that. Anyway, according to her, Satils used to seize goods and property in payment for unsatisfied debts. Is this related to that?"

"Yep. In fact, Satils had obtained land rights to the section of forest north of the capital from one of her debtors."

"That dense thicket of trees? Now that's definitely suspicious."

"She often sent carts laden with goods sold to the church up to the north. Do you think…?"

"Exactly. There's a good chance we'll find the Necromancy group's research lab up in the forest."

Dafydd had stopped by the capital just one day ago, and returned to his lab that night, only to return to the capital again the next morning. To make the round trip so soon, the lab had to be just a few hours out from the capital.

"I can arrange for a carriage. What do you think?" Welcy queried.

"That'd be greatly appreciated."

"Gotcha. But today's probably a no-go, yeah? Even if I get to work on it right now, I don't think I can get a carriage ready before nightfall."

"Hmm, I think night would be pushing it, especially coming up on a research lab."

If they didn't approach this with caution, they were done for. Flum would have loved nothing more than to go immediately, but she knew that wouldn't be wise.

"All right then, we'll leave first thing tomorrow morning. Could you make the arrangements?" she asked Welcy.

"Sure thing. Obviously, I'm going with. No objections, right?"

"As long as you understand that we can't ensure your safety, of course."

"No need to worry. I'm good at running away." Welcy winked at Flum, which did little to alleviate her anxiety.

ROLL
OVER
AND
DIE

011

Where the Miracle of Life Squirms Free

THE GROUP LEFT the capital at the very crack of dawn the next day, traces of night still lingering in the sky, and arrived at the forest four hours later. They spent a while going up and down the tree line, looking for a path where a carriage could pass.

"They're faint, but I think I see some wheel tracks over there," their driver finally said. "It'll be a tight fit but doable."

Welcy was fulsome in her praise. "Good job, Rent! You're the best driver out there!"

Though he was technically employed by a carriage company, he was one of Welcy's coworkers. Carriages were widely-used in the capital, including by the royal family and high-ranking members of the clergy, making there few better places to gather information than from a cabbie's seat. It was Rent who had uncovered where Satils' carts had been heading.

"Whoa, it's getting buummmpy!" Ink's voice shook as she rattled along with the carriage.

Obviously, no one bothered to pave a lone forest path, making for an incredibly rocky ride. The only saving grace was that no one in the cart succumbed to motion sickness.

"Bleeeugh!"

Except, that was, for Welcy.

After traveling a little further, the ground finally smoothed out.

"Huh, it looks like the rest of the way's much better taken care of. It's far from a paved road, but it's well worn."

"Seems like they tried to camouflage the entrance."

"Curiouser and curiouser."

Flum was almost certain there was a research facility nearby—meaning they could be subject to attack at any moment. But even after pressing on for another twenty minutes, she noticed no appreciable change.

"Don't be so tense," Eterna said.

"What makes you say that?"

"I didn't get the sense Dafydd was looking for a fight. Even when I didn't show up for our meeting yesterday, he didn't bother to come looking for me. It's possible team Necromancy has little in the way of combat power."

"So, no undead army?"

"Might be wishful thinking, I suppose."

"If it means Gadhio's safe and sound, I'm down with that."

Flum had prayed Gadhio would return before they left.

Life hardly goes the way we want it to. Now we're missing him and Sara...

As the carriage continued deeper into the forest, Flum's mind went back to her missing friend. She knew Sara was with Neigass, but was she really safe and sound?

She heard a sound up ahead. "Huh?"

Rent seemed to have picked up on something from the driver's seat. "There are tracks up ahead, but they definitely aren't from horses."

"Some kind of wild animals?"

"No, this is way bigger than that. Must be some kind of monster."

Even assuming none of the spiral creatures were about, they risked being attacked by other, normal but still dangerous woodland creatures. There were untold perils in this forest—of that much Flum was certain.

Ink spoke up a few moments later. "I hear footsteps."

Everyone else could only hear the rattling of the carriage wheels.

"What direction are they coming from, Ink?"

"Back and to the right. They're closing in fast. I hear two feet, like a human, but bigger."

Eterna couldn't see anything from the carriage window, but when she closed her eyes and focused in on her hearing, she could hear the footsteps. Just like Ink said, they were heavy and intimidating.

"Could it be..."

Flum had heard something like this before.

The sound reminded her of the spiral ogre under Anichidey.

A few moments later, her premonition turned out to be right on the mark. From Eterna's window, she could see a dead ringer for the beast from Flum's story. Blood spattered in all directions as the whorl of exposed flesh and muscle spasmed. Its fist was already up in the air.

"Get down!"

No sooner had the words left Eterna's mouth than a powerful tornado made contact with the carriage. The trunk was nearly completely blown away, the rear quarter of the carriage reduced to splinters on contact.

"Hey, calm down... It's okay, it's okay!" Rent was doing his best to calm the horses.

"That's one of those spiral creatures?" This was the first time Milkit had seen one. The blood drained from her face.

"Just the sight's enough to turn your blood to ice..."

As Welcy spoke, she hurriedly scribbled down a record of the events using her burn projection.

Flum drew her Souleater and leveled the blade at the oncoming enemy. She cast Scan.

Chimera Prototype: O
Affinity: Earth
Strength: 2552
Magic: 584
Endurance: 2831
Agility: 1259
Perception: 499

So this ogre is different from the other one. They may look the same, but this one's core has been suppressed to keep its power from getting out of hand.

Which could only mean someone had intentionally sent it after them. What's more, its name suggested it was team Chimera's and had nothing to do with team Necromancy.

I've gotta say, they really outdid themselves, lining up a copy of the creature Sara and I fought before. Its face is an absolute wreck, too. But...

She decided to put aside Dafydd's potential involvement for the moment. What was most important was stopping this thing before it unleashed another attack.

"Don't write me off as the same weak girl I was before! Prana Sting!!"

FWOOOSH! All of her prana coalesced at the tip of her blade before lancing outward.

The ogre shot a spiral blast from its fist at exactly the same time. What the attack lacked in grace, it made up for in power.

The two blasts slammed into each other in midair, though the ogre's attack was no match for Flum's reversal-powered spear. It pierced straight through the spiral and right into the ogre's core. The beast collapsed to the forest floor like a puppet with its strings cut.

Milkit cried out almost immediately after the ogre dropped. "There's another one coming up behind us!"

"Another one?!" Flum turned too late, seeing the second ogre punching its fist into the air over and over.

"Ice Shield!"

Eterna came to the rescue. Her shield blocked the blows from hitting Flum—though only just. Ice cracked and splintered as the spiral energy chipped away at it, but her magic was more than enough to handle it.

"Water Shot!"

Standing behind the safety of her ice shield—and out of sight of the oncoming ogre—Eterna let off a volley of bullets at the enemy that spat through the ice shield

and found their mark in the ogre's head and limbs. *Pwah pwah pwah!* Each bullet tore a hole in the oncoming creature and sent it crashing to the ground.

"Looks like we can kill them even without destroying their cores."

"There are still more...and a huge group of them this time, too!"

"What a pain..."

A pack of ogres approached from the carriage's rear. Their heavy footfalls shook the ground beneath them and carried up through their bodies, reminding Flum of a wild stampede.

"Good luck! We're counting on you!" Rent urged the horses into a full gallop, but the ogres were still gaining on them.

"Whatta scoop! Pity this image isn't really suitable for print..."

"I've never seen anything like this before..."

Both Welcy and Milkit were stunned at the horrifying scene playing out before them. The pack of ogres ran with unnatural agility—backs straight, knees lunging high with each step, and arms swaying in perfect time at their sides. The bloody messes of their faces wriggled, spewing gore with each balletic stride.

The pack stopped and raised their fists in unison. They

looked like they were readying another spiral blast. Even Flum and Eterna wouldn't be of much use in the face of this many attacking all at once.

Eterna leaned in and whispered something into Flum's ear. After thinking it over, Flum whispered back.

Welcy was starting to worry. "H-hey, everything okay? That looks like it's going to be a real humdinger!"

Flum and Eterna turned to face the enemy, their expressions composed. Even across this distance, the pulse and splatter of the ogres' cratered heads carried, until they were drowned out by the roar of the nascent cyclone forming from their combined energy. The cyclone grew exponentially, its outer edge nipping at the carriage.

Eterna climbed atop the carriage. "Ice Shield!!"

It was slightly larger than the one she cast previously, but she didn't seem like she planned any further beyond that.

Welcy started to lose her cool. "Whoa! It's coming... it's coming!!!"

Ink and Milkit, meanwhile, had faith in their friends. All they had to do was hope and pray.

Flum put her hand on the back of the ice shield and began to feed her magic into it. "Enchantment Reversion!"

This wasn't a special technique, exactly. Rather, she was using the same method as her Souleater blade or Cavalier Arts techniques to channel the unique power of Reversion into Eterna's ice shield.

The tornado tore a deep trench in the ground and sent fragments of trees in every direction as it closed in on them, but—the gale dissipated the moment it touched the shield. With its spiral power reversed, the attack lost all of its momentum.

"Time to take the fight to them."

"I'm going, too!"

The two women hopped down from the speeding carriage and landed on the soft ground below.

Eterna pressed her hand into the dirt.

"Frozen Ground!"

The earth beneath them froze over. A moment later, the frost slithered along the ground as it zeroed in on the ogre pack. The moment the frost touched the ogres' feet, it spread up their legs and locked them in place.

It was Flum's turn. She held her sword at the ready. "Hit me."

"All right then, just as we planned. Ice Enchantment!"

A layer of frost formed over the Souleater.

Flum was going to try out an attack she witnessed in Gadhio's battle with Nekt. She wouldn't be able to replicate it exactly, since she lacked his brute strength, but she did have one thing he didn't: regeneration. No matter how recklessly she fought, no matter how badly she got hurt, she would bounce back.

Flum let out a low growl and hefted her sword high. Wreathed in ice, it towered over the tree line. She could hear her bones and muscles popping. Her growl grew into a primal scream.

"Gyaaaaaaaaaaaaaaaaaaugh!!"

The occupants of the carriage could still see the colossal blade as the ogres shrank into the distance.

Flum could feel her muscles tear and bones begin to deform under the weight, though they healed nearly instantaneously. Her only concern was the pain.

"Graaaaaaaaaaaaaaaaaoooooool!!"

She swung her newly minted Jötunn Blade toward the ogre pack.

The blade tore through the pack's leading edge on first contact. When it hit the ground, the ice shattered in a massive shock wave that tore through the remaining ogres and leveled nearby trees.

The scene was drowned in fog and dust as the scattered ice sublimed, but it was clear that there were no ogres left standing. The reversal magic imbued in Flum's strike shattered their cores instantly.

No trace remained of the surrounding trees. It was like some giant's hand had reached down and carried away a fistful of the hills themselves.

"Haah...haah...haaaah..."

"We may have overdone it."

Flum tried to laugh as she struggled to catch her breath. "N-no, I think that was just about perfect. They're...they're pretty stubborn..."

Their enemies destroyed, Flum and Eterna returned to the damaged carriage and continued on their way. After about five minutes or so, they came across a sign next to the road.

"Sheol, Village of Salvation...?" Flum tilted her head to the side in confusion.

"Is that the name of the village up ahead?"

"That's strange. According to the map, there are no villages out here."

"I guess we'll just have to ask him."

Flum looked at Eterna. "What do you mean 'him?'"

Just as she asked that, the carriage came to a gentle stop.

"What is it, Rent?"

"There's a man up ahead."

A slender man in a white lab coat stood in the middle of the road. From Eterna's tone of voice, it could only be...

"Dafydd Chalmas..."

The man who oversaw the Necromancy project.

A puzzled look came over Dafydd's face at the sound of his own name as he turned toward Flum. "Our God truly is a cruel one. I never said that I was against this idea, but at least give me time to prepare..."

"Are you talking about me?" Flum hopped down from the carriage and approached Dafydd. She immediately drew her Souleater and brought the blade to his neck.

After all she'd been through with the Origin cores, it was a reasonable reaction, barbaric as it seemed. After the life-or-death battle she just finished, it was only reasonable to proceed with caution.

"Would you mind putting your sword away? I have no desire to fight you."

"Don't play dumb with me. We were just attacked by a pack of core mutants, you know."

"You fought the Chimera? So that's what that sound was. I'm sure this must sound like an excuse to you, but I assure you I had nothing to do with that."

"You're right; it does sound like an excuse."

"Chimera and Necromancy are competitors, you see. You could even call us rivals. We have no reason to use any

of Echidna's pets! Besides, the focal cores we created here in Sheol don't work well with the Chimera cores. If you let them get too close together, you might lose control over them entirely."

"Rephrase that in normal person language."

"Necromancy focal cores are used to control the Origin cores—otherwise known as Necromancy cores—used to bring back the dead. Put simply, they weaken the larger cores that are used to channel Origin's power. Chimera cores are the ones created by the Chimera team."

Flum eased up slightly at Dafydd's explanation. Just as Eterna mentioned earlier, she didn't sense anything threatening from him. She held his gaze the entire time and didn't get the impression he was being dishonest.

"Where's Gadhio?"

"He's just fine. Spending some quality time with his wife. Would you like to see him? He's expressed some concern over having left his friends back in the capital."

Welcy called out from the carriage. "Why don't you just put down your sword, Flum? I think it's pretty clear he isn't lying, and I think he'd be willing to answer a lot of our questions. There's a lot I'm hoping to learn about the church, too."

As for the rest of the party, Rent seemed to be in agreement with Welcy, while Milkit and Ink were both content to leave the decision up to Flum. Eterna, who had already met Dafydd before, said nothing.

Flum remained largely unconvinced, but she knew it was the best move for the time being. "Fine." With a little reluctance, she dismissed her sword in a flash of light.

The tension drained from Dafydd's posture. "Listen, I completely understand your grudge with the church. I appreciate your decision to stand down, really. Let me take you to Sheol. You can get back into your carriage, if you'd like. I'll lead the way."

Dafydd turned and set off.

Flum hopped back aboard the carriage, only to be met with a look of concern on Milkit's face. Perhaps she was just concerned by Flum's own annoyed expression. The thought warmed Flum's heart, and she reached out to stroke Milkit's hair.

After proceeding down the path for some distance, the forest opened up into a wide clearing enfolding a small village. Sheol, the Village of Salvation.

Flum had expected something stark and modern, but it looked just like any other settlement out in the sticks. People walked the streets, tended crops, and bought and sold wares; parents watched their children frolic. Only the great church at the village's center was out of the ordinary.

The passengers disembarked at the town entrance, leaving Rent to tend to the horses. Inside the gates, it all felt completely and utterly...normal. The only thing that seemed out of place was their little group.

"Is that church over there your lab?" Flum asked.

Dafydd nodded cheerfully. "Yes. The facility sprawls out under the village."

"I heard you were financially supported by Satils, and that this land was granted to you by another noble. Did the church build the facility?"

"My, my. You're quite well informed, I see. It's just as you say, I'm afraid."

"Why did Satils finance your work?"

"I signed a contract to grant her preferential merchandising rights to the results of our Necromancy research, once perfected."

Flum stopped in her tracks. "I knew I couldn't trust you! Trying to sell technology that could bring back the dead?! Disgusting!"

Dafydd glanced back sadly at the young women. "Trust me, I wasn't excited about the prospect of monetizing human lives, either. But I can't carry out my research or provide the people I've brought back with a place to live without money. I had to make a tough choice if I wanted to see my dream come true."

"A place for them to live? You mean everyone living here is...?"

"Correct, half of them are dead. The other half are those I have saved by returning their loved ones. What do you think? They certainly seem happy, no?" Dafydd smiled proudly.

Flum and the rest of her group looked around the village again. Try though she may, she couldn't tell who was living and who had been revived. Milkit watched carefully, Eterna thought quietly, Ink listened, and Welcy took meticulous notes.

A woman with a rounded belly emerged from the church and ran straight to Dafydd.

"Susy, didn't I tell you not to run?" he chided.

"But I was worried about you! There was that awful sound and then you went off into the forest on your own. I wish you'd at least take some bodyguards with you!"

"And this is...?" Flum queried.

Dafydd beamed. "This is my beloved wife, Susy. She was also brought back to life thanks to the core and, as you can see, we're expecting a child soon. Next month, in fact."

Susy smiled shyly at her introduction. If Dafydd hadn't just told them who she was, Flum couldn't have told them apart from any other couple deeply in love. However, the prouder he seemed about all of this, the more her suspicions grew.

"She got pregnant after you brought her back to life?"

"Flum, I understand what you're feeling. You're thinking the Origin cores only make it look like people are brought back to life. But I assure you, the child thriving inside Susy is a brand-new life. In fact, several other children have been born and raised here in this village. They're completely normal humans, with completely normal bodies. Putting aside the cycle of life for a moment, I think you can put your suspicions to rest that these people are anything other than truly resurrected."

The pride in Dafydd's voice was clear—and not without reason. His was a confidence born not just of his research but also of the many years he'd spent with his revived wife and their new friends. Flum detected absolutely no doubt in his mind that these people had been completely brought back from the dead. Even if she continued to disbelieve him, it would be tantamount to condemning the hundreds of revived dead living in the village. If it was just a few people, maybe she could do it... but there were just way too many.

No matter how grave her doubts about the project, as long as it was impossible to distinguish the living from the dead, she couldn't possibly bring herself to destroy the hundreds of cores active in the village.

So what could she do, then?

Before she could ponder this, Ink spoke up. "Oh, it's Gadhio."

She must've heard his voice off in the distance. Flum looked around for a bit before she finally spotted him walking over from a shop. Tia had her arm around his and a soft smile on her face.

"Gadhio...!"

"I'm glad he's doing well. Aren't you, Master?"

"...Yeah."

There was something about the relaxed look on his face that kept Flum from being truly happy for her friend. She'd never seen him like that before.

Gadhio's eyes went wide in surprise at the sight of his friends. A moment later, a scowl crossed his face, like a child caught doing something they knew they shouldn't. "What brings you here?"

"Well, you just kind of disappeared, Gadhio. Kleyna and Hallom are worried about you."

"Sorry. I...I didn't know what to say to them."

Tia finally broke her silence, looking deeply apologetic.

She kept her arm tightly wrapped around Gadhio's. "Don't blame Gaddy. I really should have explained things to them."

It was clear which direction the scales had tipped for him.

"I'm guessing you have no plan to come back?" Flum asked.

"Tia can't live outside this village. I could commute between the capital and here, but I don't think I could bring myself to do that."

"What do you mean, she can't live outside of here?"

"Allow me to answer that," Dafydd said.

"I'd love to live with Gaddy in the capital. I hate keeping him tied up here with me like this, but..."

"Tia, Gadhio, perhaps you can all catch up later on. I'd like to take them on a tour of the lab now."

"You're right, I think that would be best. Sorry for the interruption."

"Wait, don't go!" Flum called out to Gadhio as he began to walk away.

"You should go check out the lab," he called back to her over his shoulder. "It'll answer your questions."

With that, he and Tia disappeared into the crowd.

Ink mumbled under her breath. "He's like a completely different person."

She was right. Nothing about this Gadhio bore any resemblance to the person Flum knew. She hated to say it, but it felt almost like the weakness he'd hidden for all these years was now on display for all to see. He seemed like a fool.

Like...a coward.

"Please don't blame Gadhio," Dafydd said. "Tia is a vivacious and beautiful woman. I can only imagine how much he must have suffered from the loss of such a light from his life."

"How can you talk about this so dispassionately? Tia was killed by a Chimera! The fact that you raided Kindah and Claudia's graves tells me that an Origin core alone isn't enough to bring someone back from the dead. So how did you get Tia's body, huh??"

Eterna tensed up slightly at the mention of Kindah and Claudia's names, though Dafydd didn't seem to notice.

"Though we may be rivals, that doesn't mean we don't interact with the Chimera team. The last time I visited Echidna's lab, she showed me some preserved corpses, and Tia was among them." He chewed on his lip, seeming to think back on that moment. "My best guess is that Chimera was getting ready to use it as raw material. Once the transformation was complete, they would use her against Gadhio."

"Throwing out some unfounded accusations there, aren't you?" Eterna's voice turned harsh, though Dafydd didn't even seem to notice.

Hardly surprising, considering how casually he went about digging up people's loved ones. After all, Necromancy's research had to require a constant supply of corpses. Desecrating graves was probably just another day's work to his team.

"That's just the kind of woman Echidna Ipeila is," he said. "I imagine she was also the one who fielded those ogres. If you died at their hands, that would be one less person to bother her, but if you didn't, it would drive a wedge between you and me. She's a cold-blooded, dreadful woman. Always has been."

Dafydd's loathing for her was readily apparent. It was the first time Flum had seen him angry.

Susy took one look at her husband and offered up an embarrassed smile. "I'm so sorry. I assure you he's really a great, caring man. It's just that whenever he starts to talk about Echidna, well..."

Flum had no doubt there was something fundamentally wrong with the leader of the Chimera team. Besides, it was hard for her to believe the founder of this idyllic village could also be the creator of such awful creatures. It seemed clear to her that Dafydd was telling the truth.

Even if he is here to be with his wife, I know Gadhio must be investigating the village on his own. At the very least, this must mean he isn't actively hostile toward Dafydd and that his wife is the same person she was before. It's probably safe to assume at least that much.

Something nagged at Flum as they walked through the peaceful village. Though she usually didn't pick up on such small details when walking hand in hand with Milkit, this was impossible to ignore.

Everyone in the village was watching her.

012

Spiral Hunt

TO BE IGNORANT was to be a fool.

To be fair, the world was full of things you were better off not knowing, and Gadhio figured this was one of them. What you didn't know couldn't hurt you.

"What's wrong, Gaddy?" Tia looked up at her doting husband, her arm tightly intertwined with his.

She was so beautiful. Nothing short of perfection, as far as he was concerned. Their eyes met, and his cheeks grew warm at their proximity.

"People always called you a haughty man with a perpetual scowl, but you don't seem like that to me at all," she said.

"I hope you're not making fun of me."

"No, no, it's a good thing! I'd be in a pretty tough spot if you turned into a ladies' man before we finally met again!"

Tia was like the sun. Just having her by his side brought him unconditional warmth and happiness. Once he lost her, he was left with little else to do than focus on the blood-stained earth. With no sun left to illuminate the sky, his heart was plunged into darkness.

"But I guess I'm no perfect woman, either..."

"What makes you say that?"

"I mean, I don't want to ever let you go back to Kleyna and little Hallom. I want you here, by my side, forever and ever."

Possessiveness was a completely normal emotion. Any wife—anyone, really—might feel the same. It was, perhaps, a uniquely human trait.

Gadhio didn't know whether he could truly tell the real from the fake after he had been without his sun for so long. But as long as it was still bright, warm, and provided him with the sustenance he needed, perhaps it didn't matter if it was real or not.

"Tia..."

His goddess smiled and tilted her head quizzically.

"I love you." His voice may have been barely above a whisper, but he spoke with absolute conviction.

Tia's cheeks went a rosy pink. "I love you too, Gaddy."

Perhaps ignorance was bliss. Knowledge, by its nature, robbed you of your freedom. Gadhio knew that all too well, which was why he prayed he could be left to his ignorance for just a while longer.

The two discussed nothing in particular as they walked arm-in-arm to the house Dafydd had given them. Tia glanced over, almost unconsciously, just in time to see Flum and the rest of the group enter the church.

Dafydd and Susy stopped in front of the church.

"All right, the lab entrance is just inside. While I may owe Flum and the others an explanation, I'm afraid I can't be having any journalists coming in."

"What? How am I any different from Milkit? Listen, it's fine, I'm good at keeping secrets," Welcy objected.

"Is there anything inside that Welcy can't see?"

"Our research is still at a point where we can't make any official announcements. This is simply a measure to minimize risks."

It was clear Dafydd wasn't going to yield on this point. Welcy frowned and let out a sigh in defeat.

"Well, I didn't come here just to write up an article, so I guess it won't do me much good to try to force you to let me in. You don't mind if I look around the village, right?"

"Of course not; do as you like."

Ink looked concerned. "Are you really going to be okay alone?"

"No problem. Besides, if something does come up, I'll just ask Gadhio for help. Anyway, I guess I'll be off!"

Welcy quickly made her exit, almost like she already had somewhere to check out in mind. Flum was worried about her, but all she could do was hope she was right about being able to count on Gadhio in a pinch.

"Well then, shall we get going?" Dafydd said.

With that, the group was off to the lab.

The inside of the church, or at least what they could see above ground, looked just like any other church back in the capital or a similar-sized town. The walls and ceiling were pure white. Tall stained-glass windows shattered the sunlight into rays of color that burned across the floor.

The party walked down a long, red carpet that cut through the center of the room. Long pews lined either side of the aisle. Up at the apse stood a statue of Origin and the faith's symbol. Flum couldn't spot anything that hinted at the building's true purpose.

That all changed after they stepped through a door in the right-hand transept and made their way down a flight of stairs. Here, the floors and walls were made entirely of metal. Magic lanterns embedded in the ceiling bathed the room in harsh light—an impressive feat, considering how few there were for such a large space.

Flum and the rest of the group looked around with great interest, running their hands along the walls from the moment they entered the room. It was like nothing they'd ever seen before.

"This has been nagging at me for a while," Eterna said. "Is the technology you use here any different from the research facilities elsewhere in the kingdom?"

"These were built using construction methods based around conventional and demonic earth affinity magic, as well as a number of the kingdom's own, proprietary techniques."

"The church has adopted demon techniques?"

"As with medicinal herbs," said Eterna, "they're okay with it as long as there's no competition."

"I can't argue that point, sadly," Dafydd said. "I do wish the church was willing to share such valuable information."

Flum supposed he wasn't to blame for their close-fistedness. The church might claim they existed to bring the people to salvation, but their true purpose was more to unify in thought the minds of those they wished to.

"Why don't we start with this first room here?"

"I think I'd like to go back to my own bedroom for now."

"Ah, yes, you should rest, Susy. I'm sure Flum and the others don't mind, right?"

It wasn't like they had any real say in the matter, anyway. Susy made her exit, and Dafydd began the tour.

"Ah, right, but first a warning. We are conducting research that involves cadavers, which may be shocking to some of you. If you have a problem with the sight of corpses, I recommend you don't look."

The first room he showed them was the morgue. It was cold and filled with dozens of transparent coffins, each preserving the body of a person awaiting revival.

"Waauh..." Milkit was the only member of the party taken aback by the sight. She ducked down slightly behind Flum but didn't dare close her eyes for fear of being left behind.

The conditions of the bodies were varied, some consisting of little more than bones or gobbets of flesh—hardly recognizable as human at all. According to Dafydd, however, they could all be returned to their normal form with a Necromancy core.

"We look up particularly tragic deaths that have occurred throughout the kingdom and then work with their families to obtain permission to bring back their loved one."

Eterna fixed him with a pointed glare at the way he

portrayed this as a project born purely of compassion. "What about my parents, then?"

After a brief moment of confusion, he finally caught on to what she was saying and hurried to explain himself.

"I'm truly sorry about that. I got it into my head that I needed to win you over somehow and took their bodies without permission."

"But if you hadn't told me, I'd never have known it was you."

"As I explained earlier, after your encounter with the Children I began to fear that the top officials within the church would be in a hurry to weaponize our work. If that happened, I could no longer continue my research. I needed allies on short notice."

So you only brought Satils back to keep your cash flow safe, then? thought Flum.

All he achieved was putting himself on the bad side of the one person who could destroy Origin cores. He hadn't exactly invited her out to Sheol, anyway. Instead, he worked in the background, manipulating her friends.

"Well, let's proceed." Whether Dafydd noticed Flum's adversarial stare, she couldn't tell. He urged the group into Core Production, according to the sign by the door.

The room was lit only by a faint white glow coming from a dozen-odd clear tubes that lined the room. They

were filled with liquid with lumps of greyish tissue suspended inside.

"Are...are those brains?" Flum tightened her grip on Milkit, who was hunkered down behind her.

"These devices are called Little Origins."

"Little Origins...?"

As the words came out of her mouth, the edges of Flum's vision blurred, and she could hear a faint hiss in the distance.

This is just like what happened with Satuhkie. What is this awful feeling? It's like I'm getting déjà vu or something. Have I...have I seen this before? I...I must've just seen something similar in the facility back in Anichidey. That must be it.

"Little Origins tune into Origin's energy and ramp it up to create the black crystals known as Origin cores."

Just as Gadhio promised, Dafydd was answering all of their questions. However, Flum was taken aback at how ready he was to show them the process of making these cores.

The hiss in her head grew even louder as she looked on.

"Are you sure it's okay to show this to us?" she asked. "I'm pretty sure this is top-secret church stuff."

"Obviously, I'd be in hot water if the higher-ups knew about this. I felt this was the only way for me to really gain your trust." He didn't appear to be lying.

"In that case, I have a question. You said these tune into Origin's energy, but what does that mean?"

"Exactly what I said. Origin's body is located elsewhere, you see."

"Where is this...body?"

"That I do not know. The church hasn't revealed that to me. But I'm sure you have a guess, no?"

"The...Demon Lord's castle?"

There was no reason for someone as weak and power-less as Flum to tag along on the great journey to slay the Demon Lord. And yet, she'd been "summoned" by Origin and taken from her hometown. Their destination was the Demon Lord's castle...and the location of Origin's body.

Whether by necessity or some ineffable plan, Origin seemed to want to bring Flum to it. Maybe it had learned she was the only human that could destroy Origin cores and wanted to see this wonder firsthand.

"But why try to get me all the way out there to kill Origin? Was it really worth the risk of failure?"

"No one but Origin can answer that question."

Considering he didn't even know Origin's location, Dafydd obviously didn't have an answer to her question. Regardless, it was clear this was something Origin was dearly invested in. Realizing this train of thought was go-ing nowhere, Flum decided to put Origin's goals aside for the moment and asked Dafydd several more questions about the room, each of which he readily answered.

Before ultimately becoming Origin cores, the black crystals were completely normal gems mined in the south. To embed a nearly perfect spiral within them, they needed to be as close to spherical as possible. The brains used by the Little Origins, meanwhile, were removed from criminals sentenced to death.

Dafydd was so upfront with the way he answered her questions that it actually made Flum even more suspicious, though even she had to admit this may have been too harsh. She was beginning to understand why Gadhio chose to trust this man.

"Well, then, shall we move on? There's still much more to show you."

Leaving Core Production, the group came upon a man in a white lab coat standing in front of the next stop on their tour. Behind him was a similarly dressed woman holding a young child.

"Ah, hello, Gorne."

"Oh, are these the guests?"

Noticing the group was staring intently at the newcomer, Dafydd moved quickly to introductions. "This is Gorne Forgan, my assistant."

"Hi."

Gorne tilted his head forward in a casual greeting, which Flum returned in kind.

"Not only is he a talented researcher, but he's also been a longtime friend of mine. Unfortunately, after the tragic passing of his beloved wife, Gorne went through a rough patch and developed a drinking problem that led to ballooning gambling debts."

"Now, now, I don't think we need to go into all that."

"Hey, there's no judgment here. Anyway, I told him about my Necromancy project, and now here he is, working as my research assistant together with his wife, Luluca."

Luluca bowed her head.

Flum leaned in and looked closely at the child in her arms. "Was this baby born after Luluca was revived?"

"That's correct. As I mentioned before, all the children born here are all healthy and growing normally."

On some level, all living creatures shared a biological imperative to pass on some part of themselves. In that sense, you might say the fact that resurrected people were having children was convincing proof they were truly alive once more. It certainly seemed to serve as a great source of confidence for Dafydd. After all, Susy would soon be giving birth, as well. Assuming her child was also a completely normal human, that would further cement his beliefs.

Even Flum had to admit that the concept of those who were once dead giving life to children was an incredibly compelling argument for his camp.

"Sorry to bother you, Gorne."

"Not at all. It sounds like this was important. Anyway, I should get going."

Gorne made his exit with Luluca and their child in tow. The child stared intently at Flum as they walked past.

"The room up ahead is our research lab. This is where the real essence of our Necromancy research takes place."

A large, imposing door stood in front of them.

"This door is sealed to all but myself and a few hand-picked research staff." Dafydd put his hand on a crystal embedded in the wall next to the door.

Though similar to the switches used to turn magic lanterns on and off, the technology behind it was something else entirely. The door would only unlock after checking that the user's magical "resonance" matched that of one of the people recorded within it. Each and every person had a slightly different magical resonance, making this an incredibly secure—and incredibly expensive—system, implemented in only the most important of locations.

Whatever was behind the door was a vital state secret.

"And this here is the Central Control Room."

Once Dafydd's identity was confirmed, the door swung open to reveal an expansive chamber with a vaulted ceiling. The walls were covered in a maze of cabling. At the middle of the room was a black sphere about as big as a grown man.

"Is that...an Origin core, too?"

"I can see something swirling around inside it."

"I don't even want to think about how much energy is contained in that thing."

"Doesn't this excite you at least a little, Eterna? You must remember many of these." Dafydd walked up to the massive core and ran his hand along the surface. "This is the Necromancy focal core. It's necessary to suppress Origin's influence over the cores implanted in the people living here in Sheol."

"What would happen to them if it wasn't here?"

"Well, they would no longer be able to maintain their living bodies and fall under the control of Origin."

He spoke as if he'd seen it before.

"However, thanks to recent developments, it is now possible for them to survive in their current form for several days outside of Sheol's limits. Eventually, the focal core will no longer be necessary."

"But for now, they'll turn into some kind of creature without it?" Flum said.

"So they're not actually human. Is that what you're attempting to imply?" Eterna said.

Flum nodded. If these revived undead were only a hair's breadth away from such a tragic fate, they hardly seemed human to her.

"I'd posit that you're biased by your belief that the people living here are merely monsters going through the motions of normal human life," Dafydd said. "Those preconceived notions are distorting your perspective."

"Preconceived notion...?" Flum said. "I've had countless encounters with Origin cores. I've seen Origin's 'influence' up close. The Children and their supernatural abilities are a great example of that. Rotation, Connection, Replication... Honestly, I'd say it looks like this is just an extension of Origin's replication abilities."

Contorting, binding together, duplicating...these were the powers that Origin used to expand its power base. Flum was beginning to see the village as an enticing trap, a place that drew people to embed Origin cores in the dead of their own will.

"As you correctly pointed out, Origin cores certainly do have these characteristics. But they are, at the end of the day, merely characteristics, and..."

"Don't they give away Origin's desires?"

"Desires?"

"Origin has a will of its own. Whether it's some shapeless, thinking force or it has a body of its own, I don't really know. But whatever it is, it uses its power to corrupt and exert total control over people. No matter what way you go about it, the result will be the same: Origin will take advantage of man's dreams to fulfill its own desires."

Ink, for example, lost her sight to one of Mother's operations. While she was still a bright and cheerful girl, the Origin core embedded within her took her body's sense of its missing sight and physically manifested it as duplicating eyeballs.

"Hmm, I see. So you're saying we are a part of that process, as well? But that's what the focal core is here to prevent. There's really nothing for you to worry about."

Milkit timidly raised her hand. "But then...Origin would no longer have any reason to lend us its power, correct?"

Assuming Origin's ultimate goal was to spread its influence, it had no reason to continue to cooperate in situations like this, where it was being prevented from exerting control.

Dafydd smiled confidently. "If Origin were capable of cutting off its power on such a granular level, then we wouldn't have such an outpouring of power in the first place. I can't speak to what form it's currently taken, but taken in light of the human-demon wars and the effort expended to send a group of heroes off to the Demon Lord's castle, I can only imagine there must be a very good reason why such bothersome measures have to be taken."

"So you're saying Origin is incomplete?" This explanation made a fair bit of sense to Ink. Even if Origin was incomplete, she'd still lived for nearly ten years with an Origin core serving as her heart. Thinking back on it now, the fact that she couldn't hear "Papa's voice" could easily have been because of its fragmented power.

"At present, it's up to each individual's ability to control the degree of Origin's power and influence," Dafydd said. "As you so wisely pointed out, it's certainly dangerous, but it's also worth taking advantage of. The sum of human knowledge comes from working with, and neutralizing, dangers to create new breakthroughs. The Origin cores are but one of those dangers."

Flum fell into a thoughtful silence and gazed at the focal core. After a long pause, her shoulders finally slumped, and she let out a sigh in resignation.

Dafydd beamed. "I'm glad to see you've finally seen things from my point of view."

"I give you my word that I won't destroy the focal core... for now. You've exposed your greatest weakness to me;

that has to mean something. But I'm not going home without Gadhio."

"Well, that decision is entirely up to him."

"Correct. So I'd like to ask that you let us stay here for the time being. Is that okay?"

"You want to spend the night?"

Flum noted a brief look of concern that flashed across his face. But Dafydd carried on cheerfully.

"That's not a problem at all. In fact, perhaps this would also be a good chance for Eterna to spend some time with her parents."

"I really don't..."

Ink piped up. "I think that's a great idea! Besides, I'd love to meet your parents."

"All right, if you insist."

"Will Master and I be given an accommodation in the village?"

"Actually, I'd like to stay in the lab."

All eyes fell on Flum. Eterna, Ink, and Milkit looked at her in surprise, while Dafydd's face tensed.

"Is there a problem?" Flum said.

"No, no. If that will help convince you, then I have no issue with it at all."

She wanted to believe Dafydd, but she still had several very good reasons not to trust him.

◇◇◇

After the end of the tour, Eterna and Ink left Flum and Milkit behind in the lab. Though Eterna didn't care for the idea of everyone going off on their own, she did want to see her parents again. She and Ink would have dinner with them and then return to the lab that evening to spend the night. The party would only be briefly separated. It seemed unlikely that Dafydd would have a sudden change of heart and attack Flum in that time.

Ink, on the other hand, shared none of Eterna's concerns.

"I wonder what your parents are like. Maybe they're a lot like you..."

"Not at all. We're not related by blood, you know."

"But...but...you lived together, right? So you probably talk the same and stuff like that."

"I'm not sure about how we talk, but my mother definitely isn't as eccentric as I am."

"You think you're eccentric?"

"How about...unique? But I've always been that way, ever since I was a kid. I'm not about to change anytime soon."

"Well, I like you just the way you are, Eterna. It's always easy for me to tell when you're around!"

Eterna wasn't entirely sure if that was because of her

"uniqueness," but before their conversation could go on any further, they arrived at the home of the Rinebows. Rather than head to the entrance, Eterna immediately changed direction towards a nearby park, where several children were playing as their parents watched.

Ink tugged at Eterna's hand, noticing they'd stepped off the beaten path. "What happened? Aren't we going to your parents' house?"

"I need some time to get myself ready."

"Oh? Huh. Well, why don't we sit down?"

Eterna found a bench. A moment later, Ink hopped up onto her lap.

"Oomph!"

"Yeah!"

"Think again, kid." Eterna lightly tapped the back of Ink's head.

"What? There's nothing wrong with this. I like being close!"

"I know. You always smile whenever I stroke your hair in your sleep."

"R-really?" Ink flushed, not just at the thought of whatever goofy face she was making but at the knowledge that Eterna was brushing her hair as she slept.

Eterna felt the young girl warm slightly and wrapped her arms around her from behind.

"Th-this definitely isn't like you, Eterna."

"You said you like to be close, didn't you?"

"Nnng... I mean, I didn't expect to be this close!"

"If you don't like it, let me know, and I'll stop."

"No, I love it. Please keep it up!"

"Heh, so polite all of a sudden. Fine, I got it."

The two continued to sit there in silence for some time as Ink's body grew warmer and warmer and her cheeks flushed brighter with each passing moment. She still wasn't quite used to being hugged like that, nor was Eterna used to hugging another person. Even her own cheeks were taking on a pink hue.

"You smell really sweet, Ink."

"Where did that come from all of a sudden?! Weirdo!"

"How rude."

"Just sniffing people like that is pretty weird!"

"If you're going to be that way, I guess I'll just keep doing it." Eterna buried her face in Ink's hair and began to sniff loudly and theatrically.

"Th-that tickles!! Cut it out!!"

"Nope!"

"Start acting your age! You're supposed to listen to kids!!"

"I hardly look much older than you."

"You're pretty spoiled for a fifty-year-old kid!"

"Fifty? More like sixty."

"That's even worse!"

Eterna continued to sniff Ink's hair. She'd been joking around at first, but the more she kept doing it, the more at peace she felt. It was a unique aroma and one she'd started to look forward to every day, though she knew saying that aloud would only annoy Ink even more.

"Well, if this makes you feel better, I guess I can deal with it. Are you really that scared of seeing your parents?"

Ink seemed to catch on to what they were doing there. Voices could betray emotions even more readily than faces, and she picked up on the slight tension in Eterna's instantaneously.

"I turned Dafydd's offer down, but I was tempted," Eterna said. "Honestly, I think it would have been best if we got this all out of the way without even meeting them, but I just couldn't do that. No matter how many years may pass, I'm just too soft."

"I think kind is a better word."

"Now, now, I'm not that much of a narcissist."

"Well then, I'll say it. You're a kind person. You always take care of me and stand by my side. I think you're the nicest person in the whole wide world!"

"Ink..." Even though only a week had passed since they

first met, Ink gave Eterna strength. She squeezed the young girl tightly in her arms.

"Too tight! I don't think I'll be able to breathe if you keep that up!"

"You ground me in reality, Ink. As long as you're here with me, I know I won't get dragged back into my past."

"Huh...so you really don't believe Dafydd, then?"

Here was the source of all of Eterna's concerns.

"I want to believe him, sure. But my concerns have nothing to do with his character. There's one other point that I can't get past."

"What's that?"

Eterna's grip lightened up slightly. "Can Origin cores really help people?"

The voices of children playing in the park echoed in the distance. Were some of them also alive only through the power of the cores?

"I think Flum's picked up on it as well, but there's a great source of evil lurking within the cores. Frankly speaking, I feel like Origin and its desires won't hesitate to trample all over people and their dreams. Even with its power restricted, I have serious doubts that something like that would ever truly save people."

Ink's voice took on a sad tone. "I'm sorry, Eterna."

"What do you have to apologize for?"

"I mean...I'm one of them. I was involved. But I don't know anything about that." If she'd been able to hear its voice, as the others had, perhaps she'd know more about Origin's evil.

"That's fine. It's probably the only reason you were able to escape the Children with your life."

"You think I'd be dead if I could hear it?"

"I doubt they would have considered letting you go."

"I thought it was just because I was curious about some things..."

"If you were any slower making your move, I think things could have turned out very differently."

It was nothing short of a miracle that Ink had run into Flum and Milkit. Further, the odds that she would then come into contact with Eterna, the one person that could save her life, were astronomical.

"That's why I think it's best to just get this out of the way as soon as possible. The longer we wait, the deeper our wounds will be."

This string of miracles wouldn't last forever. Even if it did, she knew they wouldn't be able to save everyone in the village. All they could do was ride this out and push back against Dafydd's assertion that his attempts to bring back the dead were complete. She could think of few other options available to them.

Eterna lifted Ink up off her lap and set her down before she stood up. She felt recharged and ready. Hand in hand, the two walked back to the Rinebows' home.

"How ironic. We turned our backs on the government's research, and yet it's that same research that has given us this chance to see you again." Kindah and Claudia had tears in their eyes as they welcomed Eterna and Ink into their home.

"I have to admit, it's good to see you again. I don't suppose I can give you a hug?"

At long last, it was time for the family to reunite.

Claudia pulled Eterna into a tight embrace. Eterna relished her mother's scent and the warmth of her body, but deep in her heart, she knew there was something cold and inhuman about her.

The room Dafydd brought Flum and Milkit to was quite large, apparently meant for other couples and families like Gorne to live in within the research facility.

"This place is so nice, it's hard to believe we're underground. There's a bath, toilet—even a kitchen!" Milkit exclaimed.

"If it just had a window, I might mistake it for a ritzy

hotel. It's kinda hard to relax knowing we're in a research facility, though."

Flum dropped heavily onto the sofa, and Milkit sat down next to her. The two were so close that their shoulders touched. They naturally sought out each other's hands and intertwined their fingers.

"Why did you want to stay here tonight, Master?"

"I just can't fully accept what he says. I've been getting this really weird vibe ever since we got here." Not only was Flum getting weird looks from everyone in the village, but there was just something off about the way the people acted and moved. "But destroying this place will just result in further sadness for everyone involved..."

"I've never really lost anyone important to me, so it's hard to understand how they feel. But whenever I think about a day when my master would no longer be by my side, I feel a painful tightness in my chest," Milkit said.

"I don't think I could stand being without you either, Milkit. So I can definitely understand how Gadhio and Dafydd must have felt. But even if his story makes sense, there are just too many flaws in his logic to overlook."

Though she hadn't seen anything specific, Flum still had that niggling sense of something menacing lurking within the village.

"First off, if Dafydd was convinced his Necromancy method truly was perfect, then he should have had no qualms reaching out to me in the first place. I figure he must have concerns deep down that there are issues with the cores, and he was worried about having me come around and destroy all of his research."

With Susy so close to giving birth, he was probably all the more on edge. If he was as confident as he acted, he should have had no reason to worry.

"Second, I think Dafydd is biased by the same 'pre-conceived notions' he accused me of having, just on the opposite end of the spectrum."

"In a way, he *has* to believe that his own research is correct. Otherwise, he'd be rejecting Susy's revival," Milkit said.

"You think so, too?"

"Perhaps it's because you and I feel much the same, but I got the impression that Dafydd is too quick to interpret everything about Origin in the most positive light."

It wasn't hard to imagine that on some unconscious level Dafydd felt that he needed to believe in the power that returned what he lost—with interest—no matter what.

"There are a lot of holes in his story. If those correspond to real flaws in his research..." Flum said.

"Then all that power could break free at any time."

"Exactly, and we have no way of knowing when. I highly doubt it'll happen while we're staying here, but one way or another, we need to stop his research before it does."

If Flum was going to do it, it had to be tomorrow...or even today.

She had to destroy the focal core.

Given a couple more years to enjoy their life here, she could easily imagine the village inhabitants clinging even tighter to their dreamlike existence. The longer it lasted, the more painful their eventual loss would be.

"It has to be destroyed."

A voice broke through Flum's thoughts. It didn't belong to Milkit. She slowly turned to look toward the bed, where she found a young boy, sitting with his legs crossed confidently.

"Nekt?"

"Huh, I figured you'd be more surprised."

"I kind of figured you'd come."

Nekt pouted at this. "Heh, you're really taking all the fun out of this."

I Know Nothing About Myself

"**Y**A KNOW, Flum, it wouldn't hurt for you to take a page from bandage lady over there and look a little scared."

Milkit ducked behind Flum. She hadn't forgotten about her earlier kidnapping. She might have been more composed with time to prepare herself, but Nekt showing up with no warning made her react on instinct.

"It's fine, Milkit. He's not here to fight."

"I...I understand that. I just... My body doesn't seem to want to listen to me."

"Oh? You guys are really underselling me."

"If you're so great, then what're you doing out here? Trying to join forces again?"

"Nah, I've forgotten all about that. I figured since you're going to fight the Necromancy group, I may as well tag along."

Sounded like he was here to reap the profits while Flum did the actual work, but as long as he wasn't up against her, she decided it didn't matter.

"Hey, Nekt, so was what Eterna said about the third generation true?" she asked.

"And what if I don't answer?"

"I'll have no choice but to act under the assumption they exist."

"Huh, I guess there's really no benefit to keeping quiet, then. Anyway, just as the witch guessed, Mother's hard at work on a so-called third-generation. No time for us anymore."

"So now you're worried you'll be discarded like Ink was."

He didn't respond, but he didn't deny it either.

"If we ask Eterna and we can find some heart donors, I'm sure that we could turn you back into normal humans just like Ink," Flum said.

"What, and become like that defective creation?"

"Once the third generation is born, the rest of you Children are going to be treated the same way, you know."

"In that case, then isn't now the worst possible time to become a normal human?!"

"Do you have any reason to hang onto this other than for your body?"

"We're...we're still Mother's children. We can't live without Mother."

"There's a lot to find out there in the world."

"No, this is how we were raised! Nothing good would come from becoming a normal person. And besides, the church would hardly stand by and let it happen!"

Nekt felt completely powerless in the face of this choice—a feeling that went against his identity as an all-powerful being. Like a big fish in a tiny pond, he had no idea how vast the outside world really was.

"This world has no shortage of people willing to drag others down to make themselves feel superior and in control," said Milkit. "The moment you accept that you can't get away, you let them win."

"And how could we survive in the outside world without Mother?"

"There are plenty of nice, caring people out there. I think you've just given up because you can't see an easy way out."

"You talk about it like you've been through this before."

"I have. It's thanks to Master that I was able to change. I'm a living example, you could say."

Faced with living proof, there was little Nekt could

say to object. Still, there was a great gulf of isolation separating their world from his. "Just because it worked for others doesn't mean it'll work for us, ya know."

His back was to the wall—but that was only because he was stuck in the same modes of thought. Flum knew there was still a way out for him.

She stood up and walked over to the sullen boy.

"What do you want, lady? Trying to pick a fight?" Nekt lifted his head. He looked completely drained.

Flum leaned in and took a whiff.

"What the...?" Nekt eyed her suspiciously as Flum wrinkled her brow.

"Nekt, you smell."

"What?"

"Do you bathe? Regularly? And your clothes, they're filthy..."

"What're you going on about all of a sudden??"

Of course, these were all petty details, but Flum realized that the more she tried to convince Nekt, the more firmly he'd dig his heels in. Now that she'd taken control of the conversation, she wanted to turn it in a more positive direction.

"No, no, that's no good at all. A brand-new facility should have working baths, right? I mean, the church isn't putting you up somewhere sub-par, are they?"

"Of course we have them! Mother just hasn't given us permission to use them, is all."

"You need permission to take a bath?"

He replied with absolute conviction. "Of course. That's how baths work."

Flum and Milkit stared back at him, wide-eyed.

"That's...not what people normally do?"

"You mean that baths are completely off limits? No..."

"I...I see. I guess all I know is how Mother has told us to live."

"Well, why don't we take one together, then?"

Nekt practically shouted at the suggestion. "What?!"

Brat though he may have been, Nekt always maintained an impregnable shell of insouciance—and now it crumbled.

"Don't be ridiculous! Baths are to be taken alone, not with other people! And besides, you can't just show your naked body off to other people!!"

"An eight-year-old boy is no big deal, really. Do you mean to say Mother never gave you a bath, even when you were little?"

"That's different. I'm old enough to take a bath on my own now, and besides, I can't let anyone see me naked!"

Putting the bath issue aside for a moment, Flum was curious why he was so dead set against people seeing him naked. "Did Mother tell you that?"

"Oh, come on. Are you saying that normal people don't feel that way?"

"No, most people don't want to get undressed in front of strangers and only take baths with people they know."

"See? So you're the strange one here! I'm not taking a bath with you."

"Well then, I guess I'll just have to make you."

"Are you listening to me?? Get away! I'm gonna use my Connection ability! You might be able to use Reversal, but you and I both know that you need to be in contact to use it! I can easily get away!"

Flum could tell he was all bluster. He wasn't about to use his abilities against her.

She picked the young boy up and carried him over to the bath.

"No, stop! Unhand me! Let! Me! Goooooo!"

"All right, I'm gonna give him a quick scrub."

"Good luck, Master!" Milkit threw her hands in the air to cheer her on.

Giving a quick thumbs up to Milkit, Flum disappeared into the changing room with Nekt.

"Finally, you put me down and...hyaugh! Cut it out! Don't touch my clothes!"

"You could just teleport away if you hate it that much."

"I mean, I could, but certainly not dressed like this!"

"If you're not going to make a real effort to escape, then I guess you don't really hate it."

"Hey, what're you looking at?! Eyes up here, lady! Look me in the eye! If this isn't resisting, I don't know what is!!"

"And next, the pants."

"I told you to cut it out!! If you take off my... Dammit, how are you so strong for a girl?! You weren't this strong the last time we met! Whoa, hey...stop! My paaaaaants!"

Despite the ruckus, Milkit, listening outside, thought it sounded like they were having a lot of fun in the changing room.

After yanking down his pants and underwear, Flum paused.

"Huh?"

"Gah, you stupid girl..."

"Hey, Nekt...I know this is going to come off as really rude, but can I ask you something?"

"Huh? What? Seems a little late for you to worry about being rude!" His face was red with annoyance.

"Nekt...you're not a girl, are you?" Flum's voice was flat and serious.

"What in the hell are you going on about?! There ain't nothin' girly about me! What makes you think I'm not a boy??"

"I mean, you've... Well, there's nothing there."

"What's not there? I'm telling you, I'm a boy!"

And with that, it all made sense to Flum.

"What, cat got your tongue? Why so quiet?"

"It's nothing. Now let's get you in that bath."

Flum decided to think about it after they got finished with the immediate task at hand.

After getting out of the bath, Flum gently dried Nekt's hair with a towel.

"All right, I think there's something important we need to talk about, Nekt."

She'd given her a good scrubbing, which Nekt had been less than thrilled about, though her attempts to escape had been more of a gentle wrestling match than an earnest battle. Milkit had smiled as she listened to their voices coming from the other room, though she had to admit to herself that she was more than a bit jealous. But that was a conversation to be had another time.

Flum looked Nekt square in the eye, her expression serious. "You have a girl's body, Nekt. There's no doubt about it."

"You're still going on about that? I already told you, Mother told me I was a boy... A boy..."

Milkit's words came flooding back to Nekt:

This world has no shortage of people willing to drag others down to make themselves feel superior and in control.

Nekt had seen a twisted family like that before. Mother, in fact, was just such a person. It was all beginning to come together.

"So that's all this was...?"

Perhaps this, too, was one of Mother's experiments. A way of seeing how the mental state of the Origin core's host impacted what kind of effects it has on them. Or perhaps there was no special meaning behind it at all. Perhaps this was just another one of Mother's ways to toy with the Children.

Regardless of the reasoning, it had to be a massive blow to this young child's sense of identity.

"I'm...I'm a boy! C'mon, admit you're joking, lady! Are you trying to tell me this was the reason Mother made me bathe alone? Told me to never let anyone see me naked?!"

Flum's heart ached as she listened to the pain and sadness in Nekt's voice. The happiness Mother offered them had been the happiness of a walled garden; as long as they accepted Mother's word as absolute truth, they could believe they were loved. But eventually, those walls were bound to collapse. Eventually, the outside world would find them. Flum had just sped the process up slightly. Painful as it was, she felt sure it was better Nekt find out sooner, rather than later.

Nekt was still young, only eight years old. She was fully capable of choosing which path to take once she knew the truth.

"So...so that's what this all was," Nekt babbled. "Fwiss's dependency on Mother, Mute and Luke ending up the way they are... This was all part of Mother's plans?"

"I can't say for sure if it was all calculated..."

"No, it really was. Lately, it's been... Yeah, I had suspicions, but Mother really was like a mother to me, and I did everything I could to convince myself we were being cared for. But it was all for nothing. I knew it, too..."

"You know, I really think it would be best for you to leave Mother, Nekt," Flum said. "We'll support you any way we can. Do you want to try undergoing a heart transplant like Ink did?"

"I can't run away. Not alone..."

It spoke to Nekt's strength that, even now, she felt a sense of responsibility to the other Spiral Children—her siblings—as the oldest, the leader. That sense of responsibility was a double-edged sword. She could no longer ignore Mother's abuse, but nor could she leave the only family she knew behind.

"All right then," Flum said. "Why don't you bring everyone here, and we can all talk about it together? It might be a bit tough to get them all on board, but I'm sure we can come to an understanding. After all, you came around."

"I dunno if I can..."

"You can!"

"It's never too late. Ink was in the same spot you're in now, and she was able to turn her life around!"

"She and I are...different. But..." Nekt was still wavering but slowly moving in Flum's direction.

They may have committed some awful acts in the past, but Flum didn't feel it was right to hold these young children entirely responsible for what they'd done. Mother, on the other hand, was beyond forgiveness. For abusing the role of a caregiver to conduct countless inhuman experiments on these innocent children and destroying their lives in the process, Flum would make sure he paid.

The Spiral Children, however...

Nekt balled her hands up into fists.

"I...need some time to think. Connection!"

A spiral appeared in place of her face for a moment before she blinked away.

"Nekt, no!! Gah, she's gone..."

"I can't imagine she went very far," Milkit said. "I'm sure she'll come back once she's made up her mind."

"You're probably right... I hope that's the case."

At the very least, her parting words had sounded a lot closer to a yes than a no. Milkit was probably right that she would be back soon. Flum could only hope her final answer was a positive one.

Nekt warped to the top of the roof of one of the many buildings out in Sheol. Several townsfolk seemed to notice her presence, though none paid her any particular attention. She leaned back and watched the setting sun.

A short time later, the owner of the house caught sight of her. Without a moment's hesitation, he leaped high into the air and landed next to Nekt without so much as making a sound.

"I was wondering who it was before I saw your face, old man. You're pretty nimble for your size, ya know." Nekt shot an indifferent glance in Gadhio's direction.

"I guess you could say that." It was clear he didn't consider Nekt a threat at the moment. Instead, he plopped himself down at her side.

"You're unarmed. You underestimating me, old man? We were just trying to kill each other a while ago."

"You didn't look like you were in a fighting mood. What happened?"

"What, you wanna listen to my troubles now? Looks like that Flum lady keeps good company."

"So you spoke with Flum?"

"Right. And thanks to her I learned something I would rather not have. I...I always thought I was a boy. But it turns out I'm really a girl, and Mother was just messing with my head to make me believe otherwise."

"I see..."

Nekt chuckled darkly. "I guess it doesn't seem like much to other people, but... Well, it's all a pretty big shock to me."

"I think anyone would feel that way if their identity was put into question."

"So what happened to you, old man? Putting aside the fact that you're gravely underestimating me, you seem like you lost your fighting spirit."

"I feel like I'm about to lose sight of my very reason for being."

"Same."

"Guess I share the same troubles as an eight-year-old kid, then."

"Don't feel too proud of yourself. I'm still real smart, I'll have you know. Even an adult like you is no match for me."

"I see you've still got some of your childishness left." Gadhio chuckled, inciting a cackle from Nekt.

"So you saw your dead wife?"

"Yep."

"How was it? Did you sleep together?" Nekt shot a mischievous look at Gadhio.

"You're trying to grow up way too fast. You just started questioning your own gender; I highly doubt you even know what that means."

"Well, no...but that's what you do with people you like, right? And hey, don't dodge the question like that!"

"I didn't. She's Tia, of that much I'm certain. But she also isn't."

"I don't get it."

"Maybe I'm the only one who can see it. But even then, I know it's true. When you feel in your gut that there's something amiss, no matter how minute that feeling may be, it's almost certainly an indication that something, somewhere, has gone wrong."

Put another way, Gadhio was saying there was no such thing as absolute certainty of success. This was something life had drilled into him.

"Something amiss, huh..." Nekt mumbled the words as she stared up at the setting sun.

"At least, that's how I intend to live my life. Of course, you don't need to do the same."

"This is stupid! Why are you sitting here giving advice to your enemy? You're just like that Flum lady, trying to show me kindness like you expect something in return. Well, it ain't comin'!"

"I just can't leave things alone, I guess. Maybe I'm just one of those so-called nice guys? Flum probably feels something's amiss too, which is why she's acting the way she is. What about you, then? Are you happy with the life you're leading? Or have you found another path that would be better suited to you?"

"I dunno...but in any case, I don't need you preachin' to me, okay?"

"The last time we met, you were far more arrogant. You don't seem the kind to dither about."

"Heh, I guess. I'll think over what you said, old man." With that, Nekt teleported out of the village.

Gadhio tilted his head back and looked up at the sky. "I can't just let things be. You and Flum both have bright futures waiting for you."

He was hardly old enough to think about leaving the future to the next, younger generation, but old age wasn't the only force that drew warriors away from their chosen path.

Coming to the end of your dream, the loss of a place you wanted to protect, the death of a loved one...these tragedies could befall anyone, and he hoped to draw attention to them before they actually happened. It was too late for Gadhio now, but these young women still had potential.

He wanted to make sure they didn't make the same mistakes he had.

Around seven hours had passed since Flum entered Sheol. As the orange light faded into deep purples, the surrounding forest grew dark, and the night things living within it began to stir.

"The forest really is beautiful, isn't it? We don't even need to sneak around out here." Werner gazed out at Sheol through the gap in the trees. The rest of his soldiers stood watch elsewhere in the forest.

He'd had almost no interaction with Flum in the past and found the assignment largely an annoyance, but it wasn't entirely without its perks.

"I'd love nothing more than to see this despicable research go entirely to waste, but I guess it all depends on the boss." Just as the words left his mouth, a nearby bush began to stir.

A woman in a dress and high heels stepped out in front of him, her sweat running through her makeup to create rainbow-colored trails along her face. She looked entirely out of place in the forest.

She expended a great deal of energy as she pushed her way through the foliage in this attire, developing rips in her clothes and scrapes along her skin. The woman typically loathed anything and everything she considered filthy, and yet, she showed no signs of stopping as she angrily slapped branches and leaves out of her way.

"Ah, Satils Francois. So you did come."

Though Werner had never invited her to come along, he also made no effort to stop her from coming to Sheol.

"Listen, whatever you choose to do has nothing to do with us, but stay out of sight, okay? If this goes well, the boss'll really owe me one."

Almost as if by a miracle, Satils was just out of sight when Ottilie showed up to speak with Werner.

"How are things going in your sector?"

"All peace and quiet here. It's actually really boring, to be honest. Can't we just go back to the capital, and..."

"We must not let Henriette down. We will hold our position until Flum leaves this village."

Werner's shoulders slumped. "I figured you'd say as much."

Ottilie handed Werner a bright red fruit.

"What's this? Animal bait?"

"It's a gift, but I guess an unappreciative lug like yourself doesn't need it."

"No, no, I was just surprised to have something plucked from a tree shoved in my face all of a sudden. You a monkey or something?"

"Monkey?! Listen, if you don't want it, I'll happily eat it myself! They're quite delicious, I'll have you know, and something like this growing out here in nature is pretty rare! Besides, the bright red color reminds me of blood. Bright...red...blood. Now that I think about it, I suddenly want to see something bleed."

"Fine, fine, I'll eat it. Give it here!" Werner yanked the fruit from her hand and took a bite. "Let's be real here; I know it might be rare, but that hardly means it's going to be so sweet that..."

As he spoke, the pleasant aroma of the fruit and its sweet juices filled his mouth.

"Damn, this is amazing!"

"Which is exactly what I said."

"No, I mean...really! I thought you were pulling some kind of prank."

"Is there a reason I would try and pull a prank on you?"

"Me? The nicest, most honest man in the whole capital? Hardly."

"You forgot shady and dubious. Now c'mon, are you really keeping watch? It sure doesn't look that way."

Werner's response was quick and to the point. "What's there to keep watch for? Nothing's happening. I haven't seen so much as a rat, much less a person."

Ottilie couldn't detect anything suspicious about the way he was acting, nor did his expression imply even a hint of deceit. She was operating under the assumption that they were allies, after all, so there was no reason why she would assume he was lying.

"Well, that's good then. Anyway, keep up the good work." With that, she was off to check in on the next soldier.

"Leave it all to me, I got this."

Werner waved her off and watched Ottilie's figure disappear into the trees. As soon as she was gone, he let out a loud, boisterous laugh.

"Heh, looks like I'll have paid Echidna back and then some. Which means that the plan should be unfolding any moment now. Now where is that guy? He should... ah! Finally."

A man carrying bags under his arms came running out of Sheol and drove through the bushes, much as

Satils had moments before. The man was Gorne Forgan. Werner and Gorne had met multiple times in the past at a gambling hall back in the capital.

"You never change, d'ya? Betraying yet another friend for money, I see? Heh, not like I'm in any position to criticize." Werner chuckled.

The sun was setting. Soon, the village would be plunged into darkness.

014

Paradise Lost

DAFYDD PLANNED TO HOLD a lavish banquet that night at the research lab for Flum and her guests, along with Gadhio, Tia, Kindah, and Claudia. After finishing their tour, he told Flum he would come calling for her once everything was ready.

"It sure is getting late."

"I know. We'd normally have had dinner by now."

Flum and Milkit were lying side by side on the bed, chatting while they waited for time to pass. However, Dafydd still hadn't shown up. Flum figured that researchers tended to work erratic schedules, and that he probably ate dinner quite late, but even so, her stomach still rumbled in annoyance. She blushed deeply as Milkit looked down at the source of the noise.

"Hey, listen, today was really busy..."

"Being hungry is a completely healthy thing, Master. Should I make something simple to eat? There's a kitchen here, after all."

"No, it's fine. Besides, it'd be awkward if you were making something when he showed up."

"Are you sure you're okay?"

"My stomach's just a little impatient, is all. I'm totally fine." She had to be strong, even if it was only a matter of pride.

Milkit wasn't so easily deceived. "Hm."

Without any further conversation, the room fell into silence. The only sounds to be heard were those of their breathing. It was so quiet that Flum started to feel sleepy.

"You can sleep if you'd like. I'll wake you up if Dafydd gets here."

"I guess it couldn't hurt to nap for a half hour or so."

She decided to take Milkit up on the offer, slowly letting her eyelids fall closed. Within moments, she felt her consciousness begin to drift away.

"...a...ena..."

She was on the edge of deep slumber when a voice broke through the silence.

Flum's eyelids fluttered open, and she looked up to find Milkit watching over her.

"Is something wrong?"

"I heard...I heard a person's voice. Did you say something?"

Milkit shook her head. Figuring it was just her imagination, Flum was about to close her eyes when she heard the voice yet again.

"...W...hy..."

The voice kept cutting in and out, making it nearly unintelligible, but she could tell it was male.

"There it is again!"

"Oh? I'm sorry, but I don't hear anything."

Flum hopped down from the bed and closed her eyes to focus in on what she was hearing.

"...must...oh..."

There it was again. This time the pitch was higher, like that of an older woman. Flum moved slowly toward the door, where the voices emanated.

"But tha...dest..."

"The...will f..."

Flum was sure now that there were two people out there. *Why would they be talking outside our room?*

She considered throwing the door open to see what this was all about but decided it was more prudent to put her ear to the door and listen instead.

"Why should they live?" "Just destroy them." "Who cares about those lives?" "Kill." "Start with the arm."

"Cut the arm open for a taste." "Rip the skin off." "Let's put it in a box."

"It'll fit if you snap the spinal cord." "It must be done."

"Must not get away." "What's wrong with murder?" "No permission yet." "Must connect." "How will we lead?"

"Must open the vortex first." "Get inside and connect to the brain." "Become one, we all become one."

"I want to see its squirming insides, even if only once."

"We'll kill this time, then connect the next." "Cut it off." "This is not fit for connecting."

"Better to bleed." "I say we cut the stomachs open." "Where's the connection point? How should a hole be made in the skull?"

"Three, four, two, five, seven..." "We won't hurt at all."

"Aaah, it's tight, so tight." "I want the uterus." "I cut off the nail beds."

"They must suffer." "Kyiii, kyiii, kyiii." "I hear a siren." "We must take it."

"I'll stitch the arteries back up." "D-d-danger..."

"Still not enough." "Eeugh, it's...good enough..." "You must do it." "It's too late, it's all too late."

There were so many different voices that she lost count—at least several dozen, if not more. Flum felt a shiver of fear run up her spine. She stumbled forward, and her elbow banged against the wall.

The voices stopped immediately, though if she listened closely, she could still hear the ragged breathing of multiple people just beyond the door. They were still out there. Blocking Flum and Milkit's only means of escape.

Could they really get so many people into such a narrow hallway without me hearing any footsteps? When did they get here? And how??

That raised another question: were they even human?

One voice spoke up. *"Tonight."*

Another joined in. *"We will act tonight."*

The rest of the crowd voiced their agreement.

"Yes, tonight is best." "Tonight, tonight." "I can't wait any longer." "I can finally feed." "We will wait until tonight."

"Master...?"

"Stay back! Just...just wait over there, Milkit."

There was nowhere left to run.

Considering the target-rich environment, it would be easiest for her to fight them at the natural choke point formed by the doorway. Flum gripped the Souleater tightly in her right hand and grabbed the door handle in her left. She closed her eyes and took several deep breaths to steady her breathing and start building prana.

She pressed down on the handle, and the lock released with a loud click. She threw the door open in one swift motion.

There was absolutely no one there.

"Huh?"

She dashed out of the room and scanned the hall. It was completely deserted.

"What did you hear, Master?"

"You really didn't hear anything?"

"Nothing at all."

"Huh, so I guess..."

She wanted to say "just my imagination," but cut herself short. Perhaps she needed to be even more cautious about the Necromancy project than she had been. She'd had a weird vibe ever since they arrived in Sheol—to say nothing of the strange looks everyone gave her.

Were they all a part of her imagination as well?

"No, it can't be."

She knew what she was sensing was real, which could only mean there was something strange going on here. However big or small that something might be.

"There's something I want to check out. Come with me, Milkit."

"I'll follow you anywhere, Master."

Flum took Milkit's hand and fled the room.

She needed to discuss this with Dafydd or one of his other researchers, so she made her way to Experiment

Room #1. It was the biggest room in the facility, so she figured it was the most likely place to find someone.

"Hey, Gaddy, what do you think of this dress?"

Tia stepped in front of him, looking down at herself. The banquet was going to be her first opportunity to formally introduce herself as Gadhio's wife. While Gadhio planned to just go in his normal clothes, she had no such intent.

"Why don't you reply, Gaddy? I know you're looking at me. Listen, I know you've never been good with things like this, but sometimes a lady wants to wear something the person she loves picked out for her, okay?"

Clink.

Tia heard a metallic sound and slowly, hesitantly turned around.

"Ga...ddy?"

Gadhio held a black sword in his right hand. He stood there silently, his face devoid of any expression. He just stood there, cold and emotionless, like he had become one with the blade. He angled the tip toward her.

"Wh-what are you doing? Why...why would you do this to me?"

No response.

"Are you mad at me, Gaddy? I guess I can understand that, we've been apart for six whole years. But you don't need to do that! You're just trying to scare me, right?! Cut it out, Gaddy, this joke has gone too far! You're scaring me!! Just put the sword down..."

Gadhio maintained his silence.

"Please...please cut it out. I didn't come back for it to end this way..."

"Tia..."

"Wh-what?"

"I love you more than anyone else ever could."

"Then why would you do this? Is it because I'm not normal anymore?"

Now that Tia thought back on it, Gadhio had been acting strangely ever since he got back. He'd had no interest in her dress for the banquet, only providing vague responses when asked about her hairstyle or other choices in jewelry. She had no idea what had happened to make him change so suddenly, but she couldn't imagine anyone could so callously kill the one they loved.

Tia's eyes began to overflow with tears. "I'm...not normal, is that it? Was I really that strange?"

"No, it's not like that."

"Then what is it? I'm back, I'm alive again. I thought that we could finally be a couple, that I could be your loving wife once again! Sure, I'm stuck in Sheol because of the focal core right now, but someday I'll be able to leave this place! I...I'll finally have my life back!"

"No, you're finally alive again, and that's enough. You're perfect...too perfect, in fact."

Gadhio longed to cry, but no tears came. Maybe that was because he'd left her behind once before. As far as he was concerned, Tia was already dead, and his heart had been frozen ever since that fateful day six years ago.

No matter how hard he trained, he still couldn't change the past. It had all seemed so pointless. But the fact that his heart had been frozen for so long carried its own significance.

"There is one small difference. And try as I might, I can't change the fact that I know you're not the same Tia I once loved."

The way she breathed. How her fingers moved. The way she cast her gaze. How she spoke. None of it stood out individually if he didn't pay attention, but taken all together, the little differences built up.

"Just...you can overlook all that, Gaddy. You know, there are a ton of places I'd been dreaming of going once we were reunited! We can visit the ocean off to the south and relax at the hot springs in Franda! There's more, there's so, so much more to do, Gaddy!"

"I wanted to go there with you, too!" Gadhio cried. He'd hoped to just kill her without a word, but now that he stood before her, it was impossible. More than anything else, he would have loved to be with her. "I wanted to...but...that's why I can't turn a blind eye to all this."

"Gaddy..."

Tia wasn't the only person in the room suffering. She knew all too well that Gadhio had agonized greatly over this decision.

Her whole body slumped in resignation.

"I need to put an end to all this."

"...I know."

"While you're still Tia. Before it's too late..."

"Before I become...not me? I...I guess you're right. It was a tiny, nagging feeling in the back of my mind, but I noticed it. I told myself it was just part of being brought back to life, but that's not it at all, is it?"

Tia truly believed that she was Tia Lathcutt. But, much like Gadhio, she could also sense that there was something slightly off about her.

"Honestly, my mind's been fixated on the lab for a

while now," she said. "Whoever or whatever is inside of me is making me focus on it."

"That's probably because Flum's there."

"That's probably it. That thing inside me is desperate for her."

Whatever that feeling was had nothing to do with Tia.

"Dafydd told me once that you couldn't bring people back to life if all you had was their body. You needed their spirit, too. I guess that means I'm just an empty shell, huh?"

"Is that possible?"

"When someone dies, their soul moves on. All that remains is a shell. If you put something else in the shell, then that thing takes the form of Tia Lathcutt."

"That's...a completely different being."

"That's right. I...I want to believe I'm Tia, but I know that's not the case."

Now that she'd admitted it to herself, the feeling that her own skin was foreign to her crept over Tia. If things had been slightly different—if some other being had worked its way into what remained of Tia Lathcutt, maybe she could have accepted it more easily. But that wasn't what had happened. She was a failed attempt at recreating Tia, and that was unacceptable. If even she couldn't accept it, beginning to reject the core within her, the connection that kept her alive would begin to fracture.

Tia offered up a mirthless laugh. "Well, this is pretty impressive, isn't it, Gaddy? At the very least, I get to be killed by a friend this time. I guess I should be happy about that."

Her right arm started to convulse. Something squirmed just underneath her flesh.

"Your arm..."

"I think the Necromancy core can't suppress it any more, now that I've accepted what I really am."

He wanted to refute it—to hold her close—but Gadhio just couldn't do it. He had already killed his own heart.

"I'm sorry, Gaddy, I shouldn't have said all that. And now I'm making you do this, too."

"Don't apologize. This is something only I can do."

"I know our time was short, but I'm really happy we could live together again as husband and wife. Really, I was so very happy with you, Gaddy. Hundreds of times happier than any other wife ever was."

"I...I'm glad to hear that."

"That means...you're the best husband any woman could ever ask for, Gaddy. Anyone who's with you will be happier than they ever thought possible!"

Even now, Gadhio's eyes were bone dry.

"Tia, I...I...!"

Meanwhile, tears streamed down Tia's face.

"I'm still a little crybaby, I guess. But...you're just so sweet, I can't get over it. That's why I fell in love with you in the first place."

"Tia...I love you more than anyone else in this world ever could!"

This was probably the first time he'd ever expressed such strong feelings for another human being. Gadhio had always been shy. He'd barely managed to fumble his way through proposing to Tia, but she'd loved even that part of him—and now, she was overjoyed beyond words to hear him express his love with such passion.

Gadhio lifted his sword up into the air. Prana filled the blade.

He wasn't strong enough to destroy the core, but he still needed to remove it from her body.

He couldn't afford to hesitate, though reluctance weighed down his arms like a heavy chain. Gadhio let out a powerful scream and smashed through it as he swung down with his blade.

"I love you!"

As the blade tore through Tia, the prana seeped into the cut. Her body opened, and a dark orb flew out of her.

"Ga...ddy..."

She lost consciousness for the second—and hopefully final—time. A puddle of blood pooled around his sleeping princess. The most honorable and beautiful creature to have ever lived.

After wiping away the blood, Gadhio let his arms hang loosely at his sides as he burned the scene into his mind. "Wait for me, Tia. I'll be with you soon enough."

His sword never left his hand. His farewell said, his heart was set on what he had to do. His fight was not yet done.

"But it's not my time yet. There's still someone I need to face."

The word "Chimera" rang through his head. He hated everything about the church, but it was Chimera that had ripped the most important person in his life from him, and Chimera he was obliged to repay. As he stood there, steadying his breathing, he could feel anger and hatred welling up to fill in the hole in his heart.

He'd lost all hope of a bright future. The only thing that could satiate him now was seeing his grudge through to its end.

With each breath he took, his nostrils filled with the coppery scent of blood.

Opening his eyes, he gazed upon the stained corpse of

his wife, her organs spilling from her wounds. He needed the image. If he ever let himself forget it, he couldn't go on.

After some time, a man intruded upon this sacred place. Dafydd had finally arrived to summon them to dinner.

His eyes went wide at the incomprehensible scene. He was completely beside himself. "But...why...?? Did you do this?!"

Gadhio slowly turned to face him. "Yes, I did it. Did you know about all this, Dafydd?"

"Know about what?! No...no, there's no possible excuse for what you've done! I thought you were like me—I thought you, of all people, would have understood my dream!!" Dafydd could see this as nothing other than betrayal. "You loved Tia, didn't you?! How could you possibly do this to her? You're no different from Chimera!!"

Gadhio grabbed Dafydd by the collar and slammed him hard against the wall.

"You've no right to say you brought her back from the dead. She was barely more than a copy. Tia told me you knew—that those you'd brought back were just empty husks!"

"You've got it all wrong! That's all humans really are— the Origin core returns them to their original state!"

"Not quite. That Tia...thing wasn't Tia at all. I'm sure the other people living in this village have noticed, too."

"And what's that? You're mistaken, entirely mistaken about all this!"

"They're all just too afraid of waking up from this dream."

"And what's so wrong about dreaming? If you never wake from a dream, then it's no different from reality!"

"No, you're wrong! They're constantly walking on egg-shells, afraid that it'll end! But the end is already closing in, isn't it??"

"You have no proof of that! There's no way..."

As if to mock Dafydd and his denial, a loud siren cut through the air. The two men glanced outside, a sense of foreboding rising within them.

A moment later, a man slammed against the window and began to bang on the glass. "Help me! Heeeelp!!!"

A woman—likely his wife—came up from behind him and took a bite out of his neck, tearing through flesh and ripping away muscle and tendons. The man's head dangled unsteadily to the side.

"No...it can't be... That siren would only sound if... No, who would do that to the focal core?! Let me go, I must return to the lab!"

Gadhio immediately released his grip on Dafydd,

who hastily dashed from the building to make his way back to the lab.

"The focal core is in the lab..." Gadhio muttered to himself. "Flum might be in trouble."

Just as he stepped out of the house, Eterna came running up with Ink in her arms.

"Gadhio!"

"Eterna, you're covered in blood..."

"I'm guessing the same thing happened to you."

In Eterna's arms, Ink chewed nervously on her lip. Her voice was unsteady when she finally spoke. "I'm so, so sorry..."

"It's probably better it happened sooner rather than later."

"You were attacked?" Gadhio queried.

Eterna nodded. All she had to gain from giving into the fantasy was regret and guilt when it ended.

"I'm guessing this siren is coming from the lab? Flum's probably in danger."

"I was about to head over."

"I'll go with you."

The three turned in the direction of the lab. Though Eterna would have preferred to take Ink somewhere safe, it didn't seem like any such place remained in Sheol.

"Waaaugh!! Help me, someone, please!"

"Why...why?! I'm...I'm your wife!!"

"It's...nightmare...living...nightmare!"

The cries echoing through the village as the dead turned on the living put a stop to their progress. Neither Gadhio nor Eterna could turn their backs on the people in danger.

"Hyah!" With a mighty swing, Gadhio chopped a woman in half as she attacked her husband.

"Aqua Shot!" Eterna's water bullets blasted right through a man's heart as he strangled his daughter.

Both victims fell limp for a moment, but the surviving cores within them stirred their broken bodies to action. Those left among the living now had to confront their collapsing dream.

Ink heard footsteps approaching them.

"Eterna, behind you!"

One of the undead, having killed his loved one, had moved on to the next living thing he could find.

"Ice Lance!" Eterna summoned up several of her fish around her. One of the fish opened its mouth and skewered the man where he stood.

However, their problems weren't over yet. They were completely surrounded.

"Gah...I guess we'll have to take care of all these monsters first."

"I hope Flum's okay..."

The two heroes swallowed their frustration and steeled themselves to fight the swarm.

ROLL
OVER
AND
DIE

015

Wrong from the Very Start

SHORTLY BEFORE the alarm sounded, Flum and Milkit found a woman in Experiment Room #1. The name tag on her chest identified her as Clarice.

Flum decided to ask her about what happened back at their room.

"You heard a dozen voices outside your room but didn't see anyone when you stepped outside? That's impossible. You must be tired." Clarice laughed and waved off her concerns, though the look of worry in her eyes was evident.

"You know what's going on, don't you? There's no sense in lying."

"Lying?" Though her voice was harsh, Clarice averted her gaze.

Flum glared at the older woman, deciding to crank up the pressure. She could tell just by looking at her that this Clarice woman was just like Dafydd, though her conscience got the best of her.

"Do you promise to not tell Dafydd?" Clarice asked.

"I'll leave your name out of it."

"All right then, fine. Ever since you arrived, the mental state levels of all of our subjects have been going off the charts."

"Mental state?"

"The values we use to track the psychological condition of our subjects. The higher the number, the more easily excitable they are. If it gets too high, it begins to impact their body or their vital state...just like any normal, living person."

"And these values are irregular right now?"

"Right. I thought we'd addressed it, but then things have reverted back to how they were at the beginning."

"What does that mean? Will something happen?"

A dark expression washed over Clarice's face at Milkit's question. "The spiral will take over their bodies, and they will turn into creatures that attack indiscriminately."

Flum was all too aware of what such creatures were like, though she found it odd that the transformation hadn't happened already.

"And yet," Clarice continued, "the test subjects have shown no signs of changing. Their minds appear to be intact. Dafydd decided it was a calibration error and instructed us to remain quiet."

"Is that why no one showed up to call us for dinner?"

"It delayed the banquet preparations, yes, but Dafydd just left to call for Gadhio."

"I don't see how we can all just sit down and eat after hearing something like this."

Flum turned on a heel and started to walk out of the room before Clarice grabbed her elbow to stop her.

"Wait, where are you going??"

"The Central Control Room, where else? I need to destroy the focal core and put an end to this once and for all!"

"Even as powerful as you are, there's no way you can make it through that door. Besides, you realize that the dead in Sheol will transform if you do that, don't you?!"

"Tia was able to move around for a few hours without it, wasn't she? It's better to get this over with before it's too late."

"The strange readings really might just be an error! Do you know how many years Dafydd and the rest of us have toiled just to see this day?! Please, I'm begging you, don't give into impulse!"

"Don't treat me like a child!" Flum's anger was clear in her voice. "Do you guys even know what Origin cores are?! They aren't a tool to help humanity. They exist purely to bring pain, suffering, and misery to mankind!"

"Be that as it may, the difference between a poison and a cure is only a matter of dosage!"

She'd heard the same excuses from Dafydd. Flum knew it would be impossible to win this woman over. Milkit stepped up to Flum's side, joining her to shoot Clarice a stern look.

The standoff seemed like it could last forever, when a siren broke the silence.

"What...no way! Why is the emergency alarm going off?!"

"Emergency alarm? What do you mean? What happened??"

"I have no idea!"

Clang. Clang clang clang. Clang.

The three women turned their attention to the door and the erratic tapping coming from the other side. It was too quiet to be someone knocking and, what's more, it seemed to be coming from a point close to the ground.

"Who in the hell..." Clarice let out an annoyed sigh and opened the door.

A young child came tumbling in.

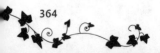

"Gorne and Luluca's kid? This is no place for children, you know. What are you doing here all alone?" Clarice leaned down to pick up the child, but the moment her hands made contact, her fingers immediately started to twist out of shape.

"Huh?"

Her fingers popped and cracked, filling the room with the sound of snapping bones as they continued to twist and break away. The deformation began to spread to her hands, up her wrists, and into her arms.

"Haugh...! Wh-what's happening?!"

"Aaah...gahahaha!!"

Flum looked over at the cackling child. A pair of pulsing, blood-red spirals filled its eye sockets. Blood spat from the gaping holes and ran down the child's cheeks like tears.

"Clarice, get away!!"

Flum drew her Souleater and prepared to attack, but Clarice was still too close to the child for her to do anything.

"I...I can't get away! I'm...I'm stuck? No, not stuck... it's like it's sucking me in!"

The disfiguration had made its way up her arms and threatened to start working down her torso, legs, and head. There was nothing that could be done to save her.

"It...hurts! Gaaaauugh! K-kill me, please!! It hurts so bad...! I can't take it!"

"Gyaaaaahahaha!"

Flum swung her sword and cleaved the child and Clarice in half, finally granting her the sweet release of death. To minimize the suffering, she cut straight through Clarice's heart.

The child she had bonded with, however, was another story. The mass of flesh and muscle began to squirm and crawl toward her. It looked more like a worm than anything human.

"Is that what the child really was?"

"I guess it was never human."

From pregnancy to birth, this thing they'd been raising was a bloody mass under Origin's control, simply copying human shape.

"That means Susy's child will be the same. Why would Origin do such a thing??"

Even as she said that, she knew the answer. Origin wanted to strengthen its influence. The closer the Necromancy project got to its goal, the more pawns it gained. That was why it went to such lengths to make it look like these people were reproducing. There was an alien logic to it, though to Flum, it just seemed an extension of Origin's desire to destroy humanity. Only a sadist would give people hope just to rip it away like that.

"We need to destroy the focal core, and quick!"

But would that also destroy all the cores of those living in Sheol? In any case, the focal core was at the center of all this—the siren, the transformed child, all of it—and needed to be dealt with.

Flum and Milkit dashed out of the room and turned toward Central Control, only to find a woman blocking their path.

"Luluca...right?"

This was the mother of the child Flum just chopped in half...or more accurately, the woman who birthed the human-like abomination. The bloody mass that was once her child crawled out of the room and slithered up her body and forced its way into her mouth, causing her jaw to dislocate and her throat to expand to an inhuman size.

It settled down into her stomach, leaving her looking pregnant.

"What, you think you can just give birth to it again now? You're supposed to pour all your love into raising a child, you know! Is this how little you think of a human life?!"

Flum rammed her sword down into the floor and unleashed a prana storm on Luluca. The prana-powered wind let out an awful screeching sound as it cut large gashes in the reinforced floor, walls, and ceiling on its way past.

It was obviously overkill. Though the cores were themselves quite powerful, these revived corpses were hardly meant to fight or withstand such attacks.

When she looked down at the blood and gristle lining the floor, revulsion welled up within her.

"This is awful, all of it!"

Her face contorted in rage as bitterness swept over her. She felt Milkit's arms wrap around her from behind.

"Th-thanks, Milkit."

"It's all I can do."

"Well, I think it's wonderful. Now let's get going!"

Reinvigorated, Flum turned her mind to the task at hand and started again toward Central Control. Though it wasn't very far, they'd have to make their way through the researchers' quarters first.

It was just as bad as she expected. Reanimated corpses played with the bodies of the recently massacred. An awful stench hung heavily in the air. The walls were covered in blood like a fresh coat of paint.

"Out of the way!!"

Flum had to put her emotions aside until the battle was over. All she could do for the time being was keep moving, destroy Origin's plans, and minimize the damage of the unfolding tragedy.

"Hya! Fwoo! Eyaugh!" She swung her blade in front of her as she ran, chopping through anything in her way. She could have taken them down with a Prana Shaker, but there was just too little room to maneuver. While it was incredibly easy to cut down each foe, the sheer number of them made for slow going, consuming Flum's limited time.

Making matters worse, their numbers were only increasing. There were so many, in fact, that Flum began to wonder where they were coming from. Many of them weren't even wearing lab coats, suggesting that they had come in from outside.

"There are just too many. The hallway's completely blocked off."

The reanimated corpses packed tightly into the hallway. From the way they moved, it was clear nothing cognizant was steering them around. She wanted to just cut them all down, but the massive Souleater wasn't suited for such close quarters.

If only I could find some sort of shortcut... I don't know much about the facility's layout. I'll just need to find a way through.

Flum's mind raced as she waded through the shuffling horde.

I could bust through a wall... No, that's going to be blocked off, too. It didn't look like there were any alternative routes, and trying to weave through these guys isn't gonna happen. The only available space is...above them.

"...Above them. That's it!" Flum wrapped an arm around Milkit and pulled her close. "Hang on!"

"Okay!" Milkit, who trusted Flum implicitly, wrapped her arms around her in a tight embrace.

"Gravity reversal... Reversion!" Flum kicked up off the floor the moment she cast the spell, landing effortlessly on the ceiling.

"Huh? What's happening??"

"I'll explain later, but right now this seems to be working, so let's go!"

Flum ran unimpeded across the ceiling and over the horde. Giving Milkit a quick squeeze, she increased her speed and ran straight to Central Control.

Flum and Milkit stepped through the unlocked door and into Central Control. As soon as she took a breath,

she wrinkled her nose. The room was filled with the smell of commingled bodily fluids.

Glancing around, the room looked nothing like it had when they were there earlier. Something—possibly human remains—was stuck to a wall, coated in a pink substance mixed with various flesh tones. Fingers, hands, legs, and arms grew around the room, fumbling and swaying. The fleshy mass was slowly enveloping the focal core.

Dafydd, who looked like he had only just arrived, stood in front of the massive black crystal. His gaze was fixed on something hanging just above it.

"That...looks like Susy's face."

Though the rest of the human limbs filling the room looked like they were hastily jigsawed together, her body was still mostly intact.

Her face was another story. Her eyes were hollow cavities, and half of her face had been consumed by a spiral mass of flesh and sinew. Her mouth looked like it had been torn open, even as it twisted into a mock-smile.

Her stomach—where her and Dafydd's child should have been—had a thick blood vessel running along it that pulsed arrhythmically. If it was anything like Luluca's child, the creature inhabiting Susy's stomach was nothing short of a monster. Dafydd's hopes and expectations would be met with little more than tragedy.

"Who do you think is to blame here?" He didn't turn around.

Flum responded immediately. "Origin."

Origin was to blame for all of this.

"It was wrong to believe in it."

Dafydd laughed bitterly. "So I was wrong all along? You're quite harsh, Flum."

"Turning your back on the truth will only cause you more suffering. I spoke with one of your researchers, and she said that your metrics were off the scale since I arrived. You knew something was going on for some time, didn't you?"

"Who can say? Then again, it looks like you figured it out in just a day's time, so I suppose I was aware too, on some level."

Even now, he wasn't entirely convinced by the evidence in front of him.

"I think I knew, even as I preached my wonderful dream to all around me. Even as I fell further into my own fantasy. But...but I just wanted to fully lose myself in that wonderful dream. I refused to believe that my Susy being alive again could possibly be a lie. It... it shouldn't have ended this way...gyahahahaha!"

And yet here they were.

All he could do was laugh. Out of sadness. Out of anger. The feelings rushing through him could no longer be named and categorized.

"And to think that this all came crashing down at Susy's hands. Who would have imagined such a turn of events?? Why Susy? Why?!"

"Get out of the way. I need to destroy it." Flum had neither the need nor the desire to listen to Dafydd's rambling.

He turned around, throwing his arms up in an attempt to protect the core and his wife.

"I won't let you touch Susy!"

"Then I'll just have to go through you!" Flum let loose a Prana Shaker.

A wriggling tendril that looked like a deformed human limb stretched out and blocked the blast.

"Susy...you protected me. That's...that's right, you really are back! I'm sorry I said all those awful things, Susy. No matter what you may look like, I still love you. I love you, my beloved Susy!"

Flum still wasn't ready to give up. "All right then, I'll just cut you down myself!"

She lunged toward Dafydd, swinging the Souleater at the tendril as it moved into her path. The massive black blade cut halfway through and stuck fast.

"Nng... What the hell?!"

Another tendril lashed at Flum. The Souleater disappeared in a flash of light, and Flum jumped clear.

"It's no use." Dafydd smiled darkly. "The focal core has accumulated so much power within it that it's now far beyond any normal core. It may not be weaponized like that of the Chimera and Children teams, but I can still make use of its massive power reserves, if I only will it."

"But...there's one...weakness you're...overlooking!! Hyaaaaaaaaah!!"

If she couldn't make it through the tendrils, she would just have to focus her efforts on the focal core itself. Flum sprang high into the air and, at the apex of her jump, shot a focused blast of prana from the tip of her blade, the Prana Sting aimed at a narrow gap in their defenses.

Another tendril whipped out of nowhere and took the blow head-on.

Flum jumped back to grab Milkit just before a tendril managed to reach her. The two tumbled across the floor, just out of range.

"Aaaaugh...aaaaaaaah...oaaaaauuuugh!!"

"Susy?"

While Flum battled for her life, Susy had began to transform, now that she'd assimilated the focal core. Her enlarged belly began to pulsate before, moments later, it burst wide open. Out came a child covered in a thick, sticky liquid.

"Susy...you've given birth to our child! It's...it's so beautiful!!" Dafydd ran to the figure lying on the floor.

"Aaugh...uwaaugh! Fhaauh! Hwaauh!" It refused to look at him. Its bloody, pulsing spiral eyes were locked on Flum.

"Lukoh...Lukoh Chalmas. That's your name, you know. Susy and I talked a lot about it before you were born. Now you're the newest member of our family."

Dafydd could care less about the form his child had taken. He felt nothing but love for it. Human or not, even as its limbs began to twist and deform—none of that mattered to him in that moment.

"Aah, you're so warm. You're all the proof I need that Susy is truly alive and back with us. You have no idea how happy I am to hold you, Lukoh."

Not only had he managed to bring his wife back from the dead and make a life with her, but now, they had a child. Perhaps he couldn't actually save anyone like he intended, but as far as Dafydd was concerned...he'd found his happy ending.

"My dear, dear Lukoh..." Dafydd held Lukoh tight to his body, rubbing his cheek against his child's through the thick mucus, blood spattering onto his face from the churning spirals.

It wasn't mucus covering his child at all.

"Nnngh...haauh...Lukoh...you... Susy and I...will raise you...together...nngaaah!!" Lukoh and Dafydd's bodies began to merge where their skin touched.

"Raise...and...nngh...happy...and...gaaaugh!"

The fusion of their bodies finally reached his brain, sending a painful shock through his paralyzed body. He could do nothing but scream as a trail of drool dripped out the side of his mouth.

"Master...look at Dafydd!"

"I don't get it! He knew these were fake, so why would he go and do something stupid like that?!"

Lukoh was still connected to Susy by a red umbilical cord. Dafydd's body slowly merged with the cord, traveling up along it toward Susy's body.

"Aaugh... Lukoh... Lukoh, where are you?!" He searched blindly with his hands while his lower body was enveloped in a warm, fleshy mass of muscle. His cheek tensed for a moment as he seemed to realize what was happening to him, though the expression quickly gave way to one of tranquility. "So that's how this all ends, I guess. We may not be able to live together, but this...this love is good enough for me. As long as you, Lukoh, and I can all live together as a family, I...I'm..."

He seemed to have given up on everything at this

point. He'd failed to save anyone, himself included, and yet, this was the path he chose.

The attacking tendrils slowed and then stopped as Susy focused her energies on consuming Dafydd.

Milkit spoke aloud to no one in particular. "Is that...is that really love?"

She wasn't expecting an answer. Nor did Flum really have the personal experience to talk about love. But she could say one thing definitively:

"No, that's not love at all. Dafydd just couldn't take the pain any longer. That's why he bought into these sugar-coated lies—to cover his own shortcomings and convince himself he was happy. This was suicide."

All the Necromancy project had really done was allow Dafydd to put off the inevitable. The moment Susy died, he lost all reason to live.

With the Necromancy project using Origin cores like they were, they were all living on borrowed time.

"Now that Dafydd's been assimilated, there's no one left to protect the core. I just hope it doesn't put up too much of a fight." Even as the words left her mouth, Flum knew she was setting herself up for disappointment.

As she raised her sword up into the air to strike at the core, she heard clapping in the background. The sound felt distinctly out of place.

A woman in gaudy attire appeared behind the now deformed Susy. She let out a high-pitched laugh. "My, my, what a wonderful show you've put on for me!"

"What are you doing here, Satils?!"

"Ngyah!"

Flum brought her sword down in a powerful strike, but Satils managed to block it with a wave of her right hand, despite the reversal magic Flum had put into the blow.

"How barbaric, Flum Apricot. But unfortunately for you, such simple attacks won't work on me—not with the power of the focal core running through my body!"

"I knew it didn't make sense for Susy to do this all on her own! So you were behind it the whole time?"

"Correct! I'm quite proud to say I wrote the whole script. It was pretty emotional when the baby popped free from Susy, wouldn't you say?"

"Wh...y...wo...uld...you do..."

Dafydd barely managed to choke out the words. He had been absorbed up to his shoulder before the process stopped—probably also a part of Satils' plan.

"Like I said, this is all my doing. I used the power of the focal core to control Susy and turn her into a monster. It's as simple as that. Lukoh being born and you being absorbed were aaaaall a part of my plan! Kyahahahaa!"

The body parts growing from the walls and floors were Satils' doing, too. Susy was as much a victim of this as Dafydd.

"That's...not possible. How...could you...this room..."

Only Dafydd and a select group of researchers were allowed to enter this room. It seemed absurd that Satils could walk right in when even Susy couldn't get past the door.

Satils face lit up at the question. "You can thank none other than Gorne Forgan for that. He's worked up a bit of a debt, you know? I thought I'd make use of it, so I put him and Echidna in touch while I was at it."

"He...gave information...to Chimera? So that's...that's why Chimera was able to...make so many advances lately!"

"That's right. They used what they'd learned about the technology behind the focal core."

"Gorne, you...you spineless...!"

Gorne was more than his assistant; Dafydd had considered him a long-time friend. Alas, that sense of camaraderie wasn't mutual. Gorne thought of Dafydd as little more than the man who wrote his paychecks.

"I must say, the look on your face is divine, Dafydd. I've looked forward to seeing it for some time. Obviously, I've been funding the Necromancy project in the hopes of bringing it to market, but I absolutely love seeing people like you, with your sugary-sweet fantasy worlds filled with love and friendship, have their hopes and dreams dashed against the rocks. It's such a splendid feeling!"

"So that was the only reason you approached me?! Just to see it all fall to ruin??"

Flum couldn't help but feel there was something strange about their exchange. No, that wasn't right. She felt that way ever since she came to Sheol and met with Dafydd.

He'd never once said anything about Satils being brought back to life.

"Did you not know that Satils was revived?" she demanded.

"Brought...back? Is that what happened? So...so that's how she gained control of the focal core. We were played from the very beginning."

Gorne, or someone from the Chimera team working through him, must have taken a core from the facility and used it on Satils. That didn't quite answer how she'd been able to live beyond the reach of the focal core for so long, but it wasn't beyond the realm of possibility that Chimera had used the information Gorne sold them to make a focal core of their own.

"Well, Dafydd, I think I'm about done with the appetizer. Let's move on to the main dish."

"You're...still not done?"

"Of course not. I've saved the best for last." Satils smiled broadly, baring her bright red gums and glossy white teeth. Her gaze, expression, and voice all betrayed her crazed ecstasy. "Your beloved wife, a certain Susy Chalmas, was attacked by two adventurers who tortured her to death. She died with tears streaming down her face, screaming your name over and over. The adventurers, Tryte Ransila and Demiceliko Radius, were real scum-of-the-earth types who turned to crime to pay off their massive debt."

"Why do you know their names? The guild wasn't able to find anything!"

"Must I explain?" She offered up a wicked smile.

Dafydd's voice quivered. He looked like a lamb ready for the slaughter. "You...you ordered her death?"

"Now, now. They *wanted* to kill Susy. I just hated the sight of her. I mean, she was always going on about what was right and just, helping people without accepting payment, and she always ruined my carefully crafted plans without any good reason. Obviously, she had to die!"

The thought that she could be wrong didn't even seem to cross her mind.

"Watching her writhe around in pain, her hands and ankles smashed, screaming your name, was absolute rapture! That's when it hit me—Susy dedicated herself to justice just so I could kill her. What a great and wondrous God we have, to put a woman like her on this planet just for my delight and delectation!"

"Is that...is that the only reason? You killed her just to satisfy your own twisted urges?!"

"I have money. I have power. There's no shortage of elites like me who feel compelled to eliminate the weak!"

"Nnnnggaaaaaauuuugh!!" Dafydd finally gave in. This was probably the first time in his life he ever felt such uncontrollable anger rush through him.

"Ah, yes, your expression is nothing short of divine! This alone makes all those years of pouring money into your project worth it. Yes, yes, my investment has truly paid off in such exquisite pleasure! Gyahahaha!" Her cackle echoed throughout the room. It was like she'd been waiting for this precise moment.

"You're sick! Rotten to the core!"

"Rotten? Hardly. This is how the world works. Anyway, I've had my fill for now. I think it's about time we say goodbye to you, Dafydd." She tapped her heel on the floor, and Susy returned to absorbing Dafydd.

"I'll kill you...kill you! You...yoooooooooou!!"

He screamed through the whole process, though this only seemed to bring Satils even more pleasure.

"It's all over for you now! You can writhe, flail, yell, scream, cry... None of it will do you any good! That Susy right there, and even your child...they only look human. Your life, and even your death, was all pointless!"

"K-k-k-kill...nngg yo...you..." Dafydd's cries ceased as his head was sucked in.

"Dafydd..." There was a certain sadness to Milkit's voice. He may have made mistakes, but she hardly felt he deserved such an awful end.

Satils' laughter broke the silence. "Well, well. Why, I need a break from all that laughter...but you two are up next. I may have been brought back to life, but I fully intend to pay you back for all the pain you inflicted on me last time."

She pointed in their direction and curled her finger back toward herself. Two tendrils flew toward Flum, trying to seize her in a pincer.

Flum grabbed Milkit and jumped out of the way in time to watch the tendrils slam into each other and twist together. Now combined, they sped up and slammed into her head-on.

"Nnngyaaaah!" Flum managed to block the blow with her Souleater. The tendrils slammed into the wall and were absorbed like a raindrop into a pond.

"It sounds like defending yourself is taking all you have.

That's quite all right—I love watching people resist the inevitable. Seeing a weakling struggle in vain is *so* very enjoyable."

"Your advantage won't last forever!" Flum gave into her anger and launched another Prana Shaker at Satils. Right before it hit, her arm transformed into a blade, and she took the attack head-on.

"You seem fixated on the idea that my body or my core are weaknesses you can take advantage of."

There wasn't a mark on her.

Satils rushed toward Flum and raised her arm. The power of an unseen spiral began to form around her hand. "This is more powerful that anything you can imagine."

She swung at Flum with her sword arm, shooting off spiral blasts. Satils followed up with an attack nearly identical to the Prana Shaker, but launched from her bare hand, and more powerful than what Flum could pull off on her own.

"Haaugh?!" Flum blocked the attack with the broad side of her sword; the sheer force of the blast blew her back into the wall.

"Hmm, perhaps I should kill little Milkit here first?"

"Not a chance in hell!"

Flum pushed off the wall with such force that she flew straight through the air at Satils. Her sword slammed into Satils' sword arm. A loud crack resounded through-out the room as Flum's reversal magic met with Satils' spiral power.

Unsure of what else she could do, Milkit tried to stay out of the way, escaping to a corner of the room. A quick look at her new surroundings revealed human limbs sticking out of the walls at odd angles, making her even more worried about what to do if another tendril appeared.

The corridor outside the room was filled with the reanimated corpses, and she imagined it was probably a similar scene above ground as well. As far as she could tell, there were no safe spaces left in Sheol.

"You realize you're using both hands while I'm only us-ing one, no?" Satils kept Flum's blade locked down with one hand as she swiped at Flum's head with the other. At the end of her swing, she loosed a blast of spiral energy from her palm.

Flum jerked her head to the side to dodge the blast, throwing her off balance. With a chuckle, Satil took ad-vantage of the moment to ram her fingertips into Flum's stomach.

Even though she didn't have the leverage to put much speed or power into the attack, it still smashed Flum upward into the ceiling. Her head slammed against it so hard she blacked out for a moment. Satils leapt to where Flum was stuck in the ceiling, yanked her up by the shirt, and threw her into the floor.

Flum used her magic right at the instant she made contact with the floor to reverse her momentum, sending her flying straight toward Satils, her Souleater stretched out in front of her.

Satils blocked this attack, too, with just her hand. "You sure like to bounce around a lot. Humans aren't supposed to be that resilient... How have you not broken any bones yet?"

"Why do you care?! You can break my bones or crush my body—it won't stop me from putting an end to you, Satils!"

Satils chuckled. "We've got a brave one here. You remind me of an adorable little puppy that growls just a bit too much. Now, I wonder what that puppy over there sounds like when it whimpers?"

"Gah, stay away from Milkit!"

"Are you really in any position to worry about others?" Satils took advantage of Flum's momentary lapse in concentration. She stretched out both hands and hit Flum with a powerful blast, throwing her toward the ground before she herself dove off the ceiling and punched Flum in the stomach while she was still in midair.

Flum's body arched in an unnatural position. Blood sprayed from her mouth as her bones shattered and organs ruptured. She hit the ground with such force that the floor groaned beneath her, and a powerful shock wave reverberated through her body.

"Auunngh!"

Even the enchantment lessening her pain couldn't fully eliminate it. Making matters worse, her body was too shattered to move; it would still be some time before her wounds could properly regenerate. Satils looked at Flum collapsed on the ground and laughed at her powerlessness, then turned her attention to Milkit.

With a wave of her hand, a tendril with a face growing from the tip sprang out of a loose arm and began to pursue the young girl.

"I'm...not...gonna let you...lay a hand...on her!"

Humans have a way of digging deeper and summoning up more strength than they ever thought possible when a loved one is in danger. Flum's bones still hadn't mended. Moving, much less standing, should have been impossible.

Should have.

And yet she was back on her feet and walking toward Milkit.

"Why, you...!"

She lunged at the tendril pursuing Milkit. Satils broke out in a wide grin at the sight.

"Stay away, Master!"

By the time Milkit called out her warning, it was too late. Flum couldn't stop. The whole room began to tremble as something tried to force its way through the facility's floor.

"Huh?" Flum felt the ground beneath her feet rise, before the floor burst open like a geyser expelling hordes of demons. In an instant, she found herself completely surrounded.

"Master!!"

So chaotic was the force swallowing Flum that she couldn't even hear Milkit's cries.

"How wonderfully exceptional to see someone give up their life to save a sub-human, a slave! Kyahahaha!"

As Satils' laughter boomed throughout the room, the newly arrived creatures rushed to bond with the focal core, engulfing Flum with their roiling bodies. Some of the creatures still retained their human forms, while others were too far gone, though all had the same spiral marking their bodies as core hosts.

"These are Dafydd's failed creations. He was too nice to just kill them outright, so he locked them up in the basement instead."

Perhaps he had held out hope that one day he could save even his mistakes.

"Fortunately for me, I can use them to further increase my power. Oh, Dafydd, what a pitiful existence you lived. It's like you were put on this planet purely for my use! In fact, I think you were! Just as God put Susy here for me to kill, it was God's plan for you to live and die just to fulfill my dreams!"

Satils threw out her arms in a declaration of victory as the creatures continued to climb out of the ground and merge with the focal core. It grew larger and larger, losing its shape.

Her feet began to transform, like they were melting away, as she, too, joined the focal core.

She belted out an ear-piercing laugh. "Well, it looks like I got rid of that annoying little gnat. I want to see your face twist in pure, blissful agony, dear little Milkit. I think I might spend some time torturing what hasn't yet been absorbed of that Flum girl to death...and you'll have a front row seat."

But then—Satils froze in place.

"Aah, yes...that's right. Of course. I guess that's what I must do."

Her previous excitement suddenly nowhere to be seen, she began to move again.

"Well, my plans have changed. I won't be killing Flum. It seems I have places to go."

"Satils...you're also one of the reanimated dead, aren't you?" Milkit said.

"You dare compare me to those puppets?! Watch your mouth! I'm different; I was chosen by Origin! If that wasn't the case, why would I be able to bond with the focal core and use its power like this??"

"All the others believed that too—that they were living and acting of their own will! But it's just Origin causing you to think that!"

"Shut up! What do you know?! The only reason you were born on this planet was to be squashed like the bug you are!!" As Satils let her anger consume her, tendrils burst to life all around the room, attempting to smash Milkit.

Milkit had anticipated that. But now that Flum had been swallowed, the only thing weapon she had against Satils was the truth. If Satils could be believed, Flum was still alive somewhere inside her body. But Milkit was too weak to fight on her own, and there was nothing she could do...

"Connection!"

The world around Milkit changed in the blink of an eye. She was now outside that cruel, deranged lab. She looked to the child who had teleported her to safety and gasped. "Haah?!"

She was mere centimeters away from blank eye cavities filled with twisting and contorting spirals.

A moment later, Nekt's face returned to normal. She pouted slightly at Milkit's reaction. "I've gotta say, it's pretty rude to look so scared of the person who saved you."

"I...I'm sorry. Thank you, Nekt."

"No problem. But it looks like I was too late for Flum, huh? Though I doubt Papa would kill her. He has plans."

"Why wouldn't he kill her?"

"By bonding with Flum, Papa would gain the power of reversal and be free of his one weakness."

"But they've tried to kill her before..."

"There's the Papa that wants her to live and the one that wants her to die. His consciousness is still split."

"There's more than one?"

Nekt's information made the situation surrounding Origin even more complicated. Before they could continue their conversation, the ground began to shake as something massive tried to burst out of the earth.

016

Creeping Crawling Malevolence

Aʙᴏᴠᴇ ɢʀᴏᴜɴᴅ, Gadhio and Eterna were giving it all they had to save Sheol's citizens.

Gadhio used powerful fire attacks to blow the reanimated dead to shreds, while Eterna used her ice powers to create Fenrir, a monstrous wolf that she rode with Ink as they escorted the other citizens to safety.

The reanimated dead continued their ruthless assault on the living. At first it was difficult to distinguish between them, but as time went on, the latter's eyes melted away to reveal Origin's mark.

Just as Gadhio was about to cleave through another dead monster, he was stunned to see it fall still.

Eterna called out in confusion. "All of the dead just... stopped moving."

Ink pressed in close to Eterna from where she sat on

Fenrir's back. She was clearly afraid. "Some...something's coming."

"Ink?"

"Whatever it is, it's really, really big. And it's coming up through the ground!"

Just as the words left her mouth, Eterna felt the earth shudder beneath her. A moment later, the roof of the church blew out as something tore up out of the earth.

"What in the..."

Rising from the hole in the roof was a tower of corpses. The reanimated dead throughout Sheol converged on the tower, becoming one with it. The more bodies it consumed, the taller the tower became, until it blocked out the light of the moon, throwing a menacing shadow over the entire village.

Gadhio looked up. "It absorbed the focal core?! And that woman up on top, that's..."

Suddenly Nekt appeared at his side. She had already taken Milkit somewhere safe.

"That's Satils."

The lower half of Satils' body had merged with the rest of the corpses, while her torso stuck out of the top of the focal core. She had lost every vestige of humanity.

"Satils? What's that deranged woman... Actually, no, we can discuss that later. Can we count on you to help, Nekt?"

"I've been out to crush the Necromancy project from the start. Besides, I can't just turn a blind eye to Flum being sucked up into that thing."

"She is?!" Ink called out from atop Fenrir's back.

"You've always had great hearing, Ink. I see nothing's changed!"

"Then we've gotta save her before we take that thing out."

"I get what you're saying, but it's pretty powerful, ya know? Just look."

Once it had absorbed all of the dead in the village, the fifty-meter tower of bodies slumped forward in an attempt to crush the heroes. The sheer sight of the thing was awe-inspiring...and full of terror.

Nekt, Eterna, and Gadhio scattered.

FWAA-OOSH!

A massive cloud of dirt rose high in the sky as houses collapsed, the earth gave way, and the undead horde fell to the ground all around it. Countless arms and legs sprouted from its sides, and it began to crawl forward.

"That's no tower, it's a giant centipede!!"

"It's heading right toward the evacuees!"

"Not a chance! Hyaaaaaaaaaah!!" Gadhio stood directly in Satils' path.

"It looks like your reputation exceeds the man, Gadhio Lathcutt!!"

The moment his blade made contact with Satils, Gadhio was blown backward with meteoric force. He tried to hold his ground, but the blow sent him sliding backwards, digging deep trenches in the dirt where his feet held firm.

"Nnng...! This thing is intelligent?!"

"I'm no mere core! I've retained my consciousness! With all my money and power, and God's love, I truly must be the chosen one!!"

"What the hell kind of logic is that?!"

Logic aside, Satils could still overpower Gadhio by an impressive margin.

I'm just not strong enough...but there's still one more thing I can try. As long as this gives me a chance to get back at Chimera, I can't worry about failure!

Gadhio had gained something important the moment he committed to ending Tia's life—the power to push past his own prior limits. But even that wasn't enough, compared to the power Satils now wielded.

"Aqua Golem, Ice Golem...go!!"

Eterna summoned up twin giants of water and ice and ordered them to grab both sides of the monster in an attempt to hold it back.

While it was slowed, Nekt launched into an attack of her own. "Get crushed! Connection!"

She teleported an empty house above Satils' head and dropped it on her.

"Your attacks are little more than insect bites to me!!"

Countless tendrils made up of human limbs reached out of Satils' torso, coming together to grab the house and mercilessly beat down Eterna's golems.

"And you—I'm going to let you die with the knowledge that you couldn't save your wife!" Satils shouldn't have known about what happened between Gadhio and Tia, but the focal core and its power over all of the Necromancy cores gave Satils greater insight into all that unfolded in the village. "Gyaaaaaaaaaugh!!"

The house came flying straight at Gadhio, who could do nothing to block the blow. If he turned and ran, Satils would pick up speed and murder the remaining survivors. He had little choice but to take the ten-ton mass of wood and stone head-on.

"You think something like that can kill me?!" he ground out.

He made it through completely unscathed, despite his lack of armor—all thanks to his prana reinforcing and strengthening his body enough to withstand the blow. In a sense, it was his very will that helped him through it.

Satils laughed. "Well, aren't you a tough bug to squash! Let's try this instead!"

She gave up on trying to smash the survivors and sent her hordes of tendrils out toward Gadhio.

"Pretty impressive for an old guy, but I think this is getting a bit hairy. You agree, old lady?" Nekt turned toward Eterna.

"I'll beat you up later, kid."

"Testy, testy. But anyway, I need you to make a huge sphere out of water or ice or something."

"Little jerk… But we don't have time for this. Ice Meteorite!!"

Eterna wasn't entirely convinced of what Nekt asked of her, but she could quibble *after* the fight. She reluctantly created a ball of ice a dozen or so meters in diameter and held it in midair.

"A little praise here, Ink, for keeping my temper?"

"You're doing great, Eterna!"

It was Nekt's turn.

"Go!! Connection!" Rather than simply teleporting it, Nekt used her power to fling the ball of ice at Satils. It hit her with such force that the shock wave alone would have thrown a normal person off their feet.

Satils made no attempt to block the blow.

And yet…

"Heh heh. Did I feel a breeze?"

She didn't even suffer a scratch.

"Unbelievable..."

"I know she's bonded with that massive core, but even then, this is incredible."

If Nekt's understanding was correct, Satils shouldn't be able to use any cores other than the focal core within her. Even if multiple cores were implanted within the same person, the interaction between them would cause a cascade effect that made them impossible to control. While it could grant tremendous power for a short while, it would tear the user apart.

Even with the effects of the focal core, she should still only be able to utilize a maximum of two cores at once. Since Satils was reanimated with a Necromancy core implanted within her, she should have only had her core and the focal core.

None of that explained how she was able to resist their attacks.

"Hngg...her power...!" Gadhio was using his sword to bat away tendrils as they came in, though he couldn't do any lasting damage. They were simply too strong. The only good side for him was that they weren't terribly fast.

Nekt finally figured out how Satils was accessing the cores.

"That's it... The dead aren't actually fused together into one massive body made up of many cores. They're

a bunch of individual bodies with their own cores, each being controlled by the focal core!"

Eterna glanced over at Nekt as she tried to protect Gadhio with a barrage of water bullets. "Meaning...what, exactly?"

"They're all moving in concert."

"So they could come apart and move around individually if they wanted?"

"I assume it's possible."

Just as they predicted, Satils' body split off right at the halfway point. The back half began to crawl on its countless arms and legs toward the evacuees.

"I'm guessing their defensive strength and power come from the power of Origin granted to each and every one of the bodies. If they can separate like this, there's just no way we can gain the upper hand with how few of us there are. I think the most logical choice would be to escape."

"There's no way we can do that."

"I figured as much. You guys didn't seem the type." With that, Nekt teleported in front of the back half. "Let's try something different this time!"

She balled her hands into tight fists, ripping trees straight from the ground and shooting them like giant arrows toward the creature. It squirmed and writhed around the trees that rained down on it as it continued on its ceaseless drive to fulfill Satils' command.

Eterna rode up next to Nekt and pointed her open palm at the enemy from where she sat atop Fenrir.

"Hydro Pressure!!" A powerful stream of water shot from her hand. As long as her magic didn't run out, she could keep the blast going as long as she wanted.

It did nothing to slow the beast down.

"I've got more where that came from!"

"I'm just getting warmed up!"

Nekt pressed on with the tree missiles, while Eterna increased the pressure of the water blast as they continued to lay into the creature.

"Just stop already!!"

Satils mumbled to herself even as she continued to battle Gadhio. "Well, if you're going to ask nicely..."

The creature went still, sending a sense of relief washing over Nekt and Eterna. Just then, however, it began to blow apart.

"It's exploding?"

"No, Eterna... I can hear voices, and lots of them!"

"It's splitting up into even smaller parts!!"

"I hardly need such a massive creature just to kill these sweet little survivors, you know. I hear you're absolutely

ROLL OVER AND DIE

amazing at fighting crowds, Gadhio, so why don't you show me your moves?"

"Go to hell, hag!"

Gadhio was too consumed with defending against the incoming tendrils to advance or retreat. It took all of his concentration just to survive.

The split-off creatures let out unearthly cries and rushed the survivors. Each moved in its own distinct way, some like crazed humans and yet others like dogs, spiders, or even worms.

"It's up to us!"

"There may be a lot of them, but they're weaker now! Here's our chance to cut down their numbers!"

Eterna summoned up a powerful hailstorm and froze the ground beneath them to hold them in place before firing off a barrage of water bullets. Nekt used her powers to connect several bodies together, forcing them to a standstill and then crushing them or flinging them into nearby objects. Despite their best efforts, it was slow going in the face of such immense numbers.

"Look here, I've prepared a little surprise for you!" The tendrils extending out of Satils' body tore a house from the ground and hurled it at the survivors. Gadhio, Eterna, and Nekt were all too occupied with their own battles to save them.

The remaining survivors came together as they watched their impending death loom closer.

"I told you to take care of this, Werner!!"

"Right-o!"

The two lieutenant generals of the royal army dove into the fray to protect the survivors.

"Vibration Claw!!" Wind magic surrounded Werner's silver claws, enabling him to easily smash through any debris flying his way.

"Take a bite, blood snake Amphisbaena!" Ottilie used her Genocide Arts to unleash two snakes made of blood. The snakes smashed their way through the remains of the home and thrashed about the interior to further weaken it.

"We'll get the citizens out of here!"

Though they would have rather stayed to fight, one quick look at Ottilie, Werner, and their contingent of soldiers made it clear they had suffered quite an ordeal fighting their way into the village.

"The army! Amazing!"

"More bugs? Well, then I'll just have to crush you, too!"

"Not gonna happen, Satils! Titan Blade!!" Stone surrounded Gadhio's sword, causing it to grow several times in length. Without a moment's hesitation, he brought it down on her head. Though she didn't suffer any damage from the blow, it did break her focus.

"I'm really growing quite tired with dealing with you! Hurry up and go join your wife!!" Satils' anger was eroding her ability to think rationally. Even as her attack on Gadhio picked up in ferocity, she became locked into the task at hand. Even the countless creatures separated from her body mere moments ago responded to her rage and formed back up on her.

"Nekt, please take Ink back to Ottilie," Eterna said.

"You want me to help Ink, of all people? Haah...I guess I don't have much choice."

"Thanks."

Nekt muttered to herself in annoyance. "Thanks for nothing. You really are dead weight, Ink...but whatever. Connection!"

She teleported Ink away.

With Ink off the battlefield, Eterna turned her attention fully to Satils. She didn't need to hold back anymore. Ottilie and the other soldiers were taken aback at Nekt's sudden appearance, but they quickly took custody of Ink. Nekt made her way back to where she'd left Milkit for safekeeping.

"Nekt..." Milkit sat behind a building on the outskirts of Sheol with her knees held tightly to her chest.

"The royal army came to rescue the survivors. You should go with them."

"Do you...do you think you can save Master?"

"I wish I could say yes, but I think our chances are pretty slim."

Though they gave Satils a run for her money, the truth was that they still hadn't inflicted any damage on her.

"Satils can use the cores embedded in all of the corpses around her to shield her entire body. It's completely unlike what my core can do. I dunno if anyone but Flum can actually tackle her."

"Even Master couldn't hurt her."

"Really...? Well, then we have no hope of winning."

"C-can you let me come along to help Master?"

"Are you serious??"

Nekt was half-convinced Milkit was completely out of her mind.

"Flum isn't just sitting inside that thing, ya know?" she said. "Sure, she's been physically sucked up into it, but being in there's like drowning in an ocean of Origin's consciousness. She's probably lost all sense of self at this point."

Nekt struggled to avoid using the word "Papa" here to describe Origin. She had thus far mostly ignored his existence, but Origin's current actions were too much for her to overlook. Nekt had only survived the barrage this long thanks to her own core.

"If I call out to her, maybe she'll come back to us," Milkit insisted.

"The real world isn't that convenient. Besides, we don't even know where she is in that thing."

"But I do! I saw Master's hand come out when I was watching the battle earlier!"

"How could you identify a single hand out of all the other ones out there?"

"If you could just get me close, I can take her hand and call out to her. She just might hear me."

"Even if she does, you know the odds of you surviving this are microscopic, right?"

Milkit didn't even blink. "Living in a world without Master is a far more terrifying fate."

She wasn't the least bit afraid to throw down her life for Flum. That much she could say with complete confidence.

Nekt sighed loudly. "You're not going to give in no matter what I say, are you? Fine, fine. I'll take you."

She laughed ruefully to herself. Apparently Milkit was having an effect on her, too.

Deep in the sea of Origin's consciousness, a lone voice called out into the void.

"Who am I?"

Countless responses came echoing back.

"I'm you." "You're me." "Me and me and me and me are all you." "I hate this." "I'm no one." "I'm what we should all be." "We're all connected, as we should be." "Get me out of here." "I always wanted us to be together." "Help." "I'm complete."

In the midst of all these voices, Flum became even more confused about where and who she was. The worst part about it was just how amazingly at peace she felt being here. The longer she stayed, the deeper she felt herself fall into it.

At the bottom of this ocean was a bed of corpses...or, rather, empty shells.

If Origin's consciousness was the water, then these shells were those that couldn't live up to its expectations. Or perhaps these were the bodies of the living who'd been devoured. Those bodies called out to no one in particular, letting all their sadness, hatred, and anger spill forth.

"All I wanted was to live with my wife again. Why did this have to happen?" "I just wanted to be reunited with my darling." "I didn't want to die. Why was I denied this simple, universal wish?" "Please, give me my happiness back."

The Necromancy project was the means through which these people hoped to have their simple, universal wish granted. They were all victims of the system. They'd known nothing of the Origin cores before trusting their hopes and dreams to it.

Flum was pulled down by all their resentment, sinking lower and lower into the depths until she reached the empty shells that blanketed the ocean floor.

She had no idea who she was, but she knew the water around her was warm and pleasant. What little she could see was fuzzy and ill-defined, though there was something distinctly familiar about the man in a white coat lying next to her.

0 1 7

Escape from Limbo

"**O**VER THERE! That arm sticking out right near the middle!"

"I still have no idea which one you're talking about, but I'll get you close!"

Nekt grabbed hold of Milkit and teleported onto Satils' corpse-covered body to make sure it was safe to actually touch it. Once she was certain of their relative safety, she set Milkit down.

Satils' laugh boomed throughout the village.

"There's nothing you weaklings can do! You're nothing more than an afternoon snack to me. Such a disgrace that you have the gall to call yourselves heroes!"

Satils hadn't caught on yet.

Milkit knelt down onto the spongy mass beneath her and shoved both hands through a small gap between the bodies. She knew pulling Flum out was impossible, but she could at least pray Flum heard her words.

"Master...it's me. You've done so much for me. It's my most desperate hope that I can also give back and be of some use to you. Please...please, just listen to my voice!"

She prayed with her entire being for Flum to come back. Nekt felt a sense of envy and admiration wash over her as she watched Milkit, realizing just how close their bond was.

"Hm? What are you doing up there??"

Satils finally took notice of their presence, craning her neck to look back at Milkit praying and Nekt standing over her. She let out a hearty chuckle.

"Oh, so you're trying to save Flum? Go ahead, pray your heart out! Believe in the power of your bond! I love it, Milkit! I'll just love crushing your dreams!!"

"I'm not gonna let that happen!"

"All right then, I guess I'll just have to smash you first!"

A tendril launched toward Nekt, though she was easily able to evade the attack by using her Connection power to throw it off course.

"How can you stand against me?! You only have one core!"

"Heh, there's more to this game than raw power!"

And yet, Satils' control over the focal core made her far

more powerful than Nekt by a large margin. In a head-to-head match using Origin's might, it would be no contest.

"Damn you!"

The next blast hit Nekt head-on, throwing her off Satils' back and through the wall of a nearby building before she finally came to rest in a pile of rubble.

Now Milkit was on her own. Another tendril careened toward her.

"Please, Master..."

"If praying was the answer to your problems, you would've never been in this position, girlie!"

"Back off, Satils!!"

"Gadhio, you're on Milkit. Ice Enchantment!"

Ice formed around Gadhio's blade as he smashed it into one tendril after the next. Though his Jötunn Blade still couldn't cut all the way through, he at least batted them off course, keeping Milkit safe for the time being.

As long as they were still standing atop Satils' back, she could easily attack them from any direction. She should have been able to wipe them out in an instant, and yet, she didn't. Or perhaps...couldn't.

Absorbing Flum—and her Reversal ability—had likely dampened Origin's power. The spot where Milkit stood must have been a spot where Satils didn't have full control, leaving her no option but to strike from a distance.

"Keep 'em coming, and I'll keep knocking them out of the way!" Gadhio roared.

"You're really becoming a pest, Gadhio Lathcutt!"

"I'll make sure you never forget my name!"

"Why, you annoying, meagre, impertinent low-life scum!!"

Gadhio and Eterna blocked tendril after tendril as they closed in on Milkit.

"Listen, we can't hold up like this forever, Milkit!"

"That's what I'm here for!" Nekt rejoined the other two in keeping Milkit safe.

Since destroying the tendrils was out of the question, Nekt grappled them and drew herself to nearby buildings, forcing the tendrils far off track.

"Why are you fools wasting your time like this?! Flum is gone now, and even if she did come back, it'd do you no good! Just give up and let me see the delicious look of defeat in your eyes!"

Milkit only continued her frantic prayers. "Master... Master... Master!!"

Flum's finger twitched.

"I..."

Discovering one's identity without any external influence should have been fundamentally impossible. And yet the empty shells lying at the bottom of the ocean of consciousness knew who they were.

"I want to see her again." "I wish we could have spent more time together." "I wish he was just left dead." "I don't want to ever experience such disappointment ever again." "I really loved him. I just wish words were enough to get my feelings across."

The empty shells held only their most passionate desires from when they were still alive. It was their feelings, their love for other people, that allowed them to hold onto some shred of self even in the depths of Origin's consciousness.

"Master, please... Master...Master...Master!"

She heard a voice. But whose?

She felt *something*. Her body started to respond. In the back of her mind, she knew she had to protect the person behind that voice.

"Mil...kit?"

It all came back at once. The name, the girl she cared for so deeply, and her own name.

"That's right, I was swallowed by...something. Am I inside it?"

Even with her newfound awareness, she couldn't move freely. It felt like an immense weight rested on top of her.

The man in front of her began to speak. "You're...Flum, right?"

"Dafydd Chalmas..."

"So, it is you. I guess you got dragged in here too, then."

"Where are we?"

"I don't know. Perhaps we're inside Origin's consciousness, or maybe this is where all dead people go."

He spoke weakly, overcome by how helpless he was.

"All these people suffered because of me. And probably others, too, assuming there are any survivors."

"I don't think all the blame rests at your feet."

"Maybe. Maybe not. In any case, it was my own arrogance that caused this disaster. I want to apologize for that, Flum."

"This is a pretty big departure from how you acted right up to your death."

"I've had time to think, and to wonder if I could have done anything differently. Living in a world without Susy was worse than hell."

Flum had no response. She didn't want to completely let him off the hook, but giving him some platitude about finding another reason to live also didn't seem right.

"You still have a reason to live. There's someone back in the other world that needs you to keep her safe."

"I...suppose you're right. She sounds like she's already crying for me."

"I'm jealous. I wonder if Susy would have done the same for me? Right now, you're being punished for the same sins I committed. But you have the power to reverse the curse."

"Lots of things. Not just curses."

"There's one favor I'd like to ask of you."

"Kill Satils?"

"Right. You're...still...alive. May...be you can...pull it off. Just...use all the weight of our grief."

All of the bodies opened their eyes in unison in response to Dafydd's call and looked toward Flum. They cried out mournfully.

If she could just reverse all of this cursed energy, she might stand a chance at breaking free.

"I was thinking the same thing. I'll break out of here and kill Origin and that woman."

"Thank you...for granting such...a selfish request. I feel like...I'll...be with Susy soon."

Dafydd's eyes drooped closed, and he fell still.

Flum felt power surge through her. It wasn't her imagination. Her fingertip twitched as she regained her sense of touch. Something small and cold deep inside Satils' body had made contact with her.

Her stats rose steadily.

"Right...that's..."

She felt a powerful curse on the object. All of the hatred flowing from Dafydd and everyone Origin had betrayed after being brought back to life, along with the many victims in Sheol, was gathered here.

Flum clasped her fingers around it, clenching so tightly her palm began to bleed.

"Haaaaah!!"

A power unlike anything she had ever known coursed through her.

"Waaaaaaaaaaaaaaaaaaaugh!!"

All of her prana and reversal magic blasted out in a massive explosion that burned a hole through all the bodies in her way. She squeezed Milkit's hand tightly and pulled herself out before pulling Milkit into a warm embrace.

"M-master!"

"I heard you, Milkit. Thanks."

Tears pooled in Milkit's eyes as she buried her head into Flum's chest. "I'm...so happy to hear that."

"Where did that power come from all of a sudden? You were completely stuck!! Why, I've never heard of anything so absurd as a prayer making someone stronger! It's absolutely preposterous!"

There were few things in this world Satils hated more than justice delivered and a happy ending. Beside herself with rage, she sent another volley of tendrils flying in Flum's direction. Their tips angled toward her and spun like drills.

Flum hefted up her Souleater in both hands and engaged them head-on.

"Why...why did you get so powerful all of a sudden?! None of this makes any sense! This kind is the kind of nonsense reserved for fairy tales!"

Flum's hands shook as she returned the tendrils' attacks blow for blow. She was holding her ground. "You brought this all on yourself, Satils!"

"Don't speak such nonsense, dearie! I am perfection! Everything goes my way!"

"Everything you've done is out of hatred for humanity! You've crushed hopes, dreams, people's love for their family and friends...all for your own twisted desires!"

"So what? What does that have to do with you getting more powerful??"

The tendrils spun even faster. The only way that she could stand so close to such a powerful enemy was thanks to her reversal power sapping their strength. Anyone else would have been ripped to shreds.

"When people have their futures ripped away from

them, it births an immense hatred in their hearts—a curse!"

The entire village of Sheol was cursed.

If Flum weren't here, this sense of anger over unfulfilled dreams and stolen futures would likely have ended up coalescing into petty cursed equipment.

"All of their cursed energy is in this ring!"

All of their hopes and dreams were now left with Flum, coalesced into Dafydd Chalmas' wedding ring.

Name: Wedding Ring of Loss and Lies
Tier: Epic
[This equipment lowers its wearer's Strength by 1,012]
[This equipment lowers its wearer's Magic by 1,072]
[This equipment lowers its wearer's Endurance by 1,053]
[This equipment lowers its wearer's Agility by 1,088]
[This equipment lowers its wearer's Perception by 1,039]

This gave Flum a combined stat value of 12,693—an S-Rank.

"This isn't a coincidence...this is the natural conclusion to you and Origin's heinous acts!" Flum batted a tendril away and unleashed a storm of prana that cut away at Satils' body.

"Ow...oww, it hurts! But you're still too weak! Whatever curses you may have working for you, it's not enough. I already told you once, girlie: there's no one stronger than me. You've just been fighting weakened reanimated corpses so far. You're back, but you still can't scratch me!"

She wasn't boasting—the Prana Storm failed to do any damage to the focal core or to Satils herself.

Nekt was up next. "Well then, what if we all attack together?"

She flickered in and out of the scene, gathering Flum, Milkit, Eterna, and Gadhio all in one place.

"Whoa... Could you at least give me a heads-up next time? Anyway, I guess I know what to do. Ice Enchantment!" Eterna wreathed Flum's sword in frost.

"Right. I'll give you my Earth Enchantment and prana, Flum!" A layer of rock formed over Flum's blade. Prana suffused the whole thing. The blade was now nearly as long as Satils' entire body.

"Hnng...!" Flum struggled to hold it aloft.

"So this is what you meant by coming together? Ha!

And what do you plan on doing with that stupidly huge sword? You can't even move it!"

"Let me help with that."

Nekt ignored Satils' taunts, teleporting Flum and Milkit high into the air. Flum knew what to do next. Milkit glanced over at Flum in confusion but decided to trust her and cling tight.

"Hang on!!"

"R-right!"

Nekt tightened her grasp. "Connection!"

She connected the Souleater with the focal core, drawing them together at blinding speed—with Flum along for the ride.

"Hyaaaaaaaaaaaaaaugh!!" Flum picked up speed until she hit terminal velocity moments before making contact with Satils.

"You think dropping down on me will do you any good?!"

Flum's reversal-infused blade made contact with the focal core. A shock wave shook the entire village.

Satils was forced into the ground with such force that the earth under her gave way, carved out into a massive crater. All the surrounding buildings were blown away or reduced to rubble.

And yet, Satils still absorbed the blow, thanks to the power of the focal core.

"Was that your best shot? Heh, and you call yourself a hero! You're nothing more than a West District street rat! You never stood a chance against me, Satils Francois, brilliant business mogul of our fair kingdom!"

"Get over yourself! You've only gotten to where you are by using others as stepping stones!"

"Is that alone not proof of my true strength? Ha!"

A crack began to form in the outer layer of prana encasing the Souleater.

"Who needs love, dreams, or hope for the future anyway?! Look at you, you even need to drag Milkit around everywhere you go! You're a little punk pretending to be a hero!"

The prana layer gave way, and the stone blade made contact with Satils. The prana didn't merely dissipate— it managed to further suppress Satils' power and finally brought a pained look to her face.

"You know nothing! If there *is* a hero known as Flum, she only exists through Milkit and my combined strength! We're a hero...together!"

"What are you going on about? Your bond? Friendship? You make me sick with all your fanciful talk!!"

Satils transformed her rebuff into a renewed attack. The stone blade twisted before it, too, gave way and shattered.

"I see you made that little plaything just for me to destroy! There's really no difference between you and that lovesick Dafydd. You'll end up dead, just like him!"

With the Earth Enchantment gone, that left Eterna's coating of ice to stab down into Satils.

Flum gripped the handle of her sword so tightly her hands began to discolor and bleed. The only thing that let her push through the pain, through the aching in her arms as the energy coursed through them, was the warmth clinging to her side.

"No...we won't lose!"

Milkit was all too aware of just how ineffective and weak she was, but she also knew Flum needed her. She had no idea just how much help she could be to Flum, but as long as Flum wanted her by her side, then she would give it all she had. She promised herself this much from the bottom of her heart.

"And what makes you so positive? Just look at what happened to Dafydd! He loved Susy right to the bitter end. Even with all your strength, I'm still chipping away at you!"

Flum groped for words, but Milkit chimed in first.

"That's because I love my Master... I love her more than you could possibly hate. That's why she won't lose to you!"

They held each other up, gave each other strength, trusted one another unconditionally, and were always at one another's side. *Love.* That was the emotion Milkit had spent her entire life searching for.

Satils cackled. "And what are you basing that on? Nothing! You think you can beat me with something silly like that? Don't make me laugh!!"

"I don't need any proof. You'll just see for yourself!!"

"Go ahead and give it your best! Look at what you've achieved so far! Your blade is breaking apart at the seams!"

A crack crept through the ice. It was only a matter of time until it, too, shattered. That would leave only the Souleater itself.

"Look, just look. It broke! With the last of your blades gone, it looks like you're pretty much at your end. Love has been defeated, and now the world will hear the inter-mingling of your cries and my laughter! Say goodbye to your happy ending!!"

"We're not done yet! Reversion!!"

Flum anticipated that it might come down to this. Satils was so powerful that she might not be able to break the core that easily. She had spent her time coming up with one last gambit.

She would reverse the eradication of everyone's combined powers.

"Gyaaaaaaaaaugh!!" Satils' body shuddered as she let out a shrill cry. "There's something...something stabbing my back! Those... Did those fragments come back?!"

After all the time she spent focusing on her test of strength with Flum, the battlefield now stretched to cover her entire back. Or, rather, all of the strength she used earlier was now coming back in force.

"This little magic trick of yours still isn't enough to turn things around!"

Even as she said the words, she could feel her concentration fading as the damage mounted. Each wound was quickly filled with a characteristic swirl—her control over Origin was weakening. This put her in an incredibly precarious position; she became less and less able to maintain the delicate balance between her own core and the focal core.

"Maybe it shouldn't be possible, but I won't let that stop me from turning the tables! I'm bringing the hopes of the living and the curses of the dead with me!"

Flum would put their magic, Nekt's connection power, and Gadhio's prana into this. And if that still wasn't enough, she still had one last card left unplayed.

The only problem was that she was getting weaker by

the second. She got right up to the focal core and poured all her remaining prana into her sword.

"You're done, Satils!" The moment the tip of the blade made contact with the black crystal, she unleashed all of her magic into it to reverse the spin of the spiral deep within. The ensuing burst of negative energy let the Souleater find more purchase and sink into the weakened focal core. A crack formed along the surface with a loud *pop* before the entire core shattered.

Flum tumbled down to the ground with Milkit.

"Yeah!"

"You did it!"

Eterna rushed over on Fenrir and scooped up the two girls. With her focal core gone, it was just a matter of time until Satils died...

Or at least, so they thought.

"You...destroyed the focal core..."

With her power source gone and her ability to co-ordinate the hundreds of corpses lost, her outer body began to fall apart. But Satils still had her own core. The one embedded within her that brought her back from the dead.

She let out a shrill laugh.

"But you see, my core is still very much intact! I can still bond with the bodies and... and... huh?!"

Satils suddenly arched her back and vomited blood. Her body was falling apart from all her earlier exertion.

Pieces of organs joined the fountain of blood pouring from her mouth.

As Satils' condition degraded, the focal core underwent a transformation of its own as a result of Flum's reversal. Were it any normal core, it would simply self-destruct, but a crystal this big began to implode, sucking things into it like a black hole.

Satils groaned in pain as her insides continued to pour out of her mouth and her body was ever so slowly pulled back toward the focal core in its vacuum-like grip. Her face distorted in a cruel mockery of its former self as her death began to unfold.

Flum and Milkit watched from their perch atop Fenrir's back.

"I'd say that's a fitting end for such a despicable woman."

"I agree."

Gadhio watched with interest as the focal core sucked in all the other corpses as it slowly destroyed itself.

"And it looks like we won't even need to take care of the bodies," he said.

"But isn't your wife's body in there, too?"

"A part of me wishes I could give her a proper burial, but there's still a risk that her body might be used for nefarious purposes again. This is probably the most fitting end. It was Origin's power that brought her body back in the first place."

Tia's body was almost completely ripped to shreds when she originally died, so it was only thanks to the power of the Origin core that her organs and brain even existed in the first place. Now that they were robbed of Origin's power, Tia—much like Lukoh had done earlier—would likely devolve back into a mass of flesh and muscle.

A small smile came to Gadhio's lips.

Besides, it won't be long until we're together again. There's no need to spend time thinking about where her body rests.

Shortly after the outpouring of negative energy died down, Ottilie brought Ink back to the village.

"Are you okay, Eterna? Were you hurt?!"

"I'm fine, no worries. I'm glad to see you're okay, too." Eterna pulled the younger girl into a tight embrace and stroked her head.

"That was quite a battle! I was watching it all unfold from under cover, but wow! I've never seen anything like it!!" Welcy approached the group, practically bursting with excitement.

"You stayed in the village?!"

"Of course I did. A scoop like this doesn't just fall on your desk every day. Once I get this all written down, this will spell the church's doom, I'm sure! I mean, sure, I almost died, but that's part of the job." Judging by her soiled clothes and mussed hair, she'd been fairly close to the action, too.

"I'm not sure if I should be impressed or aghast that you can maintain such high spirits," said Ottilie.

Flum looked toward Ottilie and cocked her head to the side. "Hey, Ottilie...what are you doing here, anyway?"

She knew nothing about their earlier arrival, so her confusion was only natural.

Werner explained their mission. "Henriette ordered us to keep an eye on you. We were keeping watch from the outskirts."

"Sis is really good at gauging things like this, you see."

"So she gave that order after I met with her...? Well, either way, thank you."

"I'll be sure to pass that message along."

As far as Ottilie was concerned, it was Henriette they should be thankful to.

Gadhio glanced over at the members of the royal army. "But how did you guys get hurt? Now that I think about it, you were already pretty beat up before you escorted the survivors to safety."

Ottilie's smile faded. "Right around the time when the dead began to attack, we were assaulted by a horde of monsters."

"They had these nasty, fleshy spirals where their faces should've been."

"We got held up dealing with them."

"Hmm, those were no mere monsters—they're the Chimera project's work. It seems like they were planning to wipe everyone here out while destroying the Necromancy team."

"Echidna Ipeila really is a cruel, ruthless woman."

Flum had heard Dafydd say something incredibly similar before. Assuming she was the one playing Gorne and Satils, Echidna truly was a force to be reckoned with. Now that Flum and the rest had drawn her attention, they would need to be more careful.

"Speaking of Chimera, I seem to recall Satils mentioning that there was a traitor inside the Necromancy team."

Milkit's words jogged Flum's memory. "Aah, right. Gorne...Forgan, I think. He was selling information to Echidna."

"That was the guy Dafydd referred to as his friend, right?"

"I remember running across his wife and kid when we were battling through the facility, but I don't recall seeing him at all."

"Makes sense that the traitor would run."

"If he left the village before things went south, he must still be pretty close. You might still be able to catch him if you give chase now."

Ottilie agreed with Eterna's suggestion and turned to Werner. "Werner, following people is your specialty."

"You want me to chase down some guy? Off in the woods? Gah, what a drag..."

Usually, Ottilie would bark back with some harsh words of her own at his attitude, but she seemed too emotionally exhausted after the day's fight to do that this time. "All right then, I'll do it."

"Wait, what?"

"Why do you look so surprised? You said you didn't want to do it, so I'll go instead. You can look after the survivors, then."

"H-hold up! Look after them? You've gotta be joking! Gah! She's already gone...looks like I messed this one up big time."

Werner ran a hand through his hair in annoyance. Fortunately, no one in the vicinity knew what he actually meant.

Within the hour, Ottilie made it back to Sheol with Gorne in tow. It had been a relatively uneventful capture. Once she was on the scene, Werner made his way back to the capital in order to secure resources for the survivors from Henriette.

Under normal circumstances, the royal army had no right to enter privately owned land without permission, but the impending emergency changed things. After performing triage and handling the survivors' injuries, destroying the remaining cores, and conducting a brief interrogation of Gorne, reinforcements arrived with the dawn.

In light of Chimera's involvement, Flum was concerned that the church knights might beat the royal army to the punch, but she was glad to see Lieutenant General Herrmann heading the royal forces. According to him, the church knights had shown no signs of mobilizing.

It made sense, in a way, that the heads of the church would choose not to involve themselves in the dispute between Chimera and Necromancy. It was for the best.

Flum decided to leave the rest up to the military and began preparing to leave.

"You know, I never would have imagined you would have done so much to help us," she said to Nekt once she found her sitting atop a pile of rubble. Even after the battle was won, Nekt had hung back to help with the cleanup, not keen on being seen by the royal army. Considering Ottilie and Werner already saw her, though, this seemed a moot point to Flum.

"I wouldn't be able to call in any favors from you guys if I left."

"So, you've made up your mind?"

"Yeah. During the battle, I couldn't help but see just how annoying Papa is. He didn't care about us at all; he was just obsessed with you and Satils. He's no different from Mother. I've got no place with them anymore."

Not having a place you belonged wasn't so different from not having a reason to exist, under the right circumstances. Nekt must have figured out her own way to give her life meaning.

"I'm going to go talk to the others. I'm pretty sure it'll take some time to win them over."

It sounded like she was sold on the idea of undergoing surgery to remove the Origin core implanted within her. There were still many challenges ahead she would need to face; Mother not the least of them.

"Well, let me know if you run into any trouble," Flum said. "I'll do whatever I can to help you break free of the church."

"You're pretty impressive, Flum. I hope I won't need to rely on you. I really don't want to have to kill anyone." Nekt stood up and beat the dirt from the seat of her pants.

"You don't want to talk with Ink about this?"

"I don't have the other Children on board yet. Besides, every time I see that bright smile on her face whenever she's with that Eterna lady, it just doesn't feel right for me to talk to her."

"I'm sure she doesn't mind."

"She's just such an airhead, ya know? You let her know that if she doesn't want to get teased all the time, she really needs to fix that about herself."

Flum could only chuckle at the annoyance in Nekt's voice.

Suddenly, her tone turned serious. "But...ya know, I really don't look down on her like I used to. We were always told she was a failed project, but she's achieved much more than any of us. Besides getting away from Mother, she's made her own place to call home. She's shown me what it's like to have a future to look forward to."

"Do you consider her an older sister now?"

"I always thought of her like a goofy, flawed older sister. I just had a really twisted way of expressing it."

Twisted seemed like an understatement. Nekt also seemed to realize there was something she needed to change.

"Anyway, I suppose we should probably make it official."

"What are you talking about?"

"This." Nekt extended her right hand toward Flum. Her cheeks went pink, and she ran her left hand through her hair out of embarrassment.

Flum smiled gently at Nekt as she squeezed her hand.

"Looking forward to working together, Nekt."

"Just remember that we're just helping each other out. It's not like we're friends or nothin.'"

"I'll keep that in mind."

"You're gonna forget, aren't ya?"

"If we're lucky."

Flum could only hope they would never need to clash again, especially after they'd made it this far.

"See you again."

"Later."

"Connection!" With that, Nekt was gone.

Milkit approached Flum as soon as Nekt disappeared. "Did Nekt really go back?"

"We'll see her again; of that much I'm sure. It seems like she's finally made up her mind to remove her core."

Now all they had to do was think up a way to source a heart between now and then. Gruesome though the topic may have been, Flum was fairly confident they would be able to figure something out.

"Well, we did everything we set out to do. Let's get going home."

"I think that's a good idea. Let's go home!"

The long night finally came to a close.

Flum left the tragic remains of the town behind and made her way back to the capital.

A Capital in Turmoil

A S SOON AS THEY ARRIVED at the capital, Gadhio bid farewell to the rest of the party and returned to his home in the East District, right around nightfall.

He made it through the gate, walked along the stone path cutting through the yard, and looked up to the front door. Kleyna was sitting there waiting for him.

She looked up at the sound of his footsteps and smiled, though the edges of her lips began to quiver, and her eyes filled with tears. After all that time she spent preparing what she wanted to say to him, no words came.

She gave up and settled on their well-practiced greeting: "Welcome home."

It stung Gadhio far worse than any angry rant ever could. He left her and Hallom behind, only to end up

killing Tia and reaffirming his love for her. What right did he even have to speak to Kleyna anymore?

The look of concern on Kleyna's face deepened as Gadhio stood there in uncomfortable silence. If it was all going to end soon anyway, then he should just cut his losses and run. But he couldn't bring himself to do that.

He offered her a warm smile. "I'm back, Kleyna."

Kleyna stood up and approached Gadhio on unsteady legs. She leaned in and pressed her face tightly against his chest. "Welcome...welcome home, Gadhio."

He gently stroked her head as she rubbed her tear-stricken face into his chest. His expression was one of pure anguish.

"We're baaaaaack!" Flum sprang through the front door and threw her arms into the air.

Milkit giggled, enjoying the sight of Flum so excited.

"Just being here has a nice relaxing effect, doesn't it?" She, too, let out a sigh as the tension eased from her body.

"This place really has started to feel like our home now."

"Yup, definitely!"

Everyone looked relaxed as they settled in and came to terms with the fact that the battle was finally over. After

throwing together a quick dinner, they all took a bath and retired to their own rooms to rest.

As soon as Ink returned to her room, she felt Eterna scoot behind her and hug her close. A moment later, she heard the familiar sound of Eterna sniffing her hair.

"Whaddya think you're doing?"

"Smelling you."

"Pervert!"

"You know, it's rude to call people that."

"I feel like we had this same conversation pretty recently."

"Welp, I guess we're just stuck with it. This is a habit for me now."

"Well, you better get on fixing it!" Despite her protests, Ink made no effort to get away—she knew it'd be of no use, with how tightly Eterna was holding onto her.

Though Eterna swore there was practically no difference between Flum and Ink, as Ink saw it, the two were polar opposites. She was little more than a normal weak little girl.

"The moment I let my guard down, it seems like you and I got pretty close, huh? But if I'm not careful, I dunno if I'll ever be able to get away from you, Eterna."

"I see no problems with that. Then I can smell you to my heart's content."

"Get off that smelling thing!"

"Sniff sniff!"

"Ewww! Cut it out! You're like a sixty-year-old kid, you old spinster pervert!"

"Hmph, you're pretty good at stringing together harsh words, kid."

"You reap what you sow!"

"You know how we deal with ill-behaved children?"

"Huh? Hyaaagh!"

A vine made of water wrapped around Ink and turned her in Eterna's grasp until the two were face to face.

"Th-this is pretty e-e-embarrassing...!"

"I agree."

"Then why are you doing it?!"

Eterna offered no explanation. She simply hugged Ink even closer to her body.

"Shh...it's okay." She started running a hand through Ink's hair.

"That's right...it must've been hard for you," Ink mumbled. "No matter what the circumstances were, you still had to kill your own parents."

"I tried to keep my feelings out of it. I felt nothing in the moment I killed them, and even all through the battle."

"But now the feelings are back?"

"I have a lot of memories here."

The image of their dying faces, mixed with all of her fond memories of this house, came together to tug painfully at Eterna's heart strings. She felt like her heart was being crushed.

"I want to overwrite them."

"With memories of our own? But aren't all your memories of this house really special to you?"

"Exactly, which is why I want to overwrite my memories of Sheol."

"Can I be here with you, then? I know I'm weak, blind, and can't really do anything useful..."

"Don't think that way. I love being around you, Ink." Eterna's usual cool, even voice made it hard to convey the enjoyment she derived from Ink's company, but the message got through to the younger girl loud and clear.

"All right then, I'll do my best to baby and pamper you until all your wounds are healed!"

This was Ink's way of paying Eterna back for all she'd done.

"Thanks, Ink. I guess the first step, then, is to get back to smelling your delightful hair."

"Whoa, hey...! Why'd you have to take it in that direction all of a sudden?!" Ink squirmed in her grasp, but Eterna only pulled the young girl closer. It seemed like the next few days would be full of similar antics.

Fwumpf.

The bandages dropped to the bed, and Milkit's cheeks went pink at the feel of Flum's hands on her skin.

She put her own hand atop Flum's as they sat down on the bed and gazed into each other's eyes.

"You know, I was really amazed by what you said while we were fighting Satils."

"Amazed?" Milkit looked confused.

"I...I mean...the whole...love thing and all that."

Flum's cheeks burned red at the mere mention, though Milkit seemed confused as to why that would be.

"Oh, that? I tried to figure out how best to refer to our relationship for a long time, Master."

"Not partners?"

"I was happy with that too, but I feel like there's a more specific term."

Now that Milkit brought it to her attention, it felt a bit off to Flum as well. The term "partner" felt too abstract.

"But while everything was happening in Sheol, I

finally found the answer I was looking for. I said it during the middle of the fight, but...do you mind if I say it again?"

"Huh? I, uh...well..."

"I guess that's...a no?" The look of disappointment was clear on Milkit's face.

After one look at that face, Flum could hardly say no.

"I mean, of course! I'd love to hear it."

"Oh, good. Well then..."

She brought Flum's hand down from her cheek to her heart. She could feel Milkit's heart beating underneath the slight swell of her chest.

Milkit looked straight into Flum's eyes. They were just as beautiful as the they were the first time Flum gazed into them, but now the luster had returned to Milkit's silver hair, and her skin carried with it a nice, pink hue. She even began to fill out a little more and gain some feminine curves.

Flum felt her heart skip a beat at just how beautiful the girl sitting in front of her was.

Slowly, Milkit's peach-colored lips began to move as she spoke. "I love you, Master."

Flum's brain ground to a complete halt as she focused on the warm smile facing her.

Love...like...romance.

Love...meant a partner. And not just any type of partner, but like a husband-and-wife kind of partner.

"W...wa...wa...w-w-w-w-w...wa!" Flum's face was bright red at this point.

"Wa?"

"W-wait, Milkit! It's all so soon, I just don't even know how to respond to this, and my brain's all turned to mush, and...!" She clapped her hands to her cheeks in a desperate attempt to cool her face down, though this only got her palms hot.

In a last-ditch attempt, Flum threw her face into the pillow.

But not her own.

A wonderfully sweet scent filled her nostrils.

This pillow smells amazing... I feel a lot more relaxed now, but my heart's still racing. Hey, wait, is this Milkit's pillow?!

Her body temperature rose even further, and her heart beat like the wings of a hummingbird. Warm blood pulsed through her entire body.

"Eeek!" Flum let out a shrill cry and ducked her head under the comforter.

"Was...was what I said that strange?"

"It wasn't...it wasn't strange, really. It was just...really sudden. I mean, love is...ya know... I was surprised."

"Surprised? But love is really the best word I can find to describe how I feel about my master."

Flum kept her face firmly pressed into the comforter, only glancing out to look at Milkit. She knew she probably looked like a complete idiot being all flustered like this, especially considering how unabashed Milkit was about the whole thing.

"Huh?"

Something stood out to Flum. Perhaps this "love" Milkit was speaking of wasn't in a romantic sense at all.

"Hey, Milkit, ya know…"

"Yes?"

"When you say love, do you mean like…that you want to be lovers? Or something else?"

"L-l-l-lovers??" It was Milkit's turn to blush. The blush went all the way up to her ears and down her collarbone, making her look like a giant strawberry. "How did you come to that conclusion?!"

"I mean, that's what love usually means…"

"Really?? No, I…well…you know…"

Her voice grew quieter and quieter until Flum could no longer hear her. Milkit curled up on her side till she was laying on the bed, her hands fixed firmly over her face.

"It's not like…well, of course I like you, Master, but it's just that…well… I don't know how to put this into words, and…"

"W-well, I guess there are a lot of different types of love, ya know. Like between family or even friends! In that respect, I think I..."

Flum couldn't let Milkit be the only one to say it. She sat up straight, put her hands firmly on her thighs, and clenched her jaw to keep a straight face.

"...love you, too."

If asked if this was a familial love, Flum could definitively say no. It also went beyond love between friends. What kind of love it was, however, she couldn't say.

"I'm happy to hear it. But...well...it's really embarrassing."

"Hey, saying it is even more embarrassing."

"I'm really sorry for forcing you into such a situation, Master. But...I really was at a loss as for how to express my feelings to you."

And yet now that she found an answer, this opened the door to even more questions. Milkit still didn't know any other descriptors for this beyond love.

Flum crawled over to her and put her hands on Milkit's cheeks.

"Master?" Milkit risked a peek between her fingers.

Flum's face was still red as a tomato, but she looked much more composed than before. She was smiling, too.

"I really like you, Milkit." Flum's heart pounded in her chest and felt like something was squeezing it at the same time. She enjoyed the sensation. "Let's go with 'like' then, huh? Love might come on a bit strong."

It was still a bit embarrassing, but she felt like it was something she could say a lot more easily.

Milkit's cheeks still burned a bright pink, and she still looked a long way from regaining her composure, but she finally locked eyes with Flum. "Then...then I like you, too."

Flum nodded and let out a bashful laugh.

She felt a sense of elation wash over her at being able to express their feelings to each other.

Milkit smiled. "I like you a lot, Master."

Flum pulled Milkit into a tight embrace.

This mere conversation, an exchange of words, brought her more happiness than she ever thought possible. This feeling was not what she felt for her family or friends. It was a warm sensation that seeped down to the very depths of her heart—a sensation she'd never experienced before.

When Milkit came into her life, she'd gained an irreplaceable treasure. With each and every interaction they shared, something beautiful, like a flower, grew a little more within her heart.

Flum didn't know what to call this sensation yet, but she figured that was fine for the time being.

Nekt returned to the underground laboratory in the capital before the others even had a chance to leave Sheol.

"I'm hoooome."

Though she'd been gone longer than normal, she was all but certain Mother wouldn't care, having lost all interest in the second generation. What did surprise her though, was that none of the other Spiral Children—Mute, Luke, and Fwiss—were there to greet her. In fact, the entire facility was dead silent.

"Hey, where is everyone? If you're playing hide and seek or somethin', I'm not it."

She continued into another room, full of books unrelated to research and toys to play with. Fwiss and Mute had spent a lot of their time playing in there.

"What the..."

The room was in complete disarray. The bookshelves were knocked over, toys were smashed, and there was thick, red liquid staining the floor.

Nekt hurried to Mother's lab.

There, too, she was met with more destruction. Broken lab equipment littered the room, and writing scrawled in blood marred the walls. Unlike the previous room, however, the walls, floors, and ceiling were deformed into a single uneven surface.

"Was there a fight here? It's hard to imagine some creature strong enough to take them on could make it here. Flum and the others must've just gotten back, so that could only mean..."

A shadow in the corner of the room moved. Nekt tensed up and prepared to fight.

As soon as she saw the werewolf step forward, she knew it was no normal monster.

"Chimera, huh? So, the church's turned its back on us, too. If only you gave us just a little more time...!!"

Welcy's article on everything she'd witnessed was published and distributed throughout the capital the following morning. The story sounded like it came out of a third-rate gossip tabloid, but fortunately she was able to back it up with all the materials she managed to recover from Satils' manor and the research facility, along with firsthand accounts of survivors from Sheol.

Of course, the church was expected to immediately deny the story, but the city took the news far more negatively than anyone could have expected. Anti-church groups that had been lying low were quick to arrange demonstrations outside the main cathedral. The same was true for the churches in the other districts as well, which attracted large crowds and speakers denouncing the church.

It was a matter of timing—recent price hikes for healing had already harmed the church's image. With nuns, pastors, and members of the clergy pressured to take responsibility, the Pope called his cardinals together for a meeting at the cathedral.

Pope Fedro Maximus sat at the head of the table dressed in white garb with gold embroidery. Atop his head sat a polished gold crown.

He was the first to speak. "It seems Necromancy has fallen."

His hair was long and white, matching his pale skin. There was something ephemeral about his appearance. His soft voice and the kind smile affixed to his face felt wholly uncanny.

"How unfortunate. I had high expectations of Dafydd."

There was no change in his expression. He looked pleased with his death.

Toitso spoke next. "We are born to give our lives to the cause."

Talchi continued on, maintaining the same tone as the

other speakers. "He fulfilled his role as a true believer in his death."

Slowanach continued the trend. "Dafydd was a martyr. Perhaps he couldn't truly understand the words of Origin, but death has made him complete."

It was like a one-way conversation broken up among several people.

"However, I believe that he was able to complete his research. What say you, Satuhkie Ranagalki?"

Cardinal Farmo smiled and turned to Satuhkie, who stared down intently at the table.

Satuhkie raised his head and turned to address Fedro. He let his boisterous personality shine through, making no attempt to remain quiet and reserved like the speakers before him.

"I'd say that the answer is apparent without my opinion." He cast a glance toward a lone woman standing in a corner of the room. Echidna Ipeila brought a hand in front of her mouth to cover her laugh.

"What a bully, Satuhkie. You know I don't know anything." From the way she moved, it was clear she already knew the whole story.

"I summoned her here for one reason. We've been working hard to find the best way to make use of the great powers Origin has bestowed upon us, and it is finally time for us to decide on our path."

Echidna let out an excited gasp, as if she had been waiting for this moment for a long time.

"I believe that the Chimera project is perfectly suited to serve as the spear tip in the church's holy war."

A round of applause erupted from the cardinals.

Echidna let out another exhilarated sigh.

"Tell Mich that the Children project is to be terminated with immediate effect."

Farmo, the cardinal charged with overseeing the Children project, agreed swiftly. "Understood."

Satuhkie, however, raised an objection. "Your Holiness, I don't think he'll be so quick to agree to his research being terminated..."

Echidna responded, "In that case, why don't you let me take care of the Children? It will serve as a good proving ground for our abilities. Two birds with one stone, and all that."

"You want to unleash those weapons in the capital?"

"We have complete control over the chimera. In a place the size of the capital, we can control them down to their individual movements. Without us, they are living statues, all thanks to the Chimera project's perfected approach."

"And yet I hear that your informant has been captured

and that you were unable to get your hands on the fundamental technology behind the focal core."

Echidna's face tensed up for the briefest of moments before shooting back to put an end to Satuhkie and his arguments. "I've no idea what you're getting at, Satuhkie, but even without those things you speak of, my Chimera is still far superior to both the Necromancy and Children projects in terms of production volume and functionality. I'd say it was a foregone conclusion that we would win this contest, no?"

She conveniently made no mention of the fact that the focal core was still incomplete.

"That's enough, Satuhkie. Stand down."

The Pope had clearly decided they would use the Chimera project, leaving him little interest in the specifics. All Satuhkie could do was click his tongue in annoyance and surrender.

"Well then, Echidna, we will leave it to you if we are unable to convince Mich to terminate."

"It's a great honor, your Holiness. I'll begin making my preparations now."

As far as she was concerned, the conversation with Mich Smithee—Mother—was as good as doomed. The Children project's destruction at the hand of Chimera was a near certainty.

That wasn't what Satuhkie was so concerned about. When an animal is cornered, it is at its most dangerous— and the Children were not weak. Once they no longer had anything left to lose, he feared that they could wreak untold havoc on the capital.

The Pope and cardinals had to know that. And yet, they accepted this as the cost of doing business.

They're barbarians...

Satuhkie kept his annoyance to himself. The church, after all, was filled to the brim with people like them. Echidna was a prime example. She would kill without a second thought if it meant getting closer to her goals. Satuhkie could tell that nothing but trouble awaited them, due to her complete lack of patience.

Before the day's meeting was even held, the chimerae were already sent out to destroy the Children project.

It was nothing short of a miracle that Satuhkie had been allowed to become a cardinal himself, in light of all the chaos that thrived in the church. There were already some who were expressing concerns about the current state of the church among his supporters. It was thanks to them he'd made it this far.

"I noticed some kind of ruckus going on outside the cathedral." Finally, Pope Fedro addressed the protest going on outside.

"Some cheap tabloid leaked the details of the Sheol incident to the public."

"Well, that's certainly unfortunate. Do we have a way to shut them up?"

Talchi responded. "I have an excellent idea, your Holiness. Now that our duties are complete, why don't you sentence Farmo and myself to death?"

Talchi and Farmo had been in charge of overseeing the Necromancy and Children projects. Now that they'd formally decided to adopt the Chimera project, their jobs were finished.

"What a wonderful idea. More humans will need to die to create the perfect world as envisioned by Origin, anyway, so this will help make way for his plans." There was no hint of dishonesty in Farmo's response. He seemed truly pleased.

"All right then; I leave the rest to you, Huyghe."

"Absolutely. I will take their heads at once."

The execution of cardinals, an event that should have been a massive change within the church of Origin, had been discussed and settled in only a brief exchange.

All Satuhkie could do was clench his fist beneath the table and sit there quietly as he watched the insanity play out unquestioned around him. As a cardinal and loyal follower of Origin, he had no choice but to keep up appearances for those around him.

"Justice Arts, Scotch Maiden Cleansing Blade!" Rays of light reflected off Huyghe's steel blade as he swung it through the air. Despite the distance and lack of any physical contact, Talchi and Farmo's heads dropped to the floor. Their bodies collapsed in their chairs, pouring bright red blood out onto to ground.

"Impressive as always, Huyghe."

"I am honored by your kind words." Huyghe remained as calm as ever.

"Actually, now's a good time to discuss that issue I brought up before, Huyghe. I just received authorization from Dian."

This Dian the Pope so casually referred to was none other than King Dian himself. It was clear the Pope considered him to be in a subservient role.

Huyghe's eyes lit up. "So that means...!"

Fedro's expression softened. "Correct. From today, the royal army now belongs to the church knights."

"We've got a problem!" Ottilie barged into Henriette's office without even knocking. Her face was pale, and she was clearly in a panic. "Cardinal Talchi and Cardinal Farmo's heads were hung in front of the cathedral!"

"Did this satisfy the protesters?" Henriette gazed out the window at the protest in the plaza in front of the castle.

"Yes. It seems the church was hoping to put an end to the unrest with this."

The idea that two cardinals would be killed likely hadn't crossed anyone's minds. It was probably fear at such extreme measures, not satisfaction, that had made the crowds go quiet.

"The royal army can't just stand by and let that happen. Henriette, we can't stay silent any longer, and..."

"We have no other choice. We've no power to do anything else." Henriette wasn't her usual energetic self. Her voice was quiet and distant.

"W-what's wrong?"

Ottilie hesitated for a moment, and Henriette turned and approached her. She pulled Ottilie into a tight embrace.

"Huh? H...H-Henriette? You, I mean...this is all so sudden! We shouldn't...!"

"Calm down and listen."

"No! I mean, we can't! Of course you smell so lovely and your sweet, gentle touch is nothing short of divine... and your chest... I mean, your chest...no! I can't think such awful things!"

"I want...I want you to resign from the army."

"Resign? What? But why??" Ottilie's exuberant mood came crashing down almost immediately. "Why? Why would I do that?? I joined so I could be with you! I'll be by your side always and forever, in life and death, whether in this life or the next!"

"You never change, do you? I'm honestly impressed that you joined the army just for me and managed to rise to the rank of lieutenant general. But that's exactly why I'm asking this of you."

"If you're going to ask something of me, then ask me to be by your side forever! I don't care if it's as a slave or even a chamber pot, whatever I need to do!"

"No, you and I are kindred spirits, Ottilie. We've stood side by side in our fight to defend the kingdom. But that was only because the King himself was of the same mind."

"No...it can't be. The King agreed to merge the royal army with the church knights??"

"It's not a merger. We're being assimilated. I'm no longer a general, and I don't know what will become of me within the church knights."

The army existed to enforce the status quo across the kingdom. With the army gone, overzealous nobles would be free to seize land as they pleased. In short, by assimilating the royal army into the church knights, the Pope had acquired unfettered control over the entire kingdom.

"I can only let go of one person prior to the assimilation. Werner and Herrmann will probably hate me for it, but I want that person to be you, Ottilie."

"B-but...I...I don't want that."

"I'm sorry, but I'm confident that you and the heroes can come together to continue to fight for the kingdom."

"This is an awful position to put me in! You know I would never turn down a request from you, don't you??"

Henriette only offered up a sad smile in response.

"Well, then," said Ottilie, "there's one thing I want to ask of you."

"And that is?"

"If we manage to bring the church back in line and I...I can return back to your side, I...I want you to h-ho-ho... no, that's too much. I...I want you to hug me!"

It was a relatively humble request. Henriette could have easily shaken her head no, but her reply went a completely unexpected direction. "If you come back to me alive, I'll even give you a kiss. In fact, I'll do whatever you ask of me."

"You...you have my word!"

The two intertwined their pinkies and swore on it.

With the dissolution of the royal army, the church knights first needed to conduct a selection process in order to carry out their assimilation. Those former members of the army who had no place in the church knights were brutally murdered in front of their former comrades. The numbers were said to be in the hundreds. This was done to break the spirits of those men and women who had been singularly faithful to their country and bring them in line with the Origin faith.

Any soldiers who showed resistance underwent a "baptism" involving brainwashing through torture and drugs.

All of these events were held in secrecy within church-run facilities and only made it out to the people in the form of rumors. What was known was that no one ever saw the army's former leaders after the assimilation.

The day after the execution of the cardinals and the announcement of the army's merger, a lone green-haired man visited the West District guild. Y'lla, who had shown up abnormally early for once—even before Flum

and Gadhio—perked up slightly from where she was daydreaming at the counter when the man walked in.

He was tall, handsome, and quite famous.

"Linus Radiants??" Y'lla smiled brightly at his arrival. She felt suddenly light-headed as she brought her hands to her chest, but unfortunately, he was here for business.

"I heard Gadhio can be found here?"

"Unfortunately, the guild master hasn't arrived yet." Everything about him was her type, so Y'lla played up the sweetness.

"Huh, I guess I'm a little early. Why did he suddenly decide to start being a guild master, anyway? He always said that it was all just kind of foisted on him, and he'd ignored it until now."

After returning from the land of demons the night before, Linus had a lot to take in from what had happened over the past few days. His head was spinning just trying to process it all.

In fact, he came out to ask Gadhio directly in order to find out the truth of what had really gone down. Something told him his ex-teammate was somehow involved.

"I figured it had something to do with Flum Apricot being here, honestly."

"Huh? Why would Flum be here?"

"I don't know anything about that. She has a slave mark on her cheek for some reason or another, so I figure something big must've happened."

"A slave mark...?" Linus's face suddenly went serious.

This made Y'lla's heart skip a beat, but Linus wasn't interested in that at the moment. He'd always thought it odd that Flum would suddenly decide to return to her hometown, but now things were coming together.

He turned to the exit without a word.

"What about the guild master?"

"Tell him I came looking for him. Another thing just came up."

With that, Linus stepped back outside.

"That stupid son of a..." He ran so fast that he looked like a blur to everyone he passed.

His destination was a foregone conclusion: he was heading to Jean Inteige's room back at the castle where he was casually conducting research.

ROLL
OVER
AND
DIE

Lamentable Boundaries

THE WEST DISTRICT was not as well organized as its eastern counterpart and lacked any defined parks for the local children to play, leaving them with little other than lots left empty due to the relatively high crime rate in the area.

While there were usually a fair number of children playing in the lots on any given day, a different group of people were engaging in an unusual type of play on this given morning.

"You look exhausted, Flum."

"Nah, I got this!"

"If you say so. We have limited time as it is, so no breaks!"

"Got it!"

Flum dashed forward and heaved the Souleater at Gadhio.

He spun away, his coat swirling in the wind, and parried the blow with his own black blade. The force of the blow knocked Flum off balance and sent her tumbling backward.

"Gah..."

"Remember what I told you: there's a difference between aggressive and reckless."

Gadhio didn't let up and followed through with a kick as Flum fought to regain her balance.

"Eyuagh!" His foot connected, knocking all of the air out of Flum's lungs and making her see stars, though she still managed to keep herself in the fight.

She swung her sword through the air and let loose a Prana Shaker.

He's just too good...but no, maybe I can hold him back with a feint!

Watching her movements carefully, Gadhio read Flum's next move. He didn't even bother taking a defensive posture, instead letting his prana surround himself and taking Flum's attack head-on.

There was a thunderclap as the two forces met. Their respective prana abilities canceled each other out, and Gadhio lunged straight toward an unprepared Flum.

"You're done!" He raised his sword in an attempt to put an end to the fight once and for all. But Flum wasn't done quite yet.

She threw her gauntlet-ed arm in the way, taking the force of the sword's blow entirely in her right arm.

It was all for naught.

There was no way her arm could withstand the force of such an attack. What's more, the loss of her dominant hand ensured she could no longer stay in the fight. For a mock battle, it wasn't necessary for her to go that far.

In the moment his sword made contact with Flum, Gadhio understood just how dedicated she was.

I thought she just did that on impulse, but no—she fully intended to throw her arm in the way. With the way she angled her arm, she meant to deflect the blow, not block it completely. So she still intends to stay in the fight, then!

Gadhio pressed the attack. His sword hit the gauntlet in a shower of sparks. Flum's arm made a wet snapping sound like a breaking tree branch as a bone gave way under the force of the blow.

"Master!!"

"What's happening now, Eterna?"

"She broke her arm. That's gotta hurt."

Milkit, Eterna, and Ink were at a loss for words from where they sat watching on the sidelines.

She was lucky to get away with such little damage. Flum's plan to parry the attack paid off, even if it hurt.

Though her enchantment reduced much of the pain she felt, it was still excruciating for what should have been a mock battle. No matter how many times she broke her arm, a chill always ran up her spine when it happened. An electric sensation ran through her muscles, goosebumps formed across her body, and she felt her blood drain away. It was all she could do to overcome the natural reaction with sheer force of will.

"Hyaaaaaah!" Flum brought the Souleater down on Gadhio with a left-handed slash. Gadhio considered blocking the blow, but decided on another approach at the last moment.

He slammed his sword into the ground and used the hilt as a handhold to vault over Flum's attack. Landing behind Flum, he pulled his sword from the earth.

"That was pretty impressive." Gadhio held his blade just shy of Flum's neck. He clearly won this round.

Flum let out an exhausted sigh and slumped to the ground. "So even that wasn't good enough..."

She felt pretty good about that attack, but she still wasn't good enough to beat Gadhio.

"Master!!" Now that the mock battle had come to a close, Milkit stood up from the bench and ran to her

master's side. She looked at Flum's right arm, the worry clear on her face. "Are you okay? Does it hurt?"

"No biggie, it's already healed anyway." Flum opened and closed her right hand, much to Milkit's relief.

It didn't last. A moment late, her cheeks puffed out in a rare display of anger. "Still, you should try not to push yourself so hard on your day off!"

"Sorry, sorry. I figured it was the only way I stood a chance at beating Gadhio."

"You really hung in there, kid. I have to admit, I was really surprised to see you sacrifice your own arm like that, even if the move was a bit rash."

"Yeah, you're probably right. I should probably hold back from stuff like that in the future."

"If it were anyone but you, Flum, I would've just called it there. But in real life-and-death combat, I have to say your willingness to sacrifice your own limbs in battle is an amazing asset."

Milkit felt conflicted at Gadhio's praise.

"Honestly, I just don't have the experience to compete properly, so that's my only choice," Flum said.

"And that's why I didn't stop. However, as I said earlier, you need to be mindful of the difference between being aggressive and being reckless. If your head or heart are destroyed, you're done for, so you need to train yourself up to be able to protect those two parts at any cost."

"You're still able to fight, Gadhio?"

"It's fine, Milkit. I was the one who asked him to help me train, after all. I rarely have a chance like this as it is, and besides, the stronger I get, the better I'll be able to protect you." Flum brushed Milkit's cheek with her hand before wrapping her finger around a strand of hair and stroking the younger girl's earlobe.

Milkit's heart was a sudden maelstrom of emotion as she felt the ticklish, warm, and gentle caress come together to send her cheeks burning. "I guess there's nothing I can say to that, but please be careful. Your pain is my pain, Master."

"Gotcha, I'll be more careful."

Eterna and Ink sat on the bench and waited as the conversation between Flum and Milkit took place beyond earshot.

"They sure are friendly..."

"It seems like they've grown even closer ever since they got back from Sheol, don't you think?"

"I think Milkit's grown. Learning that she can rely on Flum has really boosted her confidence."

Ink giggled. "So you think they're ready for the next stage, then? That'll really get on your nerves, Eterna!"

"What're you so happy about?"

Despite their teasing, it was evident Eterna and Ink were growing quite close.

Milkit finally returned to the bench. Though she hated the idea of Flum getting hurt, she would at least agree to sit by and watch on to offer her emotional support if this was what Flum had to do to improve.

Shortly thereafter, the second round of their mock battle began.

"Hyaaaaaaaah!!" Flum lunged straight in. Gadhio coolly deflected her blows.

Even after the scolding she got from Milkit, Flum threw all that out the window now that the battle started, accumulating cuts and gashes as the battle wore on. Though Flum expected it on some level, she was taken aback at how Gadhio treated this like a real battle, not daring to hold back.

They had no choice—there was little time left. The Children, Chimera, or even the church knights could act at any moment. There was no guarantee that peace would continue into tomorrow...or even today. Gadhio had a limited amount of time to teach Flum everything he knew.

So there was no holding back. Even if that meant getting hurt, it was all necessary for Flum to protect those who were most important to her.

"Whoa, awesome!" A small crowd of children gathered around the park to watch the battle.

Flum didn't really think letting these kids watch her get hurt like this was good for their healthy development, but she wasn't exactly in a position to stop at the moment. In any case, the children were having a great time watching a "real" battle take place right before their eyes.

"Why you beatin' her up like that, grandpa?! You go girl!"

"You got this, lady! That old guy can't beat you!!"

There was something about how badly Flum was getting beaten down that turned the kids against Gadhio. Not like it had anything to do with their training, of course.

Flum and Gadhio ended the fight just before noon to head back to their own houses for a short rest. Milkit invited Gadhio to come back with them for lunch, but he still felt guilty about making Kleyna worry so much about the Sheol ordeal and figured it best to go back home for the time being.

Shortly after leaving the empty lot, Eterna turned to Gadhio. "You know, you seem pretty down. Did something happen?"

"Do I?"

"Yep. It's pretty obvious."

"Well, actually…it's a bit embarrassing." This seemed very unlike him. After scowling for a bit as he mulled it over in his mind, he finally decided to say what was on his mind. "Am I really an old man?"

Flum and Milkit stared blankly at Gadhio while he averted his gaze. Meanwhile, Eterna chuckled loudly at this. Her reaction seemed to make Gadhio even more insecure, and he began to brush at his hair absentmindedly.

"Uh, it's nothing, really. Just forget about it."

"No can do, I can't forget something like that. Honestly, I'll probably be laughing about that for the rest of my life."

"You're a strange one, Eterna. Always have been, always will be."

"I see my reputation precedes me."

"Try not to puff up your chest about it."

"You saying I don't have a chest?"

"I never said anything of the sort."

"Hmph."

"Y'know, now that you brought it up…you don't seem so cheery yourself, Eterna."

"You really are insufferable…"

Gadhio rubbed his temples.

Flum spoke up. "I think you're still pretty young, Gadhio."

"That's hardly something a young person can judge."

Flum clammed up at Eterna's pointed criticism.

"Eterna's right. I guess I'm over the hill now. After 32 long years on this planet, I guess that's just how it is."

"Well, I think you're a great old man, Gadhio! I'm sure any man you ask would love to be just like you when they get old."

"That's right, you have a definite swagger in the way you hold yourself. I'd say you're more like a well-aged gentleman than an old man, really."

Milkit and Ink's praise hardly improved his mood. One way or another, he just didn't want to accept the fact that he'd gotten older. Gadhio parted ways with the group with the same glum expression still firmly entrenched on his face.

Gadhio took the main thoroughfare toward his home in the East District. Along the way, he ran into Kleyna doing her shopping.

"Well, if it isn't you." She smiled brightly at the sight of her friend and moved over-excitedly to greet him, sending her red ponytail swinging wildly from side-to-side.

"Ah, Kleyna. What brings you here?"

"I was just shopping for lunch."

Gadhio reached out and took the shopping bag from Kleyna's hand without even thinking.

"Thanks."

This kind of interaction was routine between them.

"Where's Hallom?"

"She's out playing with her friends."

"Such a spirited girl."

"As per usual. Thanks to you, she's really coming into her own."

"You really give me too much credit. Hallom has a great mother watching out for her. That's all there is to it."

"You're way too humble." Kleyna stuck out her lower lip and pouted before the two fell into step with each other. She was finished with most of her shopping at this point, so the two headed back to their house in the East District.

Though it was only a brief moment spent together, Kleyna fancied this time as something of a date. The fact that Hallom wasn't there only helped build on the idea. Gadhio wasn't oblivious to what she was thinking. He felt a deep sense of regret fill his heart every time he felt her body press against his as she walked excitedly next to him.

He thought of Tia and what he had done.

"Why the long face?"

"Ah, I was practicing with Flum earlier." Gadhio changed the topic entirely to avoid answering the question. "These kids that were watching us practice called me an old man, and I started to think that maybe I really am old."

"Strange, you don't seem like the type who would care about something like that."

"You're still a bit younger than me, so of course you don't really care about these things yet."

"It's not that I don't care. One of my friend's kids was running around like a bat out of hell and called me an old hag when I told him to calm down. Can you believe that??"

"Heh, best to not think too much about what kids say."

"I know that, but you just kinda think about these things after hitting thirty. It's the same for you, isn't it? Even if I told you I thought you were the greatest guy I knew, you'd still be worrying about it."

"You're right there."

"You've just gotta figure that this is our fate. All we can do is try our best to age as gracefully as possible."

"Age gracefully, huh?" Gadhio smiled as a distant memory came to mind.

"Hey, Gaddy, what kind of person do you want to be when you get older?"

They had this conversation shortly before they got married.

"You've got a baby face, a slim body, and a cool demeanor. I can see you turning into something of a scholarly gentleman with time, I guess. Me, on the other hand... I'm not really sure if I'll be a suitable old lady to be by your side. Heh."

"Don't talk like that, Tia. No matter how old you get, you'll always be beautiful to me."

"You really think so? I hope you're right."

Everyone holds out hope for their own future. At that point in time, they had no reason to believe it might not come true.

"You're thinking about Tia again." Kleyna's voice brought him back to reality.

He didn't bother denying it. "Yeah, I was. I just remembered we had a similar conversation."

Kleyna didn't look hurt or particularly bothered by this. She smiled softly. "I guess I'll just have to work on making myself a pretty fine lady if I ever plan to get your head out of the clouds. I'm really trying to be your ideal woman here, and you won't even give me the time of day."

"You're a wonderful woman, Kleyna. Too good for me."

"Don't talk like that; that's just going to encourage me." Kleyna gave a good-natured laugh. The look on her face reminded Gadhio of the times they spent going out on missions together. "I'll tell you right now, I don't plan on giving up. I'm going to keep on being the best woman I can, until I finally get a little attention from you. Right now, I figure that'll take at least another ten years or so. I hope you're ready for that."

Kleyna picked up the pace slightly, gaining a short lead ahead of him like she was trying to escape out of embarrassment. Her ears flushed a bright red.

Gadhio felt a pang in his chest at the sight. There was no way that he could allow himself to be with such a perfect woman. Not when his own life was marching toward its inevitable end.

"Ten years, huh?"

He still had too much fighting ahead of him to entertain the thought of such a far-off future.

Gadhio looked up at the sky and whispered to himself, "That's a long way away…"

The rays of the bright afternoon sun illuminated all of the living figures as they moved about their day within the capital. For a man who had already accepted his own impending end, it was hard to feel a connection to those around him.

Afterword

WELL, IT LOOKS LIKE the slow life has come to a brutal end. (Anyway, time for an introduction.)

Hello, this is kiki, the author of *Roll Over and Die: I Will Fight for an Ordinary Life with my Love and Cursed Sword*. Thanks for picking up Volume 3.

How did you find Chapter 4, the Necromancy arc? There were a lot of words here that never even appeared in the web version, and I've been throwing a lot of unsettling details into the story, so where it goes from here is anyone's guess. Even I, as the author, am looking forward to where the story will take us!

Sunao Minakata's manga version of the story is continuing along nicely, and it's absolutely amazing. Flum is just so cool, and I love Milkit's flat reactions in the beginning of the story! And Y'lla... Wow, she's beautiful! Dein? What a jerk! I get annoyed every time I see him.

To be honest, a lot of rewriting was needed to get the first chapter in shape for a manga version. There are a lot of added scenes that didn't appear in the online or book versions of the story, and the artist does an excellent job fleshing out Flum and Milkit's interactions. It's absolutely amazing, and I implore you to go read it!

And, once again, I realize just how hard it is to write an afterword. To kill time, I guess I'm left with the usual option: having myself interact with the characters.

GADHIO: "Hmph, you know, I'm really not good at these afterword things."

TIA: "But at least it gives us a chance to talk, right, Gaddy?"

GADHIO: "You have a point there. I suppose I should thank the author for giving us this moment. Thank you, kiki!"

TIA: "See ya, kiki!"

This is what happens when desperation takes over.

Last but not least, I'd like to thank all those responsible for bringing this book into being.

Kinta once again came on board in Volume 3 to really bring all of these characters to life. Every time I saw the cover work or any of the art inserts, I would punch the air in glee at just how perfectly you captured the characters' expressions. Thanks a ton.

Then of course there's my editor, whom I've caused untold amounts of trouble with all my wordy passages and insistent requests. You've been an amazing help and really saved my hide. I really appreciate it.

And of course, there were the many other people working in publishing and you, my dear readers, who also deserve a lot of credit for making this book a reality.

I truly am in your debt.

I hope to see you around again if I'm granted the opportunity to write another book. Next time, we'll be following the story of the Children arc!

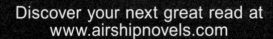